POINSETTIA GIRL

JENNIFER WIZBOWSKI

HISTORIUM PRESS

POINSETTIA GIRL

This is a work of fiction inspired by historical events and family stories. Names, characters, places, and incidents are products of the author's imagination or are used fictitiously, with some names changed to protect privacy. While certain historical elements are based on true events, the narrative has been fictionalized to explore themes creatively and is not a literal account of history.

DELUXE EDITION: 978-1-964700-45-8
HARDCOVER ISBN: 978-1-964700-44-1
PAPERBACK ISBN: 978-1-964700-43-4
EBOOK ISBN: 978-1-964700-42-7

First Edition
Historium Press, a subsidiary publishing house of
The Historical Fiction Company
New York, NY / Macon, GA USA
www.historiumpress.com

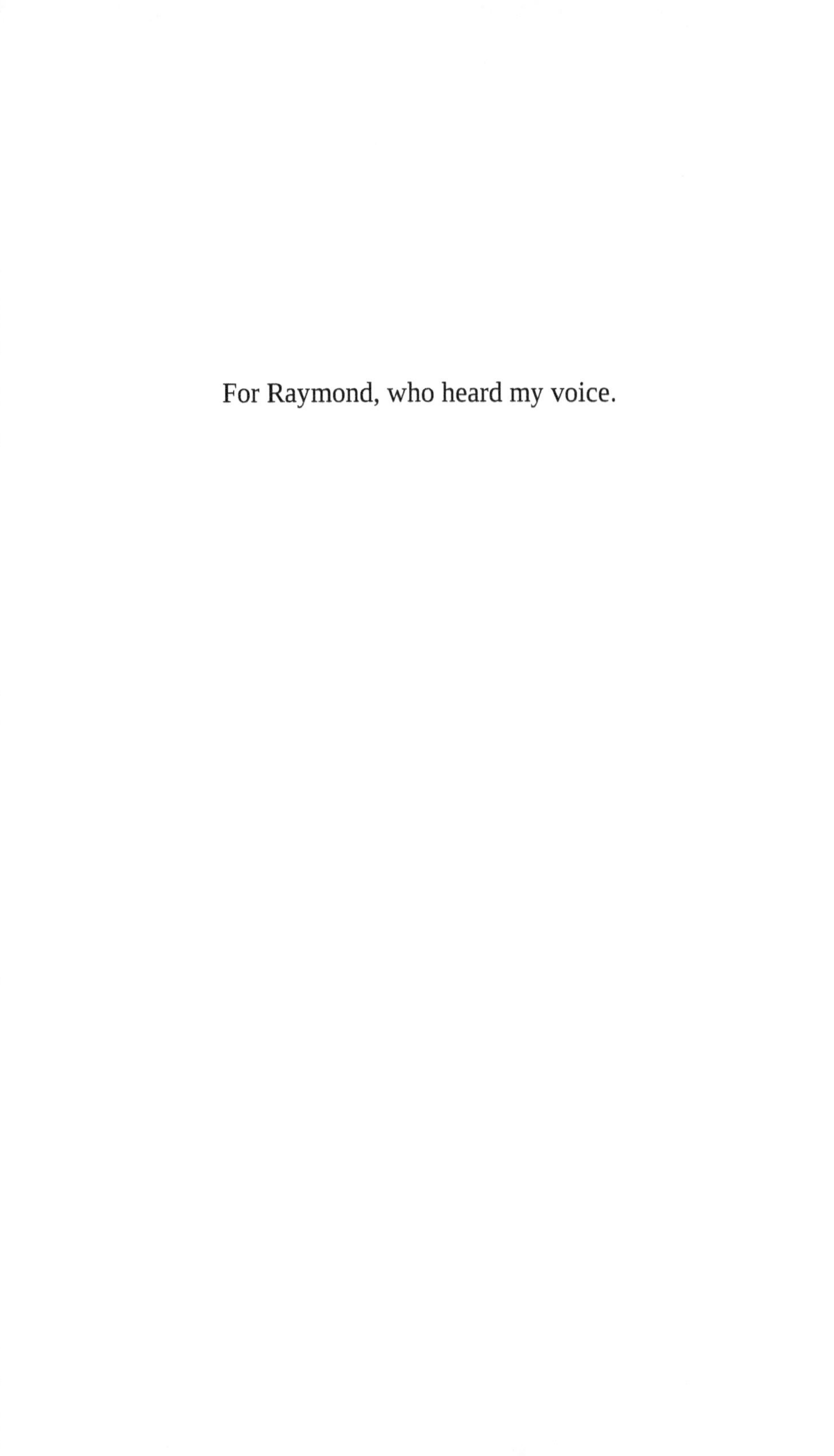

For Raymond, who heard my voice.

"HE WHO SINGS, PRAYS TWICE."

SAINT AUGUSTINE

(Refer to Glossary at the end of the book
for Italian word translation)

ACT ONE
SAN CANCIANO

1

AGATA

September 1710

The sky was stark, stale, and gray. The air, cold.

Ten-year-old Agata walked in a shuffle, keeping up with her Nonna's determined steps. The moisture in the air sat in the crevices of storefront windows, like the tears that welled in the corners of her dark brown eyes. She didn't want to look up and acknowledge where their footsteps would lead, but Nonna's short legs directed them forward. Ahead of her, she saw her father Pietro, his long black hair tied back, revealing the top of his thin neck. *Maybe today he'll be on his best behavior.* Pietro and their neighbor, Nico Sellas, reached the canal where a group of their neighbors gathered.

"Heave!" the two men grunted in unison as they placed her mother's wooden coffin into the gondola. They had made the same procession Agata had taken from the front door of Nonna's bakery house with the narrow box held in the curve of their arms. She'd run hundreds of times through the corridor of her neighborhood's colorful shops, but today, every cobble felt bumpy, jarring the soles of her narrow feet. The only reason she made it this far was because of Nonna's warm shoulders rubbing against her own. Nonna was steady and safe and always took a strong lead.

An unfamiliar priest stood ahead at the canal's edge. His black robes swelled from the wind, and a large black hat sat crooked on his head. The small crowd of neighbors tightened around him.

Nonna looked at her with her shiny black eyes, "Come, Bellissima, the priest is waiting."

Nonna's arms tangled in Agata's, guiding them toward the dock. Their neighbors, huddled in clumps, raised their eyes to greet her, saying her name quietly as if in prayer. Faustina Sellas stood by the boat dock awaiting her with an arm full of jasmine and eyes full of tears. It was good to have her mammina's best friend there. Faustina was like a jovial aunt, always appearing at the right moment, bringing cheer with her. Today, the wind waved her dependable brown bun loose, and her usual joy smudged by her drooping eyes.

Agata felt Faustina inhale deeply as she reached to hug her, placing her cheek against hers. She exhaled in a whisper. "My poor, sweet child." Faustina handed Agata the aromatic bouquet.

Next to Faustina was her eldest son, Gabriele, Agata's childhood playmate. The two children, just a month apart in age, were plopped down on the floor together from Agata's first days of life while their mothers chatted, fussed, and laughed. The friends grew tall together. Their former days of running barefoot through their campo became walks of small talk, always ending with their feet swinging at the edge of their neighborhood dock, him making her laugh with his jokes.

Today, he stood awkwardly, his gangly legs stiff, his usually mischievous face squeezed.

Agata looked past Gabriele. A funeral gondola mounded with white lilies, lacey star jasmine, and white camellias bobbed gently on the water. Beauty, peace, and emptiness taking over their place of childhood play.

She felt her lesser-known neighbors peering out their windows at her misfortune. Agata had the urge to run away from all of it. She tucked her head against her shoulder, hoping it would deter their stares.

"Do you think we'll get a concert?" a man's voice echoed down.

"I thought he had to be drunk for that," another woman taunted.

"Ohhhh, so we'll get a free show tonight as he's stumbling through the square!" another voice mocked.

Nonna squeezed Agata's hand and sucked in her breath.

"Never mind them," Nonna said.

It calmed her to see that familiar defiance in Nonna's black eyes.

"It's time to get in." Nonna pulled her to the edge of the dock. Agata stepped into the rear seat of the faded black gondola and reached for Nonna's hand to help her. The sweet smell of flowers inches away from her made mammina seem as near as ever. It hardly felt real that she was gone, though the heavy pain Agata had carried for weeks reminded her, sitting like too many sweets in her stomach; that and the black fabric, the black everywhere. The priest boarded behind them.

Her father, Pietro, stepped last onto the gondola. Agata eyed his tightly clutched violin case and how he cradled it against his body for support. His angled cheeks and heavy dark brows gave him the permanent glower she'd come to recognize him for, such a contrast to her mother's gentle disposition. The boat wobbled and shook with him as he got on. His hair tie fell into the water, spilling his matte ebony locks across his shoulders like a cape. The gathered crowd watched his every move from the shore as if they all held their breath, waiting. Agata turned away. Nonna gave her hand a hug with her own.

Two gondoliers also occupied the narrow boat, wearing sheer black scarves around their necks in honor of the deceased. The men maneuvered their oars, thrusting the vessel away from the dock. Their strokes moved heavily and quietly in a slow, plodding march. The priest stood at the gondola's bow, facing the canal ahead and clearing his throat. He began to chant in Latin, mumbling words of prayer. His small thurible of incense billowed around him with the boat's movements. He straightened his shoulders and balanced the high hat on his head, competing with the jerky start of the vessel. Agata looked back at Gabriele, standing on the dock, who usually would have made a funny face at such a sight to make Agata giggle. Instead, he offered a slight one-sided grin, his lips turning up on the same side of the unruly chocolate brown curl that always flopped in front of his eye.

It didn't take long for her Papa to take over the moment. Out of nowhere, he released his cries, weeping so loudly that it drowned out the priest and even the sounds of the water splashing off the oars. The neighbors started their whispers. *He should cry!* It was his fault, after all, that Agata's mammina couldn't be buried at their home church in San Canciano. Agata's thoughts drifted wistfully back to that church. Its pale pink interior reminded her of the sugar-glazed taralli cookies Nonna made her at Easter time. She liked the squeak of the pews whenever she swung her feet to make the time pass more quickly during Mass. B*ecause of him*, they had to bury her mammina in a strange church that sat far away, almost at the end of Castello.

The clouds, gray and immeasurably thick, continued to cry silently in the gentle mist. The sky measured Agata's sadness and clutched it in its heavy, vast grasp. Agata looked back at her friend, to the campo and those she knew and who knew her. Gabriele held his palm up in a static wave. Agata had nothing left in her to give him back.

A wave of anger washed over her sadness, blurring everything inside because *of him. Her own father.*

The small vessel found its glide. It wound through the narrow canals lined with rust-colored buildings and gray ones with wooden shutters. They veered to the Rio di San Marina with its many small pontes stretching over the water. Venetians crossed over these bridges to walk to Mass, glancing over the edge to take in the water and who was on it. Agata lowered her head back onto her Nonna's shoulder, which felt heavy beneath the weight of their stares. It was hard to fathom after her significant loss that the world could still awaken to a new day. The long boat, which carried her father's loud cries and the priest's Latin ramblings, subsided its moans to the soft tumble of oars in the water.

Creak, whoosh, creak, whoosh.

Kamelia Agnella Farusi may have seemed a simple woman to anyone else, but to Agata, she was grace, calm, and truth. The stabilizer in their home. The song that woke her up in the mornings and the smile that stretched through her day. She pictured her mammina and her golden hair weaving with the thick clouds above, seated on a great throne, gazing down at her. The wind touched Agata's cheek, sending a shiver down her spine, and she looked down at the wooden box at her feet. All she had left of her was the smell of the flora. Agata made a promise to herself that she would pray daily to her mammina, picturing her in her mind, as her spirit rose out of the dark, coffin box and now sat up in the clouds gazing down on her.

Among the quiet of the priest and the business of her thoughts, a violin began to play. Agata turned to find her father, Pietro Farusi, gazing back at her. She didn't inherit her mother's golden hair; hers was lighter than her father's, a chestnut shade of brown. As Agata aged, she grew into long legs like her Papa's she also inherited his thin long neck. She thought herself gangly, not elegant like her father or pretty as her mother; she was somehow in between. Her Papa wore an elaborate black cloth around his neck that rippled and waved in the wind. He propped one leg against the wooden box and shut his eyes.

The bow played a solitary note that suspended itself in the moment. It seemed it would never find its end. It gave Agata a terrible, terrible feeling that his crying would never end either.

She bore her brown eyes into him, furrowing her brows, hoping to pierce him with her anger. But she couldn't compete with her father's aura. That long, lonely note hung in the gray air.

The note took a deep breath, and the bow began to persist, playing rapaciously. It was movement and crying, anger and sadness all at once. Papa's emotions floated off the gondola and encircled them as the river reverberated the sounds off the pale buildings and out again. The notes swirled in a whirlpool around them. People began to notice. Eyes peered over bridges and out of windows; women stared while pretending to water plants or beat a rug on their balcony. Others leaned out and ogled with no shame.

It no doubt caught people by surprise. It was beautiful but loud—always so loud.

The gondola made its final turn onto Rio Della Pietà. The waves bounced between the small vessel and the dock, where it soon parked. A man was waiting there with red hair and wearing a bright red jacket. He looked important and appeared to be waiting for them. Was it someone Mammina knew? Or Papa?

Papa stepped off the gondola and approached the man with the red jacket, who whispered to him. Agata watched Papa's shoulders tense. Nonna grabbed her arm, cueing Agata to get her help off the boat. Agata turned back around to see the red-haired man drop coins into the gondolier's palm.

Agata and Nonna walked together to a large church, which sat on a much larger campo than theirs. The church had a white circular window at the top, and she wondered what birds made their homes inside that window. Agata counted with her finger in the air: one, two, three bells. Her church in San Canciano only had one.

"Bragora Church," Nonna whispered, not letting Agata pause any longer to look.

Nonna led her through the dark double doors and turned in to locate the stoup, making the sign of the cross across her shoulders with the scented water. Agata imitated her Nonna's gesture, almost forgetting what to do in the distraction of a new church. Nonna trudged to the front pew, her dark grey skirt sweeping the harlequin stone floor. Agata followed, self-conscious of a new place and anyone else who might be in the room. But beyond them, the church stood empty except for the black-hatted priest and the flower-covered coffin.

A ruckus of shoes scuffled at the back of the church. Agata sighed in relief, recognizing her neighbors. Benedetta Betranozzi huffed out a breath as she pulled her friend, Alba Sellas, into the chapel.

"Oh, I think we're late," sighed Benedetta.

"Calm, it hasn't started yet," scolded Alba.

Nonna's two closest friends, Benedetta Betranozzi and Alba Sellas, had made the walk to Bragora to meet them—and they looked haggard from it. Alba's long knitted shawl, which usually hugged her shoulders, dragged on the ground behind her. They sank into their seats with a squeak and an exhale, positioning themselves in the pew directly behind them. Agata watched Benedetta place her hand on Nonna's shoulder. Nonna squeezed it with her own.

"Where is my seat?" Papa appeared, staring at Nonna with a pitiful look, his violin hanging limp at his side.

Agata, who was still watching Nonna's friends, saw Benedetta's head give a sharp, judgmental turn. Agata could practically hear her eyes roll. Benedetta, her Nonna's oldest friend, was never afraid to share her thoughts. You always knew what she was thinking because she wasn't scared to tell you. She liked things out in the open. Her Nonna was much more reserved, her actions subtler. Nonna responded to her son-in-law with a sigh as she moved over to accommodate him, patting the seat beside her.

The parish priest spoke, prayed, sang, and then spoke some more. Her Papa stood heavily next to her, making no sound. The women of San Canciano sniffled and patted their tears behind her. Although her Nonna was weeping *soto voce*, she still stood strong and firm beside her. Agata's tears, while taking it all in, were quiet ones, too.

As the priest continued, Agata was looking around, saddened that the church was all but empty, when she caught a glimpse of color. Way at the back sat the man in the red jacket. He looked at her softly, like he had been waiting for her to notice him—as if he had a secret to tell. *Who is this man?* she wondered.

He replied to her gaze with a pursing of his lips and the beginning of a smile, his eyes crinkling slightly. She turned back around, uncertain how to respond.

Her Papa's silence was short-lived, replaced by cries that quickly rose in volume. He leaned into her as if her small frame could uphold his tall body.

"Oh, Aggi…," he wept. His long black hair covered her face.

She gave him an obligatory hug, tucking her small arm loosely around his waist. *He is sad, too,* she tried to convince herself.

The priest stood before them all, book open in his hands. "We commit to You the body of Kamelia Josella Farusi in the Name of the Father and the Son, the Holy Spirit. Amen."

He shut his book with a snap and looked directly at Agata.

The three exterior bells clanged loudly. Agata looked up at her Papa, released her arm, and slid her right foot, followed by her whole body, into the plush arms of her Nonna. The final bell signaled their goodbye.

How will I live without her?

2
AGATA

The September sky filled with clouds that could tell stories of their own. They provided a scrim for the pinkish morning glow dappling across sleepy buildings and sneaking into corners of campos, where shopkeepers scuffled out to greet their neighbors at the community well. Behind every morning coffee was a diligent woman first awake in her home to welcome her family with the aroma of a new day.

In the campo of San Canciano sat a bakery house, especially loved by its neighbors. Inside, Guilelma Josella, with hunched shoulders and thick hands, made her way back into it with a whole bucket of water. "Nonna," as she was known to Agata, shut the front door behind her and put down the bucket. She stared out the window as if lost in her thoughts. Dark gray circles cradled her eyes.

The bakery had a door that led to an inner hallway lined with hooks for coats and a stairwell in front of it that went up two flights to their living quarters. Inside the second floor was Nonna's humble, warm apartment, with a long plank table at its center. Black mourning fabric hung over its entrance and the doorway to its single bedroom, which Agata had not left since the day of her mother's funeral.

Dreams came and went. Agata could see the outlines of her mammina, her light, wavy hair floating and fairy-like as if she were a mermaid submerged in the sea. Mammina's big brown eyes sparkled with affirmation and laughter.

Agata looked around, startled. She could hear her voice—she sang so lightly and beautifully. But as soon as Agata heard it, it began to fade.

"Mama?" she called out desperately. "Mama?"

Then the dream darkened beneath strips of black cloth waving, a cacophony of fabric blanketing the windows and mirrors, and the sound of Papa's violin whirring and playing erratically. She heard him yelling in the background to stop their laughter.

"How can anyone concentrate?! Do you know what it takes to make sure you have food in your mouth, ribbons in your hair?"

The violin stopped. Papa's yells grew to a roar. "Stop laughing."

Her songs became quietened. A whisper, a hush.

"I'm still here, my darling girl," her mother's voice echoed softly in the dream.

Then came the flash of red. Blood streamed down the hall and onto the floor. So much blood. Her Nonna screamed as she came in the door from the *fornari*. "I'll just be a bit…"

Agata, sobbing and rubbing her forehead, looked down at her mother's head lying in her lap.

"Mama, Mama…" She turned to Nonna. "I only went outside for a second, Nonna. I promise, I promise."

Agata's eyes opened wide. Her entire body stiffened from the shock of the dream and then relaxed. She looked around, recognizing her Nonna's room. Her stomach hurt. Her head throbbed. Her body softened in the familiarity of her bed. Then the pain returned with the memory of yesterday: Mammina was gone. Agata's face squeezed tightly as the sobs came in a rush.

Agata forced herself to sit. Her stomach rumbled. How long had she slept? She needed to help her Nonna with the water for coffee. She got up, left her room, moved past the empty table, and headed out the apartment's front door.

Her footsteps creaked at the top of the stairwell. Nonna was at the bottom of it, sweeping.

"Madre Benedetta," Nonna shrieked and dropped the broom, startled by Agata's sudden appearance. She gathered her long rust-colored skirt and rushed up the stairs to her. "Agata! It's so good to see you up. Now, you mustn't rush. Let's come back in and sit for a minute at the table, and I'll get you something to eat." Nonna straightened to hide her crying, all her focus on her granddaughter's needs. Gray and brown strands of wavy hair slipped out of her bun, framing her pale, full face. *Oh no, how much sleep had Nonna lost?* "Oh, Holy Maria, this way, this way. Sit," Nonna prodded, aiding her along and into the kitchen.

She urged Agata toward a seat at the kitchen table. "Now you must get some food in you. It's been days, and you've hardly had a thing. You're hungry, yes?"

Nonna had a way of suggesting what a person wanted even if they didn't know what it was. Agata swallowed and nodded. As Nonna busied herself in the kitchen, Agata sat shivering in her thin nightgown, which felt damp and clung to her too tightly. She found herself having to forcibly blink herself awake, her gaze trying to keep up with her grandmother's sharp, busy movements. Nonna placed a sweet brioche on the table before her, Agata's favorite, then sat down with her granddaughter for just a moment before popping up again.

"Let's get you some simmered milk then. Something to wake you up from the inside," Nonna said with a wink, getting up as if Agata had asked for it to be delivered to the table quickly.

Nonna fiddled with the copper pots on the stove, moving aside a bubbling pot of soup as she searched for the right-sized container to heat the milk.

Agata examined the room from the long-planked table where she sat chewing the brioche, mesmerized by the billowing, black fabric fixed across every window and mirror, moving wildly as if possessing its own will, waving with the breeze, drifting through the open shutters.

Nonna looked up from her fiddling. "Faustina, it's you!" Nonna exhaled sharply as their neighbor came through their open door.

"Sorry to burst in. I was panicked when I saw the abandoned broom at the bottom of the stairwell," Faustina said as she delivered the broom, leaning it against the doorframe.

"She just got out of bed... ...first time in three days." Then, in a whisper just loud enough for Agata to overhear: "She's still a bit sad, I think...as am I."

Faustina nodded in reply to Nonna's short admission and bowed head while sneaking in small glances toward her.

Nonna crumbled up her apron in her fingers and tensed her shoulders, a sign to Agata of her nervous agitation.

"Have you seen him at all?" Faustina mustered.

Nonna rolled her eyes, then shook her head before turning to her granddaughter. "Agata, dear, are you okay with getting yourself a clean dress from the trunk while Faustina and I get the water ready for some coffee?"

Agata nodded, and the ladies continued. Agata walked away to her room, then peeked out her bedroom door to listen and spy on them through the open kitchen door.

"He's roaming the streets for all I know," she overheard Nonna report to her friend. "He was a whimpering mess the entirety of the funeral and wouldn't put that damn instrument down; the shame of it. All of Castello, whispering and making faces." She sighed loudly. "I thank God it wasn't here in San Canciano. What would the neighbors say?" She looked from side to side as if someone might be listening before continuing, "He will ruin us, I say. My Niccolo had such *buono fame*, a reputation for honesty and hard work. But him..." She paused before adding emphatically, "It's hard to temper the talk. The water rolls in and out of these canals, swirling any bit of gossip. It can only make its way back to you. It's too tempting not to join in. You know what they say?" Nonna paused, "The character of the Venetian people is like the tide."

Faustina joined in, "*Sei mesi, sei mesi.*"

A light from the bedroom window distracted Agata from eavesdropping. She walked over and flung it open, allowing a whoosh of warm air to blow in. She closed her eyes and let the breeze skim over the top of her head, moving a few of the loose brown hairs on top that tended to tendril and clump when in need of washing. A sudden streak of light moved across her eyes, and she blinked them open.

The morning sunlight glinted against the blue shutters opening at the window across the alleyway. In the vacancy of the opening, two long gray ears rose slowly, revealing two matching dark buttons below them. The little flat rabbit puppet appeared before being jerked back down again. Its eyes and ears quickly reappeared, barely peeking over the edge of the windowsill. A smile crept onto Agata's face as Gabriele revealed himself, holding the rabbit. He, too, let his familiar flicker of a grin show with a playful glint in his eye to match.

"You, okay?" Gabriele asked, leaning over his windowsill.

The Sellas family's lute shop stood directly across from the bakery. Gabriele's and Agata's windows, both two stories up, faced each other, with the narrow calle below them.

"I'm not sure," Agata replied, shrugging and nodding at the same time. Gabriele shook his rabbit's cloth head before bobbing it up and down in a nod, jesting with her.

Gabriele and Agata had made a series of puppets from scraps and bits of things they gathered from their homes; the lute shop was full of fascinating leftovers of wood chips and snippets of dried string. Most of their puppets were animals made to represent one family member or another, or a few notorious characters in San Canciano. Because both families owned shops, they always overheard funny stories about their neighbors. That was how the two of them first connected, chatting between chores and helping their families with their shops. The puppets became a way to tell each other about their days.

"Hi, Aaaaagiii." Gabriele's little sister, Sophia, popped up next to Gabriele to peek at Agata. Agata took care of her as she would an older sister, and Sophia tended to follow Agata around every chance she got.

"Hi, Sophia," Agata said

Something unclamped in her as she spoke. Gabriele always made her feel at ease. Even so, she didn't have much to offer in response. She felt too raw, achy, and shocked. Children somehow picked up on such "unspokens" when together. Adults were different, needing descriptions, vocalized feelings, and long sentences. Children knew better —that playing it out while not saying a lot about anything made one feel more normal for a while, as if the biggest shock in the world didn't just happen. Sophia grabbed the rabbit from her brother, and he bent down to tickle her, eliciting a giggle from his sister.

Agata realized her Nonna and Faustina had stopped talking. She made herself still—then heard his angry steps banging across the wood floor of the quiet apartment.

"Papa!" Agata gasped in a whisper. Her small body tensed, and she turned back to look at Gabriele. The fear on his face mirrored the chill in her body.

3
GUILELMA

Tucked inside her beloved bakery house, Guilelma recounted how thankful she was for the Sellas family. It was no surprise that Faustina liked to check in on her and Agata regularly, though it remained a comfort. Faustina had always been Kamelia's dearest friend. Guilelma and Alba Sellas had shared a friendship long before they had daughters.

That day, Faustina was still talking when Guilelma heard the loud stomp from upstairs. She had to get back down to see whether a customer had come.

"Guilelma! Where's my daughter?" Pietro shouted at her, eyes flashing.

"Now? He comes now, just when we got Agata out of bed?" Guilelma huffed as she looked at Faustina.

They looked up as Pietro tromped in defiantly through her open apartment door.

Guilelma knew she couldn't back down and retorted, "She has been here, in my care for three days, so that she wouldn't be alone, which you might have known if you could have paused your feelings for a moment. Where else do you suppose a ten-year-old girl in need of comfort would go?"

Pietro looked unconcerned. "Well, I'm tired. I've been through a lot. I would think you might have more sensitivity. I didn't realize I had a curfew on my grief," grumbled Pietro as he approached her. "I want to see my daughter and be in my bed."

Guilelma had a lot she wanted to say in return. She was smart enough to know that Pietro became a bear whenever he felt he wasn't in charge. She gave him a long, hard stare instead, and he gave her one right back. A moment of tension stuck in the room.

Faustina broke the quiet. "I've got to get back to the house. Matteo will be wondering where I am." She reached out and touched Pietro's shoulder on her way out. "How are you, Pietro?"

"Doing the best I can," Pietro muttered.

In truth, Guilelma viewed Pietro as an entitled child. He hadn't paid any rent for all the years he and Kamelia lived above them. How could she charge them? Kamelia was her daughter. What would he expect now that Kamelia was gone? Guilelma was afraid to leave him with Agata alone, considering her vulnerable state.

Guilelma looked through his tantrum and saw the weakness behind it. He was hungry and tired. She double sniffed at the air. He was definitely unwashed. God knew where he had spent those three days after the funeral. He might be the musician in the family, but after so many years, she had learned how to play him. Today, she would play the compassionate mother-in-law, utilizing her best *dolce manière.*

She spoke directly and emotionlessly to calm him. "Agata is tired and misses her mother. She needs her rest and someone who can attend to her throughout the night," she persuaded. "You are tired as well. You should let me take care of her so you can rest. You've been through such an ordeal. You must be exhausted. Let me send you up some soup and wine to help you sleep."

She paused to let Pietro navigate her challenge. Guilelma parted her lips while giving her eyebrows a subtle raise as she moved away from him, gathering and convincing.

She continued. "I was starting a bath for Agata. She has spent three days in bed. We've had an anxious wait, and finally, an hour ago, she woke up. The poor girl *has* lost her mother," she said, her hands exclaiming for her. "She is out of sorts, too." She then turned her back on him and moved toward the cupboard. "I've got a half bottle of wine and a loaf, of course."

She pushed the bottle of wine to the end of the table nearest him. It rotated slowly and deliberately down the planked surface, coming to a complete stop when it met the knuckles of his hand.

He closed his eyes and tightened his lips. Guilelma listened as he released a long sigh before glancing down at the bottle. Her bread and the smell of *sopa de spessati* filled every corner of her little house. She watched as Pietro took the bait. He grasped the bottle. She had won.

"I'm here, Papa," Agata called out to him, revealing herself from where she hid in Guilelma's room.

Pietro turned from Guilelma and spread his arms wide, the wine in one hand and his instrument still dangling off the fingers of his other.

"My Aggi. Come here. Hug your father."

His smile looked forced. Guilelma huffed to herself.

Aggi walked into his arms.

"My girl, my girl, we will get through this," he said and rubbed the back of her head hard with his thumb as he balanced the violin on his fingers.

Agata stood rigidly and looked at Guilelma for help. Guilelma immediately moved to the stove and scooped the warm, hearty pea and pancetta soup into a bowl.

"Take this," she directed Pietro, extending the soup bowl toward him. "Enjoy it while it's warm and get to your bath and your bed."

Heat rose up her body to Gulielma's heart as she watched Agata's pallid cheek press against Pietro's chest. His violin, still in his grip, pushed against her back. He let go of Agata, stuck the bottle of wine under his arm, and grabbed the bowl with both hands.

"Take care of my Aggi," he instructed her and then moved one available finger down the side of his daughter's cheek. He clunked upstairs with the loud proclamation he'd exuded on his way in.

Guilelma let out an exasperated sigh and clutched her chest.

Agata waited until her father's stomping had receded, then ran to her. "Nonna, please don't make me go with him. I want to stay with you forever."

"Oh, my dear," Guilelma replied. She took her granddaughter in her arms. "Someday, you will see that you are capable and strong enough to live all on your own. But for now, you needn't worry. Your Nonna has enough snap in her, and you will stay right here where I can protect you."

Guilelma gave her a big smooch on the forehead and held her tight. As she rocked her granddaughter for a while, a wash of anxiety spilled from the top of her head down to her tightening chest, where it spread and pooled. She hoped to God that she could keep her promise for as long as Agata needed her.

Weeks passed as they did when the cadence of life ticked on. Guilelma rose early every morning to fetch water, sweep out her shop, and stock her shelves with her bread. She would take her loaves to the *fornari* just a block away, who baked them in his ovens. She was proud of her neighborly relationships. She and her husband, Niccolo, had built them together over many decades before he passed. Guilelma felt she honored him by them and the lifeblood he poured into them. Eventually, she would pass all of that down to Agata. It was all on Guilelma to make sure that happened.

While their schedules got back to normal, she wondered whether Agata ever would. Could she heal from the loss of a mother when so young? She had already been such a serious girl compared to her Kamelia, whose smile entered the room before she did. Agata's dark brows hung low over her eyes, much like her father's, and she did not give away her smiles so easily.

A bell chimed at the front door, interrupting her thoughts.

"*Bondi*!" rang out Benedetta Betranozzi, her faithful old friend who walked in the open doorway.

Benedetta and her husband, Franco, lived around the corner from her bakery, which was also home to their print shop. Franco was quiet but not serious. He had a large mustache and inky hands. His wife was tall for a woman her age, her hair faded from a dull red, her small dark eyes constantly flashing. Benedetta was like a loud carrier pigeon, gathering news from this corner and that, and always stopping to deposit it at Guilelma's bakery counter.

"Everyone knows Guilelma's bakery is the place to pick up *ciacole*, as well as their daily *pan bianco,*" Benedetta would always remind her in not-so-quiet whispers.

Because the bakery was central to their community, Guilelma's neighbors frequented the shop to check in on her. She was grateful for them, the business that kept her hands moving through bivolo dough, and the endless tasks needed to keep up the bakery. She especially cherished the Betranozzi's, her emotional support and business confidants.

"How's our Agata?" asked Benedetta, who then glanced over at the empty bench where the girl would often sit.

"I don't know, Benedetta. She is up every morning and faithful to help me where Kamelia used to, but she is quieter than she was. She is more herself when Pietro leaves," answered Guilelma.

"Is he still staying upstairs?" asked Benedetta. She put her elbows on the counter, closing the space between them.

Guilelma nodded, trying to ignore the chaos his name alone brought on her. "He's in and out like the wind. I assume he has work commitments, or he feigns them. Kamelia used to confide in me that most churches stopped hiring him. There are a slew of brilliant violinists in town. I'm sure any one of them would be easier to deal with." She paused. "Tsk, but that violin never leaves his side."

"Franco mentioned it has been weeks, and you really should go over The Book," Benedetta recommended. "You can always bring Agata with you."

"No, no. Both Faustina and Alba insist she can stay and play with the children anytime I need her to." She nodded. "You're right. I should do that and get back to the norm. It will help."

Guilelma's words were more to convince herself than just a simple reply to Benedetta. Two more women then entered the shop, doubling the noise with their conversation.

"It *will* help. See you Friday." Benedetta winked and threw a kiss, and Guilelma watched her skirt, and her certainty whirl out the door.

Guilelma prided herself on being a savvy businesswoman. After the death of her husband, she was determined not to let any part of their business slip. She could not leave her fate to chance. She had a trusted friend in her, Nico's confidant, Franco Betranozzi. Every Friday, after the noon rush, Guilelma swept up the bakery and sent Agata across the alley to the Sellas family. Guilelma made her way down to Betranozzi's print shop. Franco was usually seeing the last of his customers off at about that time, right before putting his closed sign up on the exterior door. She'd wait for him to change out of his dark apron, and then he'd carry out for her what looked like a large mass of papers: the Farusi Bakery Libro Segreto—their secret book, and master ledger for the bakery. Franco took time to go over the open page line by line as she showed him her expenses for the week: the number of loaves and bivolo sold and the amount owed the *pistori* and *fornari*. That happened only after he'd poured each of them a generous cup of red wine. Benedetta was never around for these Friday meetings. She would pop in after an hour with a snack but made a point to keep the conversation business-focused. She respected her friend, making such an effort in a man's world.

"How are you doing, Mina?" Franco asked. His ink-stained fingertips topped off her wine glass.

"You are looking tired today."

"This life. I worry so about Agata. The girl was already quiet. She was so close to her mother. It's Pietro. I can hardly bear to look at him. I am quite certain that I caught him fumbling around looking for this." She tapped the top of the ledger with two fingers. "He feigns he desperately needed a warm meal, 'the least you could do for me in my state '." She let her anger vent in her friend's presence.

"Hmmm," replied Franco. He folded his hands near his face as he listened.

The sun had set outside, and the darkness lent an atmosphere of purposeful isolation between the friends. His lips parted with an audible smack.

"There are ways to protect you and the years of work you and Nico have put in. But more importantly, we must come up with a way to protect our Agata."

He put his middle fingernail to his lips and began to tap it in double time, looking lost in thought. Franco then moved his head toward hers, gazing at her through his bushy eyebrows.

"I think I have an idea!" he declared in a whisper.

"Why, that secret book must be a book of secrets! We are hush-hush around here," announced Benedetta, who'd appeared and placed a plate of *cicchetti* of *polpette* and olives between them.

The aroma of cooked meat wrapped around the room, mingling with the smell of ink. Benedetta placed her hands on her hips and gave her husband a sly wink. He arched his eyebrows. "Don't be quiet on account of me," she replied flirtatiously.

Franco wrapped his arm around his wife's full waist. "Oh, just bread and ledgers, my love. What goes in and what comes out. Nothing for you to be concerned with," he teased. "Sit with us, and let me pour you a glass of wine, my dear. Those meatballs smell divine."

4

AGATA

gata awakened to the sound of the *Marangona,* the morning bell.

It's time to fetch the water, she thought. The women in her campo would be up early to warm up kettles for morning coffee and soup to stew for the autumn day. Agata stretched her arm across the mattress and felt the cold blanket with her palm. Nonna had already left her side of the bed.

She jumped up and grabbed a long, gray sweater she'd laid across the top of the trunk at the foot of her bed. She put it on and ran her hands down its length. She'd worn it so much the fibers were pulled in some places- it was her favorite since her mammina had knitted it for her. Agata's feet hit the cold floor, her mind more awake than her eyes, and the morning more awake than the sun. The big orb hid beneath a low, gray mist, not having seen fit to find its way through for several days.

She knew it likely wouldn't be that day either.

It was November in Venice—two months since she smelled the bloom of a camellia or heard her mother's voice. Two months since Agata found her lying on the floor in a pool of blood in the hall of their beloved family bakery. After a quick scan of their quiet kitchen, Agata made her way out the front door and looked up at the closed door of her father's apartment. Not ready for another encounter, she hastened down the stairs and through the bakery to find her Nonna so she could help fetch the day's water. In the low mist, Agata couldn't see the well she knew was at the campo's center, just steps from the doorway of their shop. She decided to trust her feet to lead her there, rewarded with the quiet melody of women's voices.

On their lips was *Il canto de Natale*, a Christmas hymn:

Gesu Bambino
Nell'umile capanna
nel freddo e povertà
é nato il Santo pargolo
che il mondo adorerà.
Osanna, osanna cantano
con giubilante cor
i tuoi pastori ed angeli
o re di luce e amor.
Venite adoremus
venite adoremus
venite adoremus
Dominum.

Some of the younger women sang with such lightness, without strain. It was a wonder their buckets had any water in them. The low voices carried in the mist. She picked out her Nonna's voice: a deep alto, plain and steady. Signora Betranozzi sang louder than they all with a resonant mezzo tone, her vibrato as heavy as her usual opinions. Agata's feet halted her. She heard a pure sound that sat above the quiet chorus. The women lowered their voices so as not to drown it out. Smiles softened on their cheeks. They looked at Aggi, their nickname for her, tenderly. It was not 'til she saw them all staring that she realized it was her voice carrying through the mist and the quiet work of the women. Tears rolled off her face, blending with the low clouds, and took over the words barely whispering out. Her quiet sobs were absorbed into the aria of their voices, their protection and love enveloping her pain and carrying her song. Nonna approached her, holding her heavy bucket. She dropped it to the ground and encircled her arms around her granddaughter, continuing to sing and sway with her in union.

"Venite adoremus."

As the song's last words rang out, the women also placed their buckets on the ground and gave her a small clap.

The women continued to sing, rejoining their cycle of coming and going from the well, looking back over their shoulders with soft goodbyes and affectionate gestures. The carol drifted out to the corners of their square, finding its way into the kitchens and storefronts of San Canciano as Nonna picked up her bucket and sauntered down the lane with her granddaughter.

"Venite adoremus, venite adoremus..." they both sang together.

Agata held the exterior bakery door open for her grandmother. Once inside, she placed her hand next to Nonna's on the metal handle, and together, they managed to heave the bucket down the back hall with a childish giggle.

They continued to hum as they walked the bucket up the stairs to Nonna's apartment door. The heavy bucket landed with a plop, much more complicated than either of them anticipated. The loud splash over the sides of the bucket, wetting their dress hems, sent laughter rippling down the hall. The pair stopped when they saw the front door to her apartment hanging wide open. They looked inside, then at each other, and then back inside again, curious about the noise coming from Nonna's kitchen.

Seeing her Papa, Agata let out a sigh. He was picking up things, utensils and plates, moving them here and there as if searching for something. Their laughter must have made him realize he was no longer alone, and he began shouting.

"Where can someone find something to eat around here?" he grumbled. He picked up the large stockpot on the stove and looked under it before slamming it down.

"For God's sake, where's the coffee?"

They watched as he stammered and stumbled around. Agata took one long step backwards and slid behind her Nonna.

"It is early, Pietro," Nonna replied, shielding Agata with her hands on her hips. Usually, you are in bed, and you don't notice that water must be fetched and carried up to start the day. As for breakfast, you are welcome to a *bivolo*. They were just delivered from the ovens. Coffee will take a bit longer."

"I don't know what you are fussing over," Pietro retorted. "I work late and assume breakfast from a woman's hands should be the first thing I greet in the morning. Not you're grumbling about this or that."

"This or that is my home, my business, and my welfare. You are treading on a thin line if you think I owe you anything. You get as much as you do, so that my granddaughter is taken care of."

Papa laughed. "Old woman, we both know this place is mine. You cannot live forever. And one day, we will see what our beloved *Serrenissima* has to say about that." He shook his head and shouted, "Don't mind me. I'll be upstairs working."

He walked out, leaving her front door open so that his stomping lingered in the stairwell. Nonna's jaw clenched, and she let out a groan.

A moment of joy with her grandmother only seconds ago transformed into a hard slap of anxiety. Agata couldn't tell whether it was anger or pain that caused her grandmother to double over in front of her. Agata rushed to her as she stood half-bent, seemingly unable to move. Nonna's hand darted to her heart, and she reached behind her, trying to find the kitchen chair. Agata responded immediately, pushing the chair behind her knees.

"Nonna?" she pleaded, helping her to sit. "Nonna, are you okay?"

Agata couldn't take her eyes away from her beloved grandmother, watching as she closed her eyes and gulped in several deep breaths of air. Finally, her eyes blinked open.

"It's fine, child. I'm fine. You know your Nonna. I get so riled up by him. I shouldn't let him do that. He is your father."

"It's okay, Nonna. I want you to be okay."

Nonna reached across the table and gave her hand a reassuring squeeze. It had less grip than usual. The joy Agata was used to seeing in her Nonna's face was there, except now it cast a shadow over her eyes.

Agata swallowed hard.

The violin began upstairs, one arpeggio after another—again and again. Nonna shook her head and tried to force out a chuckle. Instead, Agata watched her lips tighten.

"Would you fetch your Nonna a drink of water from the bucket?" she asked. She gave her granddaughter a quick wink and revealed a slow, heavy smile. "I'm going to sit here a bit and catch my breath, my dear. Why don't you go get dressed?"

The days passed. Agata awoke with the sun in her room seeming brighter than usual—she must have overslept. She heard an unfamiliar squeaking noise outside her bedroom. Again, Nonna's place beside her was empty; she must have been busy with her chores in the bakery below. Agata slithered out of bed, picked up her sweater, pulled it over her arms, and tiptoed to the door of the kitchen. She stood there a moment, looked around, and noticed the other person in the room: her father. He sat with his back to her, his feet propped up on the table. He held a sheet of music up with one hand and moved his other arm back and forth like a mindless lever as he ate a cold polenta triangle, dipping it in and out of his coffee.

The chair squeaked as if crying out below him as he rocked back and forth on its hind legs, front legs suspending in the air before settling down again. Agata wasn't sure what to do. She had never spent much time alone with him and wasn't sure she wanted to. Instinctively, Agata turned to sneak back to her bedroom and change out of her nightgown, but the floor creaked, and he heard her.

He looked over his shoulder. "Well, if it isn't my Aggi? Good morning! How about some breakfast with your Papa?"

Agata stood dumbfounded and tried to find the courage to shake her head no.

"Nonna needs me for chores," she managed to mumble. She stood hidden in the doorframe, showing only part of herself to him.

"You should have some of this polenta," he invited. "Your Nonna, she is a wonder."

Agata froze, wanting to move, but her body wouldn't obey her.

He chuckled. "Have it your way, but could you fill up my coffee before you go?"

Agata didn't want to worry Nonna about seeing her Papa in the apartment. She knew he came and went, but he never stayed there long. It was different when her mama had been alive—when they would have family breakfast and dinner at Nonna's table every day.

That night, she whispered to herself before falling asleep: "*Wake up early. Wake up early.*" She hoped to miss him by waking sooner to help Nonna. Her eyes popped open the next morning; it was darker. Phew! She had done it! She got out of bed and started toward the bedroom door. But then she heard the squeak again.

"Good morning, dear daughter…," his voice trailed over to her before she could make it past the doorway.

Agata's shoulders drooped. "I have to help Nonna, Papa."

Day after day, the same routine: *Wake up early. Wake up early.* However, it seemed a little darker every morning when she did: slurp and squeak. And her continued prayer that she didn't have to spend time with him.

Agata was relieved that Papa didn't spend all morning at their table each day. As soon as she'd come back with Nonna and a bivolo from the ovens, she would head upstairs to complete her chores. She'd tiptoe quickly and quietly up the stairwell, peeking her head slowly around the apartment door —just to be sure he was gone. Agata learned over time that every move he made was a show. It was easy to hear him bumping around his apartment upstairs on the top floor. At hearing his movement, she'd run into the safety of her Nonna's kitchen and push the door shut.

Papa had always made her uneasy. He was so frequently gone working and performing with his violin that Agata, Mammina and Nonna became a tightly knit trio, like a woven braid that didn't have room for a fourth strand. Agata saw the cautious looks exchanged by her grandmother and mammina before Papa entered the room and heard their whispers after he'd left. For this reason, Agata had deemed him unsafe. Mammina distracted him from Agata when he came home. But with Mammina gone, how was she to know what to do with him?

There was an exception to her caution. One noise she couldn't entirely pull herself away from was when her father practiced his violin. He always began by tuning with a long discretionary stroke with his bow and fiddling with the pegs. She knew from the intensity in his face that he could read and interpret every moment in that singular action. He'd wriggle the same note this way and that as if he could bend it to his will. He would do this with several notes till they submitted to his desired pitch. Once satisfied, he would let loose, executing the same scales she almost knew by heart. He played them chord by chord and followed each with a series of notes that fell as if each were being pushed off the dock and into the sea.

After this, he'd play music. Agata could usually tell what kind of mood he was in by the songs that followed. Some days, he played with long, fluid strokes that sounded like gondolas whooshing and swooshing through the canal. Other times, it sounded like several sounds at once, like being in the middle of the Rialto market, his bow striking and squawking. And often, sadness haunted the melody. Not just long notes, but notes that clung together from one to the next. With these songs, he tended to pause as if taking a breath to feel the next thought. Agata thought those songs were the prettiest. They made her mammina feel near, as though she might walk in the door any second, and she could run up and put her arms around her waist as if the loss of her was just one of her terrible, terrible dreams.

One morning, as Agata worked busily with her daily tasks: making the bed, wiping down the kitchen, and sweeping the floors, she found herself with a series of notes stuck in her head that wouldn't leave. It was the same song

Papa had played every day that week. She practiced repeating the notes repeatedly until she thought she knew them, and they felt like hers.

"Wow! Very good, Agata! I have a songbird." Papa surprised her as he stood with his arms folded against his chest at Nonna's kitchen table. "I should have known with two parents like yours, you'd find the gift."

She squeezed the broom handle tight and winced. A heat spread over her cheekbones.

"Nothing to be shy about, child. The first phrase you got right, but that note right before the end is a little lower, like this." He moved his finger up and down while humming back the notes she had felt so connected to all morning.

"Now you try. Follow my finger."

Agata hummed back quietly, her eyes glued to his hand, desperately avoiding any eye contact with their proximity.

"Good. Now, keep working on it. Your mind will start to remember."

Nonna came around the corner and saw the two of them together. She gave Agata a protective look that asked *Are you okay?* Agata felt caught and didn't respond. Papa shot around and then coolly grabbed a triangle of polenta.

"Good morning, Mina," he said, chomping with a mix of cockiness and ease. "Getting a bite of food before I go."

He turned around and gave Aggi a quick wink, which made her feel that she had helped him do something wrong. After that, neither of them saw him for a week.

When he finally returned, he was a disheveled sight. His white shirt was untucked, and his black hair clumped in long, unwashed strands. Agata's guard went up as soon as she saw him walk through the door.

He met her eyes. "How's about pouring your Papa some coffee?" he asked coyly, then sat down and laid a piece of paper flat on the table. Agata set the pot she'd been carrying on the table. In a flash, he grabbed hold of her hand. She started to pull back, but he took her index finger, which she had clenched into a fist, and forced it straight. He then put his hand around hers with his index finger placed gently over hers.

"Stay with me and listen," he instructed.

Agata studied the lines and marks on the scroll.

Her Papa hummed as he guided her finger up and down across the page. When they reached the second line, she recognized the melody she had been humming only a week before. It was the song! She looked up excitedly, almost forgetting it was him she was smiling at.

"Well, *mio, mio,* she smiles! You are not only becoming the young bloom your mother was, but it also appears she has given you her gift of song."

Agata never would have sought such attention or flattery, but hearing him recall her mother in such a way lit her up inside. She pulled her hand back and fumbled with it against the other.

"I'll teach you music, Aggi—my greatest gift. I taught your mom, too, how to harmonize. Do you remember her singing? It was beautiful." He paused and stared intently into her eyes.

"Wouldn't you like to be like your mama, Aggi?"

She looked up, daring to stare back at him.

"Yes, Papa," she said with a nod. "I would like that."

"I'll make a way," he promised.

After that, anytime she found herself alone, as she worked on her chores or walked back from the square, she sought out the waves of melody—her way of finding this piece of her mother. It unlocked a part of her she had been missing and filled her with light. She wanted more of that feeling and often daydreamed that her singing sounded so beautiful that a voice would join in her mammina's, singing proudly, brought back from the dark, so Agata would never have to be alone again.

One Friday afternoon, Nonna called up Agata, telling her they were going out and that Nonna would drop her off to play with Gabriele on her way to the print shop for her weekly meeting with Franco.

Pietro followed Agata out of the apartment. Agata skipped down the stairs.

"Coming, Nonna!"

Nonna stood rigidly at the base of the steps with her arms folded when she realized the two of them had been alone together. Nona narrowed her eyes at Pietro, who stood outside her apartment door with an apple in his hand.

"Good evening, Mina!" he taunted. And then he took a large bite out of the apple, one from her table, and turned to go back to his apartment, leaving her there to simmer.

5
GUILELMA

Ugh, Guilelma thought. *What is it about that man that rankles my insides?* She grabbed her granddaughter's hand and marched them away from him using the same types of loud stomps he always sent down her stairwell. Before they got out the front door, Agata gave a quick turnaround and called, "Bye, Papa!"

Guilelma yanked Agata out the door and walked her to the Sellas hastily.

Her head was in intense negotiations with itself. *I've got to do something.* She tried to outrun her thoughts by increasing her pace to the Betranozzi's. Her short legs moved briskly through the square, brushing by people, not wanting to take the time to say hello back to those who knew her. She swung the print shop door open with more force than she thought she had in her and let out a sigh of relief as she shut the door and then pushed her back against it.

Franco stood in the shop, busy with various chores. He stopped and straightened to look at her. "Is it that bad this week, Mina? Have the wolves been chasing you?" Franco teased, letting out a chuckle.

"Oof, that man," Guilelma grumbled. "Something must be readied. I feel he is up to no good, and I can't put my finger on it. He was eating one of my apples that came from my kitchen table. Can the man do nothing for himself?! Mark my words: *"Co quando la fame vien drento pa la porta lamor va for a pai balcony."*

Franco nodded. "Well, then. It's the perfect evening then to introduce you to my gift." He set an inkpot in the middle of the table, which hit the wood with a slight thud. Franco raised his eyebrows, and his eyes twinkled. He nodded to the right, indicating the chair next to him as he sat down. Guilelma moved toward him circumspectly as he poured her a glass of wine.

The darkness outside soon combined with the lit candles, inviting an isolated purpose across the room. Guilelma had emptied her wine glass quickly, and the pair spent some time bantering over *cichetti* with Benedetta. Guilelma, realizing how late it was, excused herself and shuffled home in a hurry; she wanted to get her quill and parchment hidden under the bakery counter before she went to collect Agata from the Sellas. She let herself in. Curiously, she hadn't needed to use the key she already had out—the door had pushed right open. She stared at the door, a bit puzzled. Had she been in such a huff earlier that she forgot to lock it? Guilelma set her things down and moved back to the front door. She stopped abruptly when she detected the squawking sound. She looked upstairs, and her heart thumped. *Squeak.* She knew that noise. Panicked, she rushed quickly to her apartment door. It was dark and quiet. Then she heard his voice:

"Very good! Now let's try this."

Guilelma was flush with anger by the time she marched up the last set of stairs. Though she hadn't been inside their apartment since Kamelia died, she didn't hesitate to push the door open. She let out an audible gasp.

Agata sat in Pietro's lap. He clung to her like a child would a small toy doll, one arm tightly around her waist.

Upon hearing Guilelma's gasp, Pietro turned them around to face the door.

"Welcome back, Mina!"

His ignoble response made her already distressed heart beat faster.

"I hope you don't mind me helping you out by picking up Aggi for you. We had a meeting for a special music lesson. She is doing so well that we decided that she would move back into the apartment with me so we could focus on her music."

Nonna froze; she was stunned.

"Don't worry about a thing. I already saw to it that Aggi's clothes were moved up here."

She glared at Pietro and tried to comprehend what he was saying, but even more so what she saw. In her hands, Agata gripped the arm of a small violin, looking as innocent as a babe in the woods. Guilelma crinkled her eyes in disbelief. When she opened them, instead of seeing defeat, she saw Pietro more clearly than ever. He may have seen an old woman running out of time with no options but the one he gave her. But he didn't see the ink stains hidden on her palm. She clenched her hand into a fist.

Life was busy at the bakery. Although the days were cold and darkened quickly, one could feel a certain promise in the air. Christmas had a way of doing that. Lights and gaiety adorned the squares and shopfronts from the smallest campanelli to the largest. In Venice, the promise of Carnival added that extra dose of fervor and excitement. Carnival got its start in October, pausing with the arrival of Advent before restarting again in time for a new year.

The excitement of the festivities escalated along with the darkening skies of winter, providing the perfect backdrop of secrecy and seduction that Venice was known for. For Guilelma, it only amped up her anticipation. The arrival of Christmas and Carnival would mean a city full of musicians and entertainers looking for work. Pietro would be away from home more often than not, which gave her the perfect excuse to enact her plan. Agata was still sleeping in her Papa's apartment. It made her shudder to think of it. Guilelma needed her plan to work. She made a sign of the cross and mumbled a quick prayer to the Holy Mother. The predictability of change was always lurking around the next dark corner. Guilelma tried not to give that too much credence.

She approached Agata, who lay in the bed. "Agata, be sure to help Faustina. I will join you as soon as I finish my errand." She kissed the top of her granddaughter's head. Agata seemed irritable with her leaving. Guilelma had to admit that she wasn't usually so elusive with Agata.

Awash in a strange mix of elation and determination, she set out on her mission. The sun hid behind a mask of clouds and blew crisp, clean air through Guilelma's short curls. She almost felt young again on the inside. On her exterior, she was an old woman with a limp. She ignored that fact and pressed on. She had a long walk ahead to reach her destination in Cannaregio. She didn't look back at Agata, who she could sense was staring out the window under her heavy, concerned brows. She moved quickly, acting as unhindered as an old woman could.

Somehow, during her last month with Pietro, Agata had gotten older, stubborn even. Her responses came out uncharacteristically angry. She found her granddaughter more observant, her face always clutched. It frightened Guilelma. The thought of Agata being hurt by the same man who darkened her daughter's sparkle gave her the persistence to keep moving. She would not let him squeeze out another life. Agata was what she lived for.

Guilelma walked the main road out of San Canciano and turned north. She avoided the waterway altogether by staying on the Strada Nova, a large artery that led through the middle of five central squares. She walked through Santi Apostoli, Santa Sofia, Santa Felice, Santa Fosca, Campo Della Maddalena, and finally across a small bridge that led her over the Rio di San Marcuola to a tiny, quiet neighborhood that seemed a world away. All these squares had churches, shops, and neighbors that shared a well, but none felt quite like San Canciano.

It was fate that she and Niccolo settled in San Canciano years ago. It was fate that they made lifelong friends in the Sellas and Betranozzi families. It was fate that Agata became friends with her mother's children. What she couldn't reconcile was how fate could have led Kamelia to marry that horrible man from nowhere, a man whose countenance was as dark as his eyes. Yet there he was, trying to claim his home in theirs. He had no affinity for it. It was greed that drove him. She was determined to drive him right back out. It wasn't revenge that steamed her; it was simply saving her dowry of love from her husband to protect her granddaughter. That man didn't deserve it. He didn't recognize love when it sat in his lap, literally, in the form of his beautiful, doe-eyed daughter. And now, in the form of her deep and intelligent granddaughter. Her mind churned those thoughts, and her body was determined to keep up with them. In no time, she looked up and saw she had reached her destination.

Guilelma spotted Franco Betranozzi waiting for her on a quiet corner and didn't care for how he eyed her. She was conscious that her episodes had slowed her down. She did not want to consider herself a woman in her twilight, but stress had taken its toll on her.

"*Bondi* Franco," Guilelma greeted as she crossed the street.

Despite the relief she felt at seeing him, she got a twist in her stomach. *I'm trusting you, old friend. Don't let me down.*

"Doing well, my friend? I hope the walk wasn't too bad," Franco replied in a concerned tone. She watched him try to hide it with his chummy grin.

She nodded, out of breath. "I'm ready." Her nerves made her speech sound grumpy. He held his arm out and she grabbed onto it. Then, quietly, her old friend led her down a narrow calle. They arrived at the only doorway along its path, made of heavy wood with a window covered in rod iron and a small sign that read: *Notaio.*

The two old friends walked in and gave the wooden door a firm shut.

6
AGATA

Agata shivered beneath her blanket. Finally, she got up and put her long gray sweater on, the one her mammina wove, whose fibers were frayed and pulled; surely, it would help. She couldn't stop shaking. Her thoughts drifted to her Nonna. Agata wished that she could hear her quiet snores next to her and snuggle up to her warmth. Tears rolled down her cheeks. She felt alone, cold. Was it the cold or loneliness for her Nonna that made her feel so awful inside? She couldn't tell. Eventually, the weight of her tears lulled her into a deep sleep. She dreamed vividly of singers out on the square, men shouting for purchase of their warm chestnuts, and lights, light, everywhere. The candlelight made the scene of her dreams blurry and frayed around the edges, much like the strands of her gray sweater.

A mask appeared behind a fiery candle, moving wildly and without reason. Then Agata saw them everywhere—more masks, some calling out to her. She felt afraid and unsure, so she turned around and began to run, perspiring and breathing hard.

Then she heard him: "It's okay, sweet girl, relax."

She woke up and opened her eyes to another mask. A white one. Behind it came a familiar voice, speaking softly to her as a shape sat on the floor beside her bed.

"Relax, my little beauty. There you go. That's it."

She had her eyes closed and tried to go back to the dream. Was the male voice a part of it? It felt funny inside. She couldn't name it.

"That's it," he said again.

She peeked open her eyes, and the man with the white mask let out a low hum. She squeezed her eyes shut again, and he pulled his hand from under her covers, stood up, and walked to the small kitchen. The black-caped shadow stood with his back toward her. She felt her eyes get heavy; soon, she was back to a heavy sleep, where the Christmas candles were shining bright and brilliant, making the dull cobblestones shimmer. The streets were void, and the people were gone. All that was left was the long black cape, billowing and large, walking away, filling the small *calle* as it left.

'*Quando el pare fa carneval, I fioi fa quaresema.*" Agata heard her Nonna's voice echo through her thoughts.

There was a Venetian saying that when the father went to Carnival, the children were in Lent. Without her Nonna watching out for her, Agata felt hunger pains. It was her Nonna who went to the market and put apples on the table and bread in the barrel-shaped basket. It was her big pot that was always full. Papa kept busy with other things and never seemed to remember what Agata needed. Their apartment smelled sour, with stacks of music and dishes on every surface. Agata did her best to clean it.

She had a small bed on the floor where she slept when her mammina was alive and Papa was home from playing in concerts. During Carnival, her Papa would come and go wearing his black cape and white mask. Agata didn't miss him with her mammina there, taking care of her. It was different now that she was gone. Her Papa was so busy he would go for days at a time, forgetting to tell her he was leaving. He'd come home and say he was sorry, and he missed her.

"Couldn't we be cozy on your little bed together?" Papa would say.

There wasn't much room for him. If Agata were already asleep, she'd wake and find him there on his own. It made her feel like a shadow lived with her on the inside. All she wanted was to move back with Nonna and make the shadow go away.

Her father spent so much time away from home. She was not sure, as she thought about it, whether she wanted him around at all. When he was home, he was demanding. He wanted his food brought to him and yelled at her if she didn't realize that he was hungry. He was always grumpy and smelly when he returned. It was up to her to wash his cape, black pants, and white shirt. She hated touching them. They had an odor to them that felt dark. It made her stomach twist up. Then he would leave again for days and climb back into her little bed at night and tell her again how he missed his dear little Aggi.

The violin lessons stopped. Papa angrily huffed that if she had the gift, he would have seen more of it by now. When he was away, and it was quiet, she'd find the pieces of music left lying around and let her finger trace the ups and downs of the notes. That morning, she lay on her stomach with the music splayed out in front of her. It felt good to hear the sound vibrate inside her chest as she hummed the notes with her ear to the floor.

Abruptly, Agata shot up and remembered it was market day. She made her bed as best as she could, grabbing her gray sweater on the way out. She tumbled down the stairs to see Nonna doing something strange.

When she came around the corner, she noticed how focused and quiet Nonna was as she stared down at the counter.

"Nonna?" Agata called.

Her grandmother looked up, taken by surprise but not secretive. "Come here, child."

It wasn't until Agata stood by her side that she saw the long quill in her hand.

She gasped, "Nooo-na."

Nonna smiled proudly and waved Agata's gaze toward the marks on the paper.

"Did you make these yourself, Nonna?"

"I did," Nonna replied confidently. "This is the letter 'G' for me, Guilelma. I've been practicing. Maybe I can find out how to make an 'A,' and you can practice."

Nonna stopped to look at her as she always did when she had something Agata needed to hear.

"Having your signature, Agata, recorded on paper is very powerful. Think of all the people whom you want to tell something important, but they can't all be there to see or hear you say it. Your name, signing these things you want, is as good as you telling your truth in person, for all to hear, for generations to come." She leaned a bit closer to Agata. "For now, this is our secret, and no one will know anything about it yet."

Agata moved close to trace the "G" with her finger, then looked up at her grandmother. "Today is our market day, Nonna," Agata reminded her. "I'm ready to go."

Nonna didn't look at her right away. Agata then realized Nonna had her Sunday dress on.

"Oh, Agata, I'm sorry. I have an important errand to run today. Benedetta said she would grab a few extra staples to get us through the week. We can go for an extra-long walk next week on market day."

Agata stomped her foot on the ground. She needed her weekly outing with Nonna. The clean air washed her insides from the shadow. "Nonna, why? Why can't we go today?" It wasn't like Nonna hadn't heard her.

It made her Nonna young again when they went to market together. Nonna would talk, and they'd walk arm in arm. How could Agata explain that to her? The words wouldn't come out.

"You know how much I love our outing day together, but this can't wait. You will forget about time with your old Nonna when you are having fun with Gabriele and his sisters. Now let's walk over, child, I'm running late." Nonna pushed her gently out the front door, locking the smell of yeast and loneliness behind them.

Agata breathed in the aroma of wood and warmth as they entered the Sellas' Lute Shop and scuffled to the stairwell. It was busier than the bakery ever was, with guitars and violins dangling from the ceiling, all filling up the space like additional family members of the already large Sellas brood.

"Good morning, ladies," Signor Sellas boomed. He held a violin by its neck, carving details into it with a small knife in his other hand. "I know a little girl who is anxious to see you, Agata." Signor Sellas smiled and gave her a quick wink before setting his attention back on the elegant piece of wood.

"Aggi, come and play with me," Sophia whined from the top of the stairs.

"I'm coming, Sophia," Agata said, irritated. She didn't know why Nonna couldn't put off this errand for another day. She thought Nonna was unusually distracted. Agata watched her and Gabriele's Nonna Alba share an extra-long hug before she left; they were secretly communicating with each other—Agata was sure of it. What were they saying? First, she was missing their special day out, and now her Nonna was hiding things? Agata sat angrily at the window as Nonna walked away, trying to hide her limp. But Agata saw her. Agata saw everything.

Her Nonna had grown more tired as of late. She would doze off before finishing her small glass of evening red wine. Agata would wake her and whisper: "It's time for bed, Nonna." She would place her unfinished glass on the table, cover her Nonna with the blanket she'd drag off her bed, and then quietly walk upstairs to her bed on the floor in the apartment above before her Papa got home. He got angry when she wasn't there. Sometimes, it was the middle of the night, and he might return clanging, smelling of spirits, and come to her. There were nights he wouldn't show up at all, and she'd spend the entire night alone in that apartment. Then there were the nights she woke up and found him beside her in her tiny floor bed instead of his own, lying out long on his side. She woke up early on those nights, not comfortable with him being so close. It made her feel like night itself had climbed inside her, even though the sun was about to rise. There was no way of knowing which kind of night it would be. She made sure always to stay the same. To remain quiet, consistent, and compliant—that was what stabilized his mood, what kept him from getting angry.

It was a slow morning at the Sellas house. Usually, the business of Gabriele's younger siblings crawling all over her made her forget about time. She could feel Nonna Alba watching her closely all morning from her corner chair. It made her antsy. Faustina appeared and suggested it was time to clear out the noise and get out for a walk.

The chain of Sellas children, plus one, meandered hand in hand along the canal. Agata held on with a fingers-only clasp at the end of the chain, still feeling disgruntled about her morning, letting them pull her along. She closed her eyes, let the December air soak in, and recalled the song Pietro had taught her. Agata used her free hand to count out the rhythm on the side of her skirt and hum the notes. Something inside her was released, like a locked door that had become unlatched. When she opened her eyes, the sky was the same gray color, but she could hear the Sellas children laughing, pointing at the *presipio* in the window shops.

"Can we look, Mother, please?" Sophia, Gabriele's younger sister, pleaded.

The line of children jerked Agata forward toward the display of nativity scenes, and Gabriele turned around and smiled at her. It was the smile of a friend who knew her. She smiled back and then noticed a frail old woman limping along the canal bridge. It was Nonna! She broke away from the chain of hands and ran toward her, eager to tell her how sorry she was for being angry. All she wanted was to feel her next to her again. She was the only one who made everything right.

But then Nonna stopped hard. Her breath looked caught in an inhale and stilled. Agata instinctively threw her arms around her. Nonna's hand moved in slow motion to her heart before her feet yanked her down to the cobblestone, bringing Agata down with her. Nonna's body lay still next to hers.

"No—naaah!" She smoothed her gray hair on her forehead and kissed her.

Gabriele was next to her in an instant. "She's breathing, Agata," he assured. "It's okay. She's going to be okay."

Agata fell back on her knees and cried like she never had before.

Two nights passed with Nonna resting in her bed. Benedetta and Alba took turns sitting beside her so Agata had someone to help them both. They brought over soup and posted limited hours for the bakery breads to be sold, with each of them taking turns sitting at the counter. Nonna went in and out of sleep, and every time she woke up, one of them was there. She would snigger at them, saying she was fine before drifting off to sleep again. She woke again on the third day, looking more herself. Agata was at her side, staring at her. When Nonna's eyes opened, she said: "Come here, child." Agata curled up into her and let quiet tears of relief fall.

"I guess I don't have to ask if you've seen your father?" She patted her arm while she spoke. "How many days has it been? Well, never mind. It's just us for now. Let's enjoy the quiet." Nonna kissed her forehead.

That evening, when Agata got up to pour herself and Nonna a bowl of soup for dinner, Pietro's footsteps stomped sluggishly upstairs. He pushed the front door open to Nonna's apartment, which hit the wall with a thud. Agata's shoulders tightened, and her fingers clenched the bowl's sides. He ignored Agata and swaggered around the corner to take in Nonna, who looked very much bedridden. Black circles cradled her eyes, and her unwashed hair stuck to her head.

"You can bring my bowl upstairs," he instructed Agata, then walked back out the door without so much as looking at her.

Agata's eyes bore into his back. His feet came to a halt when she didn't give him a response. Then he turned around and smirked at her. She swore she saw a glimmer of happiness in his eyes. He turned back and around and left, not bothering to shut the door behind him.

7
GUILELMA

Three weeks had passed since Guilelma met Franco on her secret errand. She had not been the same since. She remembered Agata running in haste to catch up to her and calling out her name. Guilelma recalled her mind spinning, her lungs out of breath. *Am I lost?* she remembered thinking. But she was crossing a small bridge near home. The water beneath it had looked like a mirage, smudging the recall of her actions with her fears. It was Agata who caught her as her knees buckled and brought her body to the ground. It was Gabriele who located a sheet to carry her home in, with the strong arms of Signor Sellas leading them back to the bakery.

All her life, Guilelma was known as someone who never sat down, who never needed tending. She proudly obligated herself to her mental checklist of duties every day. Her stringent expectations made it a very long list to check off. There was always a task to complete, a meal to prep for, a neighbor she might double her recipes for and check in on, not to mention the bakery and caring for Nico, Kamelia, and now, Agata. Yet there she was in her bed, no longer able to spin around and do. All she had was this repose.

She had spent more time resting in the last three weeks than she had allowed herself her entire life. It was a difficult change for her to negotiate. Franco helped her cope by coming up with a workable plan she felt comfortable with. He would get up early to help Agata get the *bivolo* to the *fornaio* down the road. Benedetta would assist in getting them back so Franco could open his shop. He'd arranged for the bread loaves to be delivered back from the *fornaio* who exploited their situation by charging a small fee, insisting he needed it to make the situation work. And so, with her friends' help, she could sleep longer in the morning and open her shop in two shorter shifts. Guilelma could then readily take money from customers while still enjoying the chatter of her neighbors without too much strain on her body.

Guilelma didn't want to say it aloud, but she felt some relief at the predictability of Pietro's inconsistencies. His response to any affliction aimed at his tender ego, however, was less easy to calculate. He was much like Venice, which seemed easy to understand in the daylight with its charm and shimmering waters. In the darkness, behind the many closed doorways and small walkways that led nowhere, lay a prevalent enigma. Like most Venetians, she had no idea where they led. When he was in the light and she could see him, all the iniquity grew blaringly visible. The dark sides of Pietro were like the gaming rooms of Venice: dark and secretive. She had no desire to learn all that went on behind them. Still, her time was running out. The inevitable decision ahead stared back at her with every thought of her son-in-law.

From all those recent changes, a new tradition was born. On Sundays, when her two dear friends, Benedetta and Alba, would sit on her bed with her after an afternoon of food prepping for the week, Benedetta would bring wine and Alba would bring cards, lightening the mood. They had done this for years, formerly around Guilelma's table. They knew their friend well and recognized that laughter was all that could allow her to forget she was sitting. This trio of women understood that the recognition of laughter implied contentment. They were intelligent, resourceful, and knew the power of togetherness.

It was mid-December, and Venice was well into the Carnival celebrations. The days had turned cold and dreary. The chill carried in any time the door swung open and swirled its way up the stairwell to their apartments. Pietro was home less frequently because of it and had proved as unreliable as ever. He would come and go at his leisure, keeping his inconsistent hours, always with his black cape swishing behind him and his white mask firmly in place.

Venice would not be who she is without her music lingering around every narrow calle and corner. The musical ensembles in St. Mark's Square and the string quartets in private parties and gaming rooms provided the template of sound that lured people to them. Their instruments were the backbone upon which the games, laughter, and gaiety balanced to create an aura that attracted people from around the globe. Opportunities arose daily for musicians to play their instruments and meet their lustful needs, especially during Carnival season. Guilelma imagined Pietro felt connected to those urges and the necessity of indulging them in his Serene City. Pietro lugged his violin like a young child with a toy doll, so he'd be acknowledged as somebody special.

Throughout the weeks of those new arrangements, everyone did their part to keep Guilelma and the bakery up and running—everyone that is, but Pietro. She had settled into her evening chair and sipped her small glass of wine during one sunset, looking forward to the small talk of a shared close to the day. She reflected on whether it was worth all the trouble. After finishing the dinner dishes, Agata shuffled over and slumped into the chair beside her. In seconds, her sweet snores took over the conversation. Her head fell back, and her body seemed almost lifeless. Guilelma grabbed a blanket to cover her and took in her growing grandchild.

Agata has changed more than ever this last month. She hated that Pietro roamed in and out so freely into her home and business. Her Agata, much like her Kamelia, had become more reclusive and to herself. Pietro was abhorrent to be around and a thief who took advantage of her; she feared how he might rage if she tried to kick him out. She pictured the bruises on Kamelia's arms that she tried to cover with sweaters. Her eyes filled with tears at the memory. Would he do something to hurt her, an old woman, to ensure she could no longer care for Agata? Or even worse, would he hurt Agata directly? *Had he already?* She had put too much weight on the girl when she intended to make her burden lighter. Agata's face showed it. Her countenance had darkened. Guilelma knew she couldn't allow the cycle of days of the girl rising dutifully to tend to the bakery and to her father's demands to go much further. Guilelma's plan was no longer working. She clucked at the weary sight of her beloved granddaughter and then looked up, into the looking glass on the wall—the physical reality of her weariness was more blatant than she wanted to admit.

Several hours passed, and the two snoozed quietly in harmony in their chairs. Agata was shocked out of sleep by seeing her Nonna across from her and panicked.

"I've got to go, Nonna! If he comes back, he will be angry!" Agata mumbled and, while barely awake, moved quickly to the front door. Her stocking-covered feet got twisted up in the confusion and landed her firmly on the floor.

"Oh, my dear, you must be still. Why don't you stay here tonight?" Guilelma cried. "He hardly ever shows on a Saturday," she persuaded.

Agata sat on the floor sobbing like a much younger child. Now fully awake and tired, Guilelma watched her unravel in front of her. She threw her arms around her.

"I'm tired, Nonna. I'm so tired," she cooed, abandoning her shell.

Guilelma's eyes brimmed with tears, which soon overflowed in anguish at the entrapment of the mess she felt herself in. As she cradled and shushed her granddaughter, who remained on the floor of her apartment, she reminded herself that she wasn't stuck. She had a way out. It was her bakery, her home, and her family. It was time to take back control- even if it was the last thing she did.

"Your Nonna is going to fix this, so you won't ever have to be afraid of him again. Do you understand? I will make this better."

"I don't want him to hurt you, Nonna." Agata sniffed loudly.

"No one is going to get hurt, not while ol' Nonna still has some snap in her," she declared, cupping Agata's face. Agata stood up and embraced her tightly.

She persuaded Agata back into bed with her, who had no trouble falling asleep quickly, and tucked herself against Guilelma's back for security. Guilelma listened to her wispy breathing, though sleep did not come to Guilelma. Her mind was a tug-of-war of surety and apprehension all at once, arguing with one another throughout the night. The decision was troubling. Could Agata forgive her for it?

She had reluctantly succumbed to the reality that she was not well. She felt it in her tired body, in those little skips in her chest whenever she grew worried. She decided that staying home from Mass that morning was the best option. How could she disrupt Agata from the hard sleep she was in? Plus, she would have to avoid the looks and murmurs from her neighbors. She felt the grimace on her granddaughter's face settle onto her own.

Guilelma was sitting at her kitchen table when the door pushed open. Benedetta had wasted no time marching straight from her pew across the square to Guilelma's front door, leaving Franco behind with little instruction.

"What is wrong?" Benedetta scolded, pushing the door to her apartment open without a knock. Her hands fisted onto her hips; her intense stare told Guilelma her melodramatic friend was concerned.

Guilelma put her finger to her lips. "Shh!" She cocked her head slightly toward her bedroom, where Agata lay sleeping.

Alba came panting up the stair's minutes later. "You could have waited a minute for me," Alba scolded Benedetta. "My hips don't move as fast as yours!"

They settled on convening as they always did for their Sunday evening weekly cards and wine. Alba would tell Faustina to take Agata for a couple of hours so they could talk. The women wasted no time that evening, immersed in conversation before the first glass of wine was poured. While sitting with her companions, Guilelma made her confessions. Her body had grown more fatigued than ever; she was sure it was giving her a message. The only way she could think to get rid of Pietro was to remove Agata safely from his reach. It would be a sacrifice. She risked spending her last days alone, without her beloved granddaughter. She risked Agata feeling abandoned. But she knew it had to be done. So, she disclosed her heavily burdened plan to them.

"Why can't I just take her, Guilelma?" exclaimed Benedetta, refilling their wine glasses to their rims. Alba quietly set the stage with a hand of cards dealt out between them on Guilelma's kitchen table as they had done for countless Sundays.

"Pietro is not only unpredictable but also angry. Can you imagine the fit he'd throw? You saw the display he made of himself in the church at Kamelia's funeral. He's acted out in so many places, he's quite unwelcome in most of them."

Guilelma took a long breath. "Besides, it would make no sense while I am still here."

Alba began crossing herself, which prompted the other two to do the same.

Guilelma continued, "He walks in and out here at all hours of the day, either mad at the world or completely smug. God knows what he does with his money. Is he booking jobs? The only ones left for him are secular venues. I don't know who else he has offended. How would Agata eat? Who would guide her and take care of her? He cannot be counted on to provide for her. The one thing I do know is I cannot count on him. I never know how he may respond from one mood to the next. It may have been the pregnancy that killed Kamelia and took her from us, but living with him is what caused her death. He broke her sweet spirit, and I cannot risk Agata landing in his hands by some legal quandary when I am not there to defend her. I am here now."

Alba broke the pause. "I think you have your answer."

"Then I will surrender my final days with her so she can be safe." Her words came out tear-filled but final.

The three women encircled each other in a hug of trust, their heads bent and foreheads touching, weeping with their friend.

"Well, what is going on here?"

The women pulled apart; their hands still clasped.

Pietro sniffed demonstrably at the air. "Don't you ol' birds cook on Sundays? Have Aggi bring me up some dinner." He flashed a sardonic smile, with his cape wrapped around his arm and his mask hanging under his chin, he turned and stomped up the stairs.

"I could ring that man's neck," Benedetta exclaimed.

8

GUILELMA

It wasn't easy for Guilelma to tell her granddaughter that she had to leave her. Her tears and choked vow of love blanketed her cheeks and spilled onto her granddaughter's. If there were one thing Agata would know more than any other truth, it was that her Nonna loved her.

Guilelma talked skittishly while combing the sides of Agata's hair with her hands:

"You need to be braver than you've ever been. You are going on a secret adventure. And to keep you hidden and safe is this special cloak Signora Betranozzi made just for you."

"Can I wear my gray sweater with it?" Agata asked, sounding agitated and fearful.

"Why, of course," Benedetta expressed. "The cloak was made to protect your sweater, too."

Agata pulled her sweater tight around her body.

Benedetta, standing next to Guilelma as she finished with Agata's hair, shook out the dark cloak she'd been holding and placed it over her thin shoulders almost reverently. Guilelma smoothed out the sides of it, explaining how it would be like a great shield whenever it was out in the night.

Guilelma observed the girl who peered back up at her. *She looks so small.* Guilelma choked back her panic, focusing on tying the cloak around her neck.

A quiet knock was heard at the door. Franco opened it and nodded at the visitor. Agata looked up and gasped. Guilelma realized that she recognized the man in the red jacket from her mother's funeral. Guilelma nodded at him, and he pursed his lips in an attempt at a smile.

"Good evening," he said, bending at the waist in a slight bow.

The women acknowledged him with head bows and then continued to fuss over Agata. Guilelma looked up at him but wasn't ready for his entrance—or his purpose there. *How could it be time?*

Benedetta pulled out a small black mask with black lace ribbon attached on either side. Guilelma knew she had sewn in her prayers with every stitch. "The final touch for your disguise."

As Benedetta went behind her to tie it on, Guilelma took her granddaughter's face in her hands.

"I love you. I will always love you. You will have nothing to fear anymore." She kissed her small forehead and lay her head on top of hers, soaking up the last touches of her granddaughter.

Guilelma approached the man in the red jacket and handed him a scroll. He unhooked his hand, which was clasped behind him, to receive it, and his red ponytail, tied with a neat black ribbon, fell to the front of his jacket with it.

"I will see she arrives safely. Then the gentle man spoke to Agata with his quiet, airy voice. "I'm going to need you to keep up with me, Agata. Your Nonna has asked me to be your protector."

Nonna watched Agata tuck her shoulders in as if she could make her body small enough to hide in her cape. "Nonna?" she asked, her frightened eyes shifting between her and the stranger.

Guilelma swallowed hard. "You can trust him. He is an old family friend."

"Your Papa and I knew each other as boys. We learned to play violin together," the man in the red jacket spoke.

"Will you tell my father where I am?" Agata demanded.

"He will take you somewhere safe," Guilelma injected. "He knows the city better than I and wants to help us. Do this for your Nonna." She squeezed the child as close as she could get her.

Agata pulled away and looked at her for the first time. Despite the uncertainty and hurt in her gaze, she obeyed, pulling her mask down over her eyes.

Guilelma watched her granddaughter walk apprehensively to her front door for the last time. Agata looked back at her Nonna, and Guilelma could feel her questioning her through the eyes of her mask. Agata then turned and followed the man in the red jacket quietly out the door.

Guilelma instinctively covered her mouth to shush the cry that followed.

ACT TWO
FIGLIE DE COMMUN

9

AGATA

It was often said that during Carnival, the entire city is in disguise. Agata had never known that before the man with the red jacket came that night to her Nonna's apartment. The tucked-away neighborhood of San Canciano sheltered Agata from the strangers who descended upon Venice seeking out its famed excitement. She'd grown up observing it, celebrated by the neighborhood men, who regularly played table games in the square. They shook their same dice on the same rickety table night after night throughout the rest of the year—only during Carnival, they played those games with their Carnival capes and masks on. The extra candlelight, placed there for the celebration, coaxed their playing even later than usual into the night.

When their lonely wives would yell out the windows that it was time to come in, they'd respond with such comments as:

"Let me finish my cup!"

There was always a neighbor who would yell out from somewhere: "Aww, let them play their game."

And then there were those wives who did not take well to being told what to do. "You mind your business while I tend to mine!" they would scream back at the neighbors.

A smattering of giggles, alongside clamorous venting, often made its way in and out of open windows, bouncing throughout the square in response. The men's cups never seemed to empty, but the barren bottles of grappa that rolled at the foot of their chairs told their wives what they already suspected. It would be another long night.

In these months of Carnival, a lost stranger to the city might be found wandering into tucked-away campos such as San Canciano with his mask on. The men found great sport in offering a glass to incorporate another player into their game, and it was more entertaining to give directions, sometimes more reliable than other times, depending on the number of bottles hugging their feet. But San Canciano was far enough away from the main attractions of St. Mark's Square for the trappings of Carnival to reach them.

That night, like the men in her campo, Agata was in disguise. Her heart pulsed endlessly in her ears like an echo. What would strangers have thought of a masked girl following the elusive man in red? His pace quickened as he dashed from one small calle to another. She watched his fiery curls bounce on the back of his neck. Their steps connected piece by piece the maze that was their Serrenissima. As he led them over tiny bridges, she remembered mammina explaining how local Venetians had built them to collect tolls from their neighbors who sought shortcuts to the backs of campos Agata had never seen before. She pictured her papa stomping through these same alleys with his long cape furling behind him. What if they ran into him? Would he recognize her? The man in the red jacket wound her around in such a way that she would not know how to find her way back in the darkness without him. Agata breathed heavily; the mask made everything that much darker. Though she was nervous, the man's quick steps and gentle certainty made her feel she could trust him. What was more, her Nonna trusted him. *Nonna would never lead me astray.*

After what seemed a long time of only hearing her feet scuffle and her long cape swoosh across the stone, a far-off sound made its way to her ears. People... Lots of them! They were cheering and excited. The man in the red jacket moved them quickly between buildings to remain unseen. As they neared the noise, she saw that it emanated from a gathering of Carnival revelers in their masks, retelling stories of what they had just been a part of. Their laughter wound its way to her, aligning with the same frenzy she, too, was feeling. The man in the red jacket paused and breathed heavily. Surely, since this was a secret mission, he did not want to be seen. They made their way back in the direction they had come, entering a large campo that was lit up but quiet. The glow of the campo reached Agata's face, the celebratory candlelight of Carnival lighting up her vision in the dark. Her fears rested in that extra light on her face and the idea of being so near to the excitement.

Piazza San Marco was the center of the great Venetian Carnival. She had heard stories of the jugglers who balanced on their hands or each other, of the dog fights, the races, and the great alluring chaos signified in the wearing of a mask. At this moment, she would have been the only child from San Canciano who had ever gotten so close to it! She wished it were Gabriele's hand she was holding so they could dart through the streams of candlelight and find Piazza San

Marco on her own and watch it all aglow. The man with the red jacket seemed determined to keep her out of the middle of things. As their steps led them away from the large campo, she turned around to capture a glimpse of the energy she heard. Light flashed between the crevices of calle, and the *oohs* and *aahs* of a society she would never know were set in her rearview, never to be looked at fully in the face.

They came around the corner to the Riva degli Schiavoni, where a great froth of cold off the water shook through Agata, blowing her large hood right off. She gasped at the shock of it; until then, it had been so quiet. She pulled her hood back up with her spare hand. The man in the red jacket looked down to check on her as he felt her movement. He slowed next to her.

"Take care, child. We are almost there."

Their pace steadied as he led her over one last bridge that curved at the top like a church bell. On one side of her was a small waterway. As she looked to her right, past the man in the red jacket, she saw for the first time the great, black expanse that was the sea. It was so much bigger than the canal waters that protected San Canciano. As they came down the other side of the bridge, they paused at a faded white building three stories high. The man led her away from the front of the building and around the corner to a large green door.

The man in the red jacket looked down at Agata with a closed-lipped smile, revealing a key in his palm. He flipped his hand to find another to open a red door behind it. He paused and moved back from the red door. Instead, he rang the bell that hung on a string just above his head.

"We must do this properly if we want to be on the good side of the Prioress," he said.

They waited. Agata stared at the green door, and panic began to fill her. What was behind it? Why had she listened to Nonna? She should have said something. She should have stayed with her.

The green door creaked open slowly, revealing a small, pink hand pulling it open. Inside, a young maid in all white with a dark red apron stood.

"*Bueno Sera*, Maestro. Come in," said the high, tender voice.

The maid appeared surprised to see him.

The man with the red jacket returned her greeting, holding his hand up to signal her inside.

"You brought a guest?" she asked, staring down at Agata.

Agata peered up at her through the small eyeholes of her mask, unsure whether she should answer her. She was met with gentle brown eyes and tiny lips that spoke again to her on the edge of a whisper.

"I can help you take that off," the maid said to Agata.

Agata nodded and turned around so the young woman could untie the lace of her mask at the back of her head. Quick clickety steps marched behind them, accompanied by a stronger voice.

"Maestro! We normally don't have the pleasure of greeting you so late in the evening. I see you have brought..." She paused. "...a visitor?" She turned her head and spoke to the young woman before the man had a chance to answer.

"Thank you, Giapetta, for your help. You may go back to your post."

Giapetta acknowledged the stern woman with a nod, slipped back to the front door, and sat down in a small chair placed to the left of it. She snuck Agata a discreet smile before looking down.

"This is Agata. She will be a..." He cleared his throat and stuttered out, "…a long-time visitor."

Agata swung her gaze toward him. Long-time visitor? Surely, he didn't mean that. Who would help Nonna with her chores in the mornings?

"I see. Come. You'll follow me, and we will get you situated." The woman turned around, and Agata followed her quick, sure steps down a hall to another door. She wasn't sure whether she liked this woman. The red jacket followed close behind her.

"You will sit here in this chair while I check you in," the stern woman commanded Agata, directing her to step inside a small room.

"Um, I do know the girl. Well, her family. I..." Again, the man stammered, reached into his coat pocket, and pulled a few papers out of it, fumbling in the presence of the strong woman.

"It is customary for me to conduct the initial interview. You will wait outside as is appropriate," the woman announced, grabbing the papers from his hands and then shutting the door firmly, with his nose almost in it.

Agata sat up tall. This was not a woman she wanted to upset.

The woman, who was a little older, a little fuller-bodied, and a lot surer of herself than the first girl, took what seemed a very familiar seat at a small desk. She opened the documents she grabbed from the man in the red jacket and read through them. "Hmm-mm, I see."

"I am going to ask you a series of questions. Please respond to me as briefly and honestly as you can." She proceeded to dip a small, pointed quill into ink.

"What is your name?" the woman said without looking up.

"Agata Farusi," she mumbled.

"What are the names of your parents?"

"Pietro and Kamelia, but my Nonna takes care of me." Agata swung her legs, nervous with all the questions.

The woman never took her eyes off her desk, writing and asking more questions at the same time. She had thin eyebrows and flat olive skin. Agata wondered what color her hair was underneath the white cloth that was tightly wrapped around her head.

"Where were you born?" she asked as soon as Agata answered. "Child, be still. I need to hear from your mouth, not your legs." Her dark brown eyes were stern, set in place by two hard lines between them. They looked into hers, demanding an answer. "Where were you born?"

Agata swallowed and straightened. "In my Nonna's bakery house." She felt her eyes get fluttery and her nose tingly, like she might cry.

"Do you live in that same house now? Do your parents?"

Outside the door, Agata overheard someone else getting asked questions in a direct tone.

"I thought you might give me a chance to talk to you about her before sneaking her in late at night like a thief," the woman's voice reprimanded.

The stern woman stared at her, waiting for her answer.

"No, my mother is dead, and my Nonna is very sick, and my father is...gone," Agata replied. She was unsure how to explain her family situation to a stranger.

"Have you been baptized, Agata?" The woman at the desk continued to write fervently, appearing equally attentive to the conversation outside her door.

Agata heard the man in the red jacket's raspy voice respond quietly. He was her only friend here, and his voice had quickly grown familiar. She could only make bits of phrases out. She supposed he talked quietly when he thought he was in trouble, too.

"We all know from whom she came. Here... Nonna... sickly... insisted... couldn't wait a night longer."

"I am not putting the poor girl through that tonight, and she must be in shock. I do require to see her face and know who is under the roof of which, as you well know, I take great care."

The door pushed open to reveal another woman, in all white, her head also covered, her face not unkind.

"Pardon me, Signora Prudenza, for the interruption. I heard about our new arrival and thought I should introduce myself." The woman in charge looked upon her. Agata felt small, shy, and entirely taken in by the woman.

"You must be Agata. I am the Prioress here, but all the girls here call me Madonna, as I hope you will. I understand the Maestro here knows your Nonna and promised her your safety."

Agata stared, noting the woman's compassionate grey eyes that wrinkled at their corners, but couldn't make any words come out.

"I will get to know you more and ask some more questions of you as we find your place here. For now, I will let Signora Prudenza finish her questions and the nurse her examination. Then, a short bath, a fresh gown, and a bed will be what I think you require for the night. We can begin anew tomorrow. Understood?"

Agata nodded and caught the glare of Signora Prudenza, who mouthed to her *Yes*.

"Yes, Madonna," she managed.

"Very good." Madonna stood up, turned, and acknowledged Signora Prudenza.

"As always, Prudenza, thank you for your thorough work. I will be in my office until the foundling baptism, should you need to locate me." She glided her way out the door, grabbing the doorframe as if she had forgotten something. "And Agata, your Nonna needn't worry. You are safe here."

Signora Prudenza's questions went on and on. Agata felt dazed and wondered what her Nonna must be doing. Was she climbing into her bed? At some point, this Prudenza was satisfied enough to stop. She jumped up with papers in hand and said, "Follow me."

Agata obeyed and followed her deliberate steps down the same hall she had entered, then trailed her to another door. She gave two firm knocks.

A friendly voice responded after the first one. "It's open! Come in!"

A plump woman in white sat at a small table and looked up at them. Agata noticed her hat sat stiffer and higher on her head than did stern Prudenza's or Madonna's, revealing a gray-brown bun like the color of her Nonna's at the nape of her neck.

"This is Agata, Nurse Clementina. She needs her check-in examination."

"Agataaa! Welcome, bellissima. You can sit right here on this bed while I get myself organized."

"You will obey Nurse Clementina. Good evening to both of you." Prudenza bowed quickly and backed out the door.

"You survived your first test, didn't you then?" The gray-haired Clementina gave her a quick wink.

Agata immediately liked this plush, friendly woman more than the first one.

"Okay, dear, I will just have to give you a little look over and a measure to see how tall and strong you are. Let's take your cloak off." The nurse chatted away while she looked over the front and back of Agata's arms and legs, smoothing her thick hands up and down her spine and even her belly.

"Agata, are you about ten years old then?"

Aggi nodded. "Almost eleven."

"Of course, you are." Clementina took her head in her hands, showed her teeth with an "Ahhh," and tilted her head from one side to the other to check her ears. A soothing calm flowed through Agata's body as the woman's warm hands held her, firm but sweet, pressing her anxiety away. She felt overwhelmed with the need to sleep. A yawn escaped.

"Oh, dear, we must get this finished and get you to bed. Up we go." She grabbed Aggi's hand and sat her up, leading her away from the bed.

"Just wait here, dear. Nurse Laura is a kind soul, and she will get you all warmed and clean for a good night's rest." Clementina placed her warm, thick hand on Agata's upper arm, squeezing it. "Welcome to the Pietà, my dear," she whispered. The nurse shuffled off, fading into the dark hall.

Agata's stomach rumbled as she sat in the low-lit hallway, waiting to be fetched for her bath. She looked down at the lace mask in her hand and squeezed it tight. How could it be that only hours ago her Nonna and her friends had circled her, touching and affirming her with their familiar hands? Now she sat alone in this hallway, led through one door and then the next. How many more could there be for her to walk through? Her thoughts stirred until she was gently shaken awake by Nurse Laura.

"Agata, wake up. It's time for your bath."

Nurse Laura was kind to her. She held up a great big sheet while she undressed and got into the warm tub of water. Quickly, Nurse Laura picked up Agata's clothes off the floor and began folding them.

"My cape. My mask," Agata exclaimed, hesitant about them leaving her sight.

"You won't be needing those tonight. We will get you in a dressing gown for bed."

Agata, not convinced, let the nurse bathe and assist her with her night clothes.

"We've all had our first night here, *piccolo*," she said. Nurse Laura squeezed the excess water from her hair off her back. Her voice was deep and calm. "Most of us just don't remember it."

Another knock came, and a new voice gave an announcement. "I am here to take up the new girl." A lanky girl with alder skin like her Nonna's wood countertop and tight blondish-brown ringlets that stuck out each side of her head spoke loudly enough to be heard, though she faced the door, allowing them their privacy.

"Poeta, thank you. I can't leave Nurse Maddalena alone with the little ones too long." Nurse Laura looked down at Agata, gave a short smile, and hurried off.

Agata watched Nurse Laura leave and stared bewildered at this new person outside the door.

"No reason to stare. I am Poeta. You can follow me."

The two went down a long hall; several more rooms were attached to it. Agata looked back into one and saw Nurse Laura holding a tight bundle in her arms, bouncing and walking at the same time.

Poeta whispered, "Those are the other new foundlings here. Just like you."

Agata was both disoriented and overwhelmed by Poeta's comment when she realized she was back where she had started in the large round entry. She looked at the door, searching for the first shy girl still sitting in her chair, her hands in prayer. Agata followed the new one, Poeta, who paced with certainty toward a large, curved stairway, and wondered how she hadn't noticed it when she first arrived.

Things already looked so different with her mask off and time with these women.

Poeta rounded her way up one level and then a second one. Agata looked down to see how high they were and remembered the man in the red jacket. He was no longer there.

Poeta opened a dark room with many empty beds.

"Here, I snuck some out of the kitchen. You'll soon learn the cooks don't like to be off their schedule; no one does."

She pulled a wrapped piece of bread out of her pocket, then walked Agata into the room and pointed to the bed by the window.

"I thought you might like to look at the moon. It always makes me feel better knowing that God hung this big light in the sky. We don't get many chances to see it from in here."

Agata looked up at the sky and turned around when the young woman spoke again.

"Good night, Agata. Welcome to the Pietà." The door shut with a click, the moon her only companion.

10

AGATA

Agata sat on the edge of the bed, chomping her bread hungrily. It wasn't much of a dinner. She shot under the covers with the last bite and rolled into a ball, trying to shut out the emptiness in the room. She wept. Her stomach growled as she turned one way and flopped another. She was sure she didn't sleep a wink. She rubbed her finger over the bumpy lace of her mask back and forth, back and forth.

Her eyes abruptly opened to a room full of bright light. It was the room that Poeta, the girl with the alder skin and blonde ringlets, had led her to. The room had a window, and four small beds arranged in a square. The beds were empty. Her hands were as well. She remembered one of the ladies in white saying she didn't need the mask anymore. Oh, no! Panicked, desperate for the return of her mask, she cried out, "Nonna, where are you? What did you do?" She sucked in air through her sobs, sitting straight up in bed, fighting the last vestiges of her dream. "Where am I?"

"Mamma Mia, maybe they let you sleep too much," exclaimed Poeta as she opened the door. "You're okay. You must dry your eyes and get dressed. The Prioress is ready to see you."

"You mean Madonna, the lady in white?" Agata asked. She rubbed the back of her hand over her eyes, embarrassed at her childishness.

Poeta giggled.

"The lady in white. We are all in white. Yes, Madonna. Here, let me help." Poeta approached Agata, pulled her nightgown over her head, and grabbed the white dress at the foot of the bed. Agata didn't see it blended in with her sheets.

"Will she tell me where my Nonna is?" Agata asked, enthralled by the girl's yellowy tight curls that stuck straight out of the sides of her white cap.

Poeta balled the sheets up and left them on the bed. "She's expecting you. Let's be quick."

Agata dressed quickly, then followed Poeta's brisk steps back out of the long hallway and down the round staircase. The high walls were creamy-white like Nonna's bivolo before it was sent to the ovens. A heavy gleam reflected light off them, making the ceiling appear far away and the sun close. Agata wondered how it could be so bright when she didn't see any windows on the way down. Poeta seemed to accelerate her pace with each step. Agata did her best to keep up, wondering if they always walked so fast there. Poeta turned off the next level; they passed several closed doors and many other women. Poeta was right—the ladies who roamed the halls all wore white garments, robes, or dresses with red vests or aprons over them. Some walked solo, some in pairs. They all moved quickly and quietly as if on an important errand. Poeta stopped abruptly at a closed door, smoothed out her apron, and tucked her loose hair into her cap. She poised her chin up and lifted a hand to knock when the door opened abruptly. Signora Prudenza backed out toward them.

Signora Prudenza turned around and regarded Poeta with a frown. "Finally, you're here. The Prioress has a tight schedule. We cannot abide tardiness." Prudenza turned her gaze down toward Agata, her eyes as stern as the night before. "Did you not think to brush the girl's hair? Why is her…? Why is your face red?" she finished, asking the question directly of Agata for the first time.

At a lack of reply, Prudenza made an angry sound that blew air out of her nose, her glare returning to Poeta. "You are excused," she reprimanded.

"I'm sorry, Signora Prudenza," Poeta replied and then curtsied, scurrying back in the direction from which she came. Signora Prudenza stepped close to Agata and combed her fingers through the ends of Agata's hair. Agata winced.

"This is the last time you leave your room like this. There isn't much else I can do. Madonna is already waiting for you. "She tapped Agata's bottom to steer her in the door and then stepped out.

Agata found the Prioress sitting tall and regal in a chair with an empty one placed directly in front of her.

"Agata, please have a seat." The Prioress waved toward the chair. "I trust you slept well. We keep a strict schedule here, but we had two foundlings come in around the same time you did. I knew with the shock, you needed to get your bearings, and sleep does cure all."

"Yes, M'm…"

"Madonna."

"Yes, Madonna," Agata confirmed.

"Your father..." Madonna paused before continuing, "Did he ever give you music lessons?"

Agata was taken aback. She knew he Papa? "A little. He taught me how the notes go up and down and how to hold a violin, but..." Agata fidgeted.

"Go on, child, there is no one here but me."

But Agata noticed an old woman with dark skin who stood in the corner behind Madonna, taking in their conversation. She continued, aware of her new audience, "He said I must be useless and not have the gift of music. I didn't pick it up quickly enough." Agata bowed her head in shame.

"My child. That is simply untrue," Madonna assured. "Music is practice, and practice is discipline."

Madonna looked at Agata intently. "On the exterior, any passerby can see, we are tucked away from the outside world through an outer layer of stone and iron gates. It is the inner layer of silence and obedience that protects us. In turn, this layer, which we all have the responsibility to contribute to, provides us with the path to individual inner discipline and modesty. You will find no idleness here. Work will be your haven. The thing that propels you to excellence can be the thing that brings you purpose in a way living in the outside world cannot."

The Prioress continued. "You will have your opportunity to let your work reveal your gifts and, beyond that, your purpose in bringing Glory to God and honor to our Serene City. I do believe some of these gifts may be inherited from our fathers. But first, you need to practice discipline."

Agata couldn't take her eyes off the woman and her words. It was hard to take in everything she said.

"Many girls come here, most as infants, all like yourself with a previous story. Those stories don't matter here. We leave them behind as soon as we cross the threshold at the green door. We propel ourselves forward toward renewal by taking new chances. We don't spend time discussing our pasts. We work toward our futures. Consider it a unique gift you would never find outside of these walls, or most definitely as a young woman," Madonna paused. "Your Nonna likely baptized you, but everyone who enters the Pietà is baptized again, named with your new life, your new beginning. The name Farusi will not be spoken of here. Do you have any questions, Agata?"

Agata, stilled by her new reality, tried desperately to take in the authoritative but calm woman and her admonishment. It took all her bravery to muster: "Can I please have my lace mask back? It is the last thing my Nonna gave me, and I don't know when I will see her again."

The Prioress remained stoic. Agata had a habit of tightening her forehead when she couldn't find the courage to respond as she wanted. What could she say to convince this woman she wasn't meant to stay here for but a little while?

"New beginnings begin with an end. Let's go find your new beginning, Agata."

At that, Madonna stood and held out her hand. Agata sat in defiance for a moment, closing her eyes and willing herself to speak up. *What about my Nonna?* She had an urgency to get up, run back through the green door, and find her. But she didn't know how to find her way home, and she didn't know anyone who could help her. Instead, she stood in instinctive obedience and took the Prioress' hand.

Madonna led them to a narrow corridor that ended in the glow of stained glass. In the small chapel, three head-covered women in white sat in a pew. The Prioress sat with them as Agata was directed to the priest, who stood placidly in front of a large oval bowl.

He whispered for her to face out toward the women in white and lay her head over the bowl. She looked up past them, taking in the plain chalky ceiling, her tears mixing with the cool water that ran down her face. Images of Canciano slid with them, Nonna's bakery house full of warm bread and banter, the cobblestone walkway she ran through protected by familiar shops and the neighbors who loved her, and the small bridge that curved up from the dock where she last saw her mother, all lost in the basin beneath her. How would she retrieve them?

"I baptize you in the Name of the Father, the Son, and the Holy Spirit," the priest said.

She stood. Agata, no longer feeling the drips of water running down her back, looked behind her. A woman barely her height gently squeezed the ends of Agata's slick hair with a fabric. The woman had a brown, wrinkled face and knowing, dark eyes. She recognized her as the old woman from Madonna's office. The woman put her arm around her and turned Agata to face the women in the pews.

"I give you, Agata della Pietà."

11
MARGARITA

The little girl brought to the mysterious community of women in the dark of night had become part of something bigger than she could fathom. Agata Farusi did not exist anymore. Nor would she ever again. The girl could not grasp how Agata della Pietà would replace her with a greater story to tell while the clutches of her Nonna's hands were still so present in her young mind.

The older woman at the baptismal guided Agata out of what was called *The Infants Chapel*, a small chapel where foundling babes dropped at the green door were baptized. It was often used as a personal chapel for the Prioress to say her prayers. They exited *The Infants Chapel* through a narrow corridor to a small room where the woman picked up a brush atop a dark dresser and began speaking to Agata quietly, running the brush through the girls' damp tangles.

"You will find your way, Bambina," Margarita spoke in her low, beguiling voice. "I know it seems overwhelming now, but the Pietà is meant to be your home." She spoke on, "I don't remember much of the outside. What I do know is how protected I am here in the Pietà, and the Prioress has managed to bring calm and peace to all the girls here."

Finally, she leaned in with a smile. "There, all better." She smoothed her wrinkled brown hand over the back of Agata's hair. "My name is Signora Margarita, and I am a Discrete here at the Pietà. I am assigned to be your aide. I have been here so long that my only job anymore is to check in on girls like yourself and see that you are getting on okay."

Agata looked back at her without words.

Margarita held her chin up, dark eyes meeting hers, allowing the new foundling's gaze to fall on her. She was used to such stares, of young new girls taking in the lines of her face, trying to contemplate how many years they represented of a life spent enclosed.

After all her years in the Pietà, she had learned the greatest gift she could give them was dispensing words of encouragement that prodded them forward. Her kind words were reassurances, and she stood by them. She knew that all things tended to work out on the outside because a life spent in such confinement meant you had to face things on the inside. There were no distractions to prolong it. *And what,* Margarita thought as she looked at her, *would this child, this girl with the serious face and dark furrowed brows, have to overcome?* She knew from her paperwork that Agata's father was a musician. She also understood that an indulgent reputation accompanied him. The girl's gift of music must quickly be nurtured so she can recognize it in herself.

Margarita shifted the quiet between them. "You must be starved. It is lunch hour already. I will take you to the *caffeterria* and get you acquainted with your new schedule."

A loud stomach rumble moaned from the girl at the mention of food. "Yes, Signora, grazie."

Margarita squeezed Agata's hands and widened her eyes, hoping to give her a boost of support. And then, she released it.

"Stay close to me. I'll show you the way."

Margarita led Agata from the dark corner of Madonna's quarters to the main entry hall. They walked up the curved staircase. She had walked these steps thousands of times at the Pietà. They marked the beginning and ending of days on her way to Mass, the beginning and ending of stays for foundlings on their way to a new life. The steps held her secrets. They felt it when her feet were tired from tracking the monotony of the schedule, and they felt it when her feet grew heavy, when the weariness of carrying the hurt of forgotten souls was too much to lift. She brought all these things with her, giving them back to the steps that supported her, moving to the next one. She knew Agata's fears had already been laid three times below her. She had no way of knowing how many more steps lay before her.

Up they went one floor.

With a new foundling at her side, she viewed everything anew as if the child beside her might be seeing things for the first time. Two older women, Discrete like herself, walked together toward them, their hair wrapped up tight like hers underneath a white cloth. Their eyes met. She nodded *bondi* at them, and they nodded back. Though their faces remained neutral, the blink of their eyes told her they had acknowledged the unfamiliar face next to her. The Discrete were her workmates, but she saw them as her comrades, armed with their years of life spent in quiet together, their wisdom gathered, and steadfastness earned. Their gray-wrapped hair and lined faces were their badges of honor.

Old women on the outside, yes, but frail we are not.

Margarita was used to moving quickly. The girl was a pace behind. Hesitation? Maybe. *She will acclimate,* she thought. *She has to.*

They approached the double, wooded doors of the *caffeteria.* Signora Prudenza was halfway through her reading, which meant lunch was too. She scurried over to the kitchen to get a bowl of rice for the girl and left her to take in the room. Agata stood with her mouth gaping.

"My daughter, forget not my law; but let thine heart keep my commandments: 'For length of days, and long life, and peace, shall they add to thee. Let not mercy and truth forsake thee: bind them about thy neck; write them upon the table of thine heart.'"

The ever-serious Prudenza stood at the head of the room. Behind her, the long front table was outlined with the rest of the staff, straight-faced women in white head covers, but Margarita knew the oomph behind each quiet face. At the center of them, in her recognizable vertical stature, sat her dear friend, the Prioress, presenting as calm, ethereal, and in charge. Signora Prudenza had a way of finding herself in serious roles of leadership, especially ones where she could be heard, such as the daily reading of scriptures over meals. It was apparent she had in mind an upward trajectory to the seat of the Prioress herself. She was only one year younger than the current Prioress. She did not have her eloquence, but a stern demeanor and an uptight disposition. If she weren't heard, Margarita would cluck her tongue. The rules of quiet forced a surrender on emotional outbursts, even small ones she might enjoy.

Margarita scanned the room full of foundling girls seated at additional long tables placed in a gradual rise from youngest to oldest. They were expected to eat quietly and listen attentively to whoever was speaking to them. They were not allowed to comment, laugh, or smirk back. They, too, wore white dresses with white half-aprons tied at the waist.

Their hair was pulled back in braids or half down, depending on their ages. Margarita never tired of looking at the young ones' faces, searching less for misbehavior than missed emotions. The happier they were, the more likely they were to succeed in the cycle of the Pietà. The more successful the Pietà ran, the more likely the current Prioress would become because of it.

Although never spoken in a public place such as this, it was understood amongst the staff that Signora Prudenza was not a foundling favorite. She tended to extremes. Margarita chose balance as the higher path.

She tripped over her thoughts, forgetting where she was, placing the bowl down at an unoccupied spot next to a visually overwhelmed Agata.

"Go ahead, bambina. You are in good hands. It's time to get some food in you," Margarita whispered.

Signora Prudenza gave her a scolding, turning her head at once to face Margarita and forward again as she continued. Even whispers were not tolerated in the Pietà when someone else was speaking. Her volume increased as if to reiterate her point.

"'Thou shalt find favor and good understanding in the sight of God and man. Trust in the Lord with all thine heart; and lean not unto thine own understanding. In all thy ways acknowledge him, and he shall direct thy paths.'"

The quiet in the room was broken when Prudenza closed the book from which she was reading and proclaimed: "This is the Word of our Lord."

The entire room stood with her, making the sign of the cross and joining her in unison.

"In the name of the Father, the Son, and the Holy Spirit. Amen."

Agata shot up, bumping the table with her leg as the entire room stood. Her spoon dropped on the floor, the sound echoing around the room like a high-pitched bell. Margarita felt Agata look toward her, though her eyes were still averted down. Prudenza blinked twice, letting her anger toward Margarita be known. Margarita was well aware she did not like the focus on her to be anything less than a show of perfection and control. Nothing else was said. Prudenza, like the rest of the girls, was governed by the same rule of self-control and quiet.

Like clockwork, the standing girls, beginning with the front table, commenced filing out the door in two even lines. Agata stopped eating as the girls walked past her.

Margarita was not bothered by Prudenza's fussing. "Finish up, child. Let's not make a small thing larger than it is."

After seeing her finish her last few bites, Margarita walked out of the empty room with Agata, trying to keep up with her. It was quiet in the hall as if only the two of them were in the entire building. The girls had made their way to their next scheduled room as succinctly as expected. Margarita pushed open a door to a room full of fifty girls huddled on risers.

Elena, their teacher, softened, pleased to see her.

"*Bondi*, Discrete Margarita," Elena said. The corners of her mouth crept up modestly.

Margarita always admired her voice, so different from hers; it rang out like a dove, clear and sweet.

"Excuse the interruption, Sotto Maestra Elena." Margarita cleared her throat.

"Girls, we have a new ward joining us. Her name is Agata della Pietà. I trust you will make her feel most welcome."

With permission to take in the new inmate, all eyes turned toward Agata. Margarita sifted through their faces. "Candida, where are you, my child?"

A sprite girl with black, full braids shot her skinny arm up. "Right here, Discrete."

"Agata will shadow you this afternoon. You are of a similar age and follow much of the same schedule. I've already had her bed made next to yours."

Candida smiled as if trying to hold back her excitement. "Of course, Signora."

Margarita held her hand out to direct Agata toward the group of girls. "You're in good hands. You will see me soon."

She turned around and went back out the door. It was time to let Agata enter the race. Let her journey in the Pietà begin.

12
AGATA

Agata could never have imagined that so many girls lived in Venice. Yet here they were, all in one room. She dared look up at them. They were all looking back, studying her. She felt Margarita place her hands gently on her back and push her toward the group of girls. The little girl with the thick black braids waved her arm at Agata with exuberance.

Agata forced herself forward, and the row opened so she could have a seat.

"I'm Candida," said the girl. Her mischievous green eyes sparkled.

Agata offered a reserved smile. "I'm Agata," she replied, painfully aware of her newness.

"Oh, we know," Candida said with enthusiasm.

A few surrounding girls nodded, hiding their smiles. The number of them! Agata couldn't help but turn her head to take in all who stood behind her. Her Nonna would pinch her leg if she had done the same at Mass. She whipped her head back to the front, catching the eye of a blonde girl with long braids who sat diagonally, a row in front of her, looking back at her with a smirk of disgust. The girl put her finger to her mouth as if to shush her. Agata looked down, embarrassed. Candida gave Agata a shove with her elbow and a quick roll of her expressive eyes to tell her she was okay and lifted her upper lip in a sneer at the blonde girl.

"That's Giulia. Never mind her. She was always snippy about something," Candida whispered.

Agata tended to veer away from loud personality types but was drawn to Candida's openness. Agata looked back at the entry to find Margarita already slipping away through the door.

"You're lucky. You got a good one for your first class," Candida said.

Class? Agata mouthed back.

"Yes, class. What do you think we do all day? Class and prayer and mass and class and prayer and Mass—oh, confession! We have a lot of that, too."

"Girls, girls. It's time to begin," directed the teacher from the front of the room, a tall, young woman with dark brown hair and a thin nose. Agata took in her confidence, grace, and the small lace collar on her shoulders.

"I hope you enjoyed your lunch." The teacher spoke with softness and directness all at once. "As you've heard, Discrete Margarita announce. We have a new classmate." Her eyes fell on Agata. "Agata, welcome to *Piccolo Choir.* We train our voices together before many of us take our path to the Coro."

Candida gave Agata a kick and an affirmative nod.

"My name is Sotto Maestra Elena, teacher of voice and performance training and one of the many choral conductors here. Listen to the voices around you and do your best to follow. We can work together on where to place you later."

Agata's insides clenched, and she tightly gripped either side of her chair. Would she have to sing in front of all these girls?

"We will get started with warm-ups right away," announced Sotto Maestra Elena before she approached a wood dresser with spindled legs placed at an angle at the front of the room.

The gentle teacher placed her fingers on the dresser, and together, they produced a sound much unlike their dainty demeanor. A strong chord filled the room. Agata was stilled by the drama of many notes coming from the little dresser and the young woman who played it. She later learned Sotto Maestra Elena was playing a harpsichord, but to Agata, it was as though with her fingers alone, the teacher had commanded a great ship into movement. With one look at the girls in white, they began singing alongside her with surprising energy. Agata was mesmerized—caught up in the power of it. Until that moment, she had thought of the Pietà as a building of quiet. The girls' voices encircled her like something able to lift her off the ground. They carried her through memories like a bird flying over her past life; she looked down at the "S" curve of the canal, her father playing beautifully on the gondola, his black hair whipping in the wind, a mound of white flowers beneath him. She saw the Canciano women at the well, worn hands clutching their buckets and their song echoing off the buildings in the morning fog.

She was so overwhelmed by the sound and the images of her father and San Canciano that she didn't know how to join them. She crinkled her face to push back the tears, but they had already made their way over her eyelines. Embarrassed, she wiped her cheek, hoping no one saw. They must already think her odd. Candida grabbed her hand and held it firmly. It was clammy and stuck to her own. Agata didn't mind; she needed a friend.

The girls sang their way up a scale and back down again, much like her father did with his violin warm-ups. The choir transitioned to working on a song. Another older girl came from the back of the room and took Elena's place at the harpsichord as she moved in front of it. It was all so seamless; they knew what to do without any instruction. Agata watched the gentle Maestra's face, feeling connected to the movement of her arms, the way her expression reflected the notes that the girls pushed back in her direction. It was an exchange, a communication in melody, and they all knew how to converse.

A loud bell interrupted their singing. The Maestra brought her arms to her sides and directed the girls in a short prayer.

"God bless you as you go. I will see you tomorrow."

The girls filed back out of the hallway in the same even lines they came in. Candida went around Agata so she would have her to follow.

"Welcome, Agata," the Maestra said to her as she walked past. "I look forward to knowing you."

Agata was amazed at how quietly and succinctly this large number of girls moved when she felt so fumbly. Even their shoes moved in rhythm. She did her best to match them. It was much easier to focus on Candida's black braids bouncing in front of her. She was used to relying on Nonna. Her breathing relaxed as she joined their cadence. Once they crossed the hallway with the stairwell, the girls began diverting in different directions. Some went up the stairs, some went back down. Most, like her, followed the person in front of them to another hallway that seemed like the entrance to a new building. Agata felt the air change from cool to stuffy.

Candida slowed, turning her head back to her, and whispered, "We're almost there."

Once up another level, the girls began filing off into rooms. Agata tried to peer in and see what class they might all be heading to next, but instead of classrooms, she saw row after row of beds. One room after another was the same. The girls thinned out, and Candida's black plaits stilled as they entered the last room in the hall. Agata stayed close behind. Candida led them to their beds, three away from the window. There must have been twenty girls in there with them, lying down with their faces to the ceiling.

Candida lay down and then flipped over to face Aggi. "It's rest time," she whispered loudly. "Isn't Sotto Maestra Elena nice? You don't have to worry about crying a bit. Everybody does when they first come."

Agata winced, embarrassed to talk about it.

"What happened to you, Agata? Why are you here?"

"My Nonna is sick. She will come get me when she is better."

Candida gave her a cheeky look, one Agata didn't realize she would become quite familiar with.

"Girls only leave here when they marry. That's a long time away for us. You must focus on being a good musician, Agata. We are part of the *figlie di commun* now, but someday, I am going to be part of the *figlie del Coro*. That's what you want too. They get to wear lace collars, get extra beef in their bowls, and *dolce* on Fridays. If you make it through Coro training, you could be a Poinsettia Girl. They perform on stage with the largest lace collars and a fresh poinsettia behind their ear. Everyone comes to watch them, even the Doge and real Opera singers! That's why I am working so hard. You'll see, one day, I am going to stand on that stage not as Candida the foundling. I will be known as Candida, the Poinsettia Girl."

"I know my Nonna will come when she can," Agata snapped back. She sounded angrier than she meant to.

But Candida didn't appear bothered; she shut her eyes to rest, leaving Agata with a smile on her face. In what seemed just minutes, Agata dozed off.

A bell rang in the halls, startling her from her sleep.

"Ugh, already?" Candida complained. "I need to get to my cello lesson and then off to chores. I guess you stay here and get a longer nap before Vespers. See you later."

"Chores?" muttered Agata, worried.

"Yes, chores. We all have them, and we all hate them. Arrivederci!"

The girls in the room filed out with even spaces and steps. Some glanced over at Agata, but most ignored her. She was alone again, back in total silence.

The tall, thin window revealed a sliver of clouds and a small beam of light that shot through them. Agata pictured the sky above the familiar rooftops of San Canciano. Had the sun come out there today? She closed her eyes and saw her Nonna, with the daylight coming into the bakery, her hands busy in the kitchen, smiling and talking away with customers; she looked at Agata and gave her a wink—like she often did. Agata curled in a ball and took the corner of the sheet, methodically rubbing her thumb on the corner of it like she used to do when fumbling with her gray sweater. Her thoughts of home lured her into a deep sleep.

Agata was in the warmth of San Canciano and the gossip of Sunday night with Benedetta and Alba when she was shaken awake.

"I saw your deep sleep, Bambina, and let you miss Vespers, but now it is time for supper."

Discrete Margarita had her arm on her shoulder and a look of concern on her face.

Agata's face scrunched up. "Don't wake me up. Don't," she sobbed. "I was with my Nonna. I don't want to leave my Nonna."

"Bambina, your Nonna must be a wonderful woman for you to miss her so." She spoke in her deep, gravelly voice. "If she sent you here, to this place of all places in Venice, she must love you with such a depth as well. You are here for a reason. Your Nonna, who is getting on in years and is quite sick, can't care for you as she would like."

"No, it's just a trick on Papa. She promised me I would not have to stay with him anymore. But I can go back and take care of her."

Margarita responded gingerly, "It seems that our little flower cannot grow amongst the weeds, even in the bright sun. Your Nonna is like the great sun—full of warmth and having provided you with such growth and care. But the weeds are tall in the garden: your Papa, her poor health, your lack of a mother." Margarita paused.

"You, my dear, are meant to grow tall and bloom. You will never do so, planted in those tall weeds. Your Nonna has taken the courageous step of transplanting you here, in the Pietà, where there is a meadow of flowers for you to be among."

Agata sniffled and tried to understand the gravity of the old woman's words. "Won't I ever see my Nonna again?"

"You will feel your Nonna more and more as the years pass. It is impossible for such a great love ever to be lost. But no, you will not see her again in this life. For now, we must focus on your daily needs. Your schedule, the growth of your mind, the interactions and new friendships to be had, and for now, your dinner."

Margarita stood and reached out her hand. Agata ignored it but let the old woman grab hers and lead her away. They walked back through the hallway of empty beds and down the curved stairwell toward the empty dining hall. A slight game of tug-of-war ensued between them. *Nonna is all I have left.* Agata hesitated, pulling her arm back. *What will I do without her?* Her eyes welled up, but she was too angry to cry. The small woman had then pulled her forward. Once in the kitchen, Margarita retrieved two bowls of watery stew and rice for them. The two, one old and one young, ate in quiet together in the large caffeteria, connected by their detachment to the outside world. Their silence was an affectionate one, even without words or touches. Agata felt hollowed out but not unloved. That was all she needed to start anew.

13
ELENA

E lena stood at the door of her classroom while her Piccolo choir students filed out for rest hour. She made a habit of greeting them as they came and went. She wanted them to trust their speaking voices outside of class as much as their singing voices in class. Talk was allowed so infrequently at the Pietà, except for confession and responses in Mass. How would they ever learn to trust the exchange of conversation otherwise?

"*Bondi*, Lorenza," Elena said with a nod.

"*Bondi*, Sotto Maestra," Lorenza replied.

"*Grazie*, Candida."

"*Bondi*, Sotto Maestra," Candida replied proudly.

"*Bondi*, Agata. I look forward to knowing you."

Those sad brown eyes looked up to her own. "*Bondi*," Agata replied. Elena noted the foundling's hesitation.

Was it fear, shock, or uncertainty? It was clear God had given her a new little life that needed pouring into. Elena would make sure to find her way to her.

Sotto Maestra Elena, as she was known in the Pietà, had grown into a dependable fixture both as a musician and a young teacher. It had taken her twenty years to get there. She was left at the green door, a little girl at the age of five, by a landlord with no intention of caring for her baby sisters when her mother turned gravely ill and could no longer pay rent. She remembered standing outside the green door, the landlord's heavy breath and his gruff tone. She was greeted by the noiseless women in white. Their presence immediately put her at ease. They fed, bathed, and gave her a clean bed. All new luxuries to the life she had been living in the small room near the Arsenale. She hadn't known she needed such things since she had existed without them all. It wasn't until days after her arrival and the provision of food and sleep that she felt guilt over the fact that she had them while her mother remained without them. Thus, she had refused to indulge in such goodness.

She quickly adjusted to learning, class work, and the tight schedule the Pietà ran by. She was used to hard work and adapting. There was no one to instruct her in mothering her baby sisters or nursing her mother when she got rashes on her hands and drifted in and out of lucidity. She was a natural caretaker, but finding her way, she had come to learn, was the gift of a survivalist.

She remembered how she had tried to understand the complexity of a well-run school, how hundreds of girls could wear clean dresses and be fed daily when her mother had barely managed her and her siblings' daily needs. It had been different when her father was alive, and they were tucked inside the gates of the Jewish Ghetto. She learned that keeping up and working hard paid dividends inside the Pietà, unavailable to women outside it. She acclimated quickly and graduated to every new stage and audition on her first try. She learned to trust her ears, her affinity for pitch, and her sensitivity to sound. No wonder the outside world's noise was so brash to her being.

As the youngest assistant teacher in the Pietà, she had earned the small lace collar that distinguished her so and draped her shoulders. With only a couple more years of hard work and a successful audition, she could earn the larger lace collar representative of her ultimate goal of joining the performing Coro, or as they referred to themselves inside the walls: a Poinsettia Girl. While she no longer held the childhood worry of being cared for, she couldn't shake her propensity to care for those around her.

Like the younger foundlings, her days were full and scheduled. She shared time between teaching the younger girls in the beginner classes and taking advanced-level courses of her own. On top of that, she had Mass, confession, staff meetings, and solo practice—the only way to advance beyond her peers. There was never enough of that.

Just as the girls in the *figlie di commun*, the older girls and young women, like herself, of the *figlie del Coro* received a scheduled thirty-minute rest period. As she walked back toward the Coro dormitories, well away from the younger dormitories, she was met with a heaviness that she couldn't shake. Elena collapsed atop her small bed and stared at the ceiling. It was the little girl, Agata, in her *Piccolo Choir* class. Something about her countenance had reached inside of Elena and joined the memory of her own. The two experiences entwined somewhere deep in her thoughts. Many girls had passed through the Pietà, an established carer of foundlings for hundreds of years. The women who grew up in these halls roamed them as well. Once young girls or even foundlings themselves, those women brought stability and confidence to balance the fear and self-doubt that held onto the younger inmates and the losses that accompanied their memories. It was a certainty that for some, loss held a tighter grip on their souls.

Loss, so much of it. Every footstep in the hall had a relationship with it, a misplacement they couldn't reconcile—and that included Elena. She tried to recall her mother. Her dark curly hair, her raspy, once-vivacious voice. They hadn't had many material possessions. They lived in the Ghetto, where families like hers shared their sameness: their culture, faith, and feasts. It made her home that much richer because of it—even with two brothers to deal with. Oh, how she missed them, or at least the idea of them. Tragedy always struck without any announcement to the bearers of it. The day her father died was the day her family, as she knew it, died. Her mother decided to escape the Ghetto and find her brothers. The impression of that loss and her mother's choices was etched on her soul.

"Elena, it's time."

Elena blinked her eyes open. Two small brown eyes set deep into a narrow face studied hers.

"Cristina! I didn't realize I nodded off," she said. Elena forced herself to sit and wake herself up.

"I came in just three minutes late, and you were already snoring." Cristina laughed.

Cristina flipped her long light braid back over her shoulder as she stood. It fell back into its place at the center of her back.

Elena shook her head and laughed with her. "Sorry about that. Did you get a chance to nap at all?"

"I lay there. Some days, you fall when you drop onto your bed. Other days, your mind won't stop working," Cristina replied.

The rooming situation improved with every student's advancement into the Coro. Elena moved into Cristina's dorm after another member left the Pietà for marriage, which some considered their desired advancement. Cristina had a middle voice in the Coro when it was needed, but her true talent was playing the flute and recorder. While the Pietà was a breeding ground for competitiveness, Elena found that true friends ensured they were not late for things such as rehearsals with the director, who only came in three days a week.

"Gasparani is here today. We've got to hurry and get tuned up," Cristina urged.

Francesco Gasparini, the official music director and composer for the Pietà, came to conduct rehearsals and attend meetings related to performances. They did so in the balcony of the *Chiesa della Pietà*, the church attached to the Pietà by an overhead walking bridge. The *Chiesa della Pietà* was open to the public for performances and masses and used by the Coro for rehearsals the rest of the time. A door at the entrance of the walking bridge separated the school from the church and remained firmly locked except when Coro members needed to pass through for their weekly performances and rehearsals. Young foundlings and other members not part of the Coro were not allowed past this door except when accompanied by a teacher. The girls from both sides went to Mass in the Chapel of the Pietà, a smaller, less ornate sanctuary in the Pietà building.

The three days Gasparini came were the only ones during which the full orchestra and choir practiced together. He was busy with the ensembles at St. Mark's, working with men, the "Professional musicians." The Coro spent the rest of their week perfecting their skills in solo practice and ensembles by instrument in the Pietà building.

The two young women walked quickly through the hall.

Elena whispered, "I don't feel ready for a long practice today. I wish I could just rest. You have a lot of energy. Why are you walking so fast?"

"I don't like to be late. You know that. I don't want to disrespect Signor Gasparini like that," Cristina replied. Cristina was a full head shorter but kept Elena at a frenzied pace.

"No, you just want to hurry at a chance to see the great Signor Gasparini!" Elena teased.

"He is handsome. And so smart. Can you believe that piece he wrote we're working on now?" Cristina blushed as she answered.

"Handsome? Eww, have you seen the nose on that man? It takes the whole of his face."

"Elena, it does not—you exaggerate!" The young woman giggled but quickly looked away and quieted.

Maestra Prudenza walked by and made a point of greeting them. "Good afternoon, esteemed ladies of the Coro. Thank you for keeping your silence."

Elena and Cristina nodded in unison. "Good afternoon, Signora."

They had been caught. Chatter was a minor crime in the Pietà. More directly, indulgent or unnecessary talk in the shared spaces was forbidden. They smiled at each other, and Elena bit her lip; they were fortunate she hadn't written them up right there.

The young women quickly found themselves in the large, upper reception room off the church balcony. On its own, the reception room was a magnificent place for the audience to interact with some of the chosen musicians post-concert; today, it was merely the rehearsal space on the church's second level that looked down on the sanctuary below it. The open balcony room filled with the beautiful anticipation of group rehearsal: Lutes picked and plucked; the high pitches of the wind section trilled and warmed their fingers up and down arpeggios; the strings brought a level of complexity— some bows slowly ran across their bridges listening to the very intricacy of the pitch while others ran through a few measures of their piece; and the choir girls let their voices fall from one high note to the lowest they could go, finding their airways.

Cristina made her way to the wind section, pulled out her recorder, and placed it on her lap while she unlatched her flute case and twisted the head on. Elena walked over to the choir section and let a few notes fall before Gasparini tapped his baton on the music stand in front of him.

"Ahem, ladies of the Coro. I have something new in mind tonight in anticipation of the approaching season of Lent. Something to shock the souls and remind them of why they sacrifice their intake of meat, *ahem,* on Fridays."

Elena caught Cristina ogling at the conductor's instruction and shook her head, amused.

After their busy practice concluded, Elena spent the rest of her afternoon with a private voice lesson and a teacher meeting with the Prioress, all before Vespers and supper. Madonna met with her teaching staff once a week to discuss any changes, hear any updates from the board, listen to any concerns, and inform them of new inmates who had arrived at the Pietà.

The room was full of women. Male teachers and professional musicians came in from outside the Ospedale to teach at the top levels of musicianship, but they met with the Prioress separately. Most of the teaching staff was comprised of women in the Coro at various levels, serving their ten-year contribution back to the Pietà as Sotto—Maestros and Maestras in their respective areas of gifting.

"It is our season of Lent. I would ask before or after you go about your planned lesson, you encourage a lesson on sacrifice, a line or two, on what our Lord gave up, and of course, schedule those confession times." The Prioress raised her eyebrows and spoke with a deliberate slowing. "These are not just meant for our students. Let this serve as a reminder to ourselves to keep on top of our schedules and our tardiness. I cannot encourage you enough to admonish girls who arrive late to your classes. This first comes, of course, with practicing timeliness ourselves. If you need any help with a verse or introductory antidote, Signora Prudenza has gone to great trouble to make a list. Please see her for those details."

Elena and Cristina caught each other's eye and then avoided further contact.

"Onto other matters. We have three new babies that have arrived through the *scafetta* door this week. Please consider checking in on the nursery to relieve Nurse Maddalena and Nurse Laura—they literally have their hands full. We also have one new foundling girl, age ten. She has been placed by her grandmother due to her age and health, and she can no longer care for her. She is overwhelmed by the new situation she has found herself in, and I don't doubt other troubles may surface. This little one will need your care. I do have Discrete Margarita assigned to her, but cheerful hearts and empathetic gestures will ease her in. Please see me if more careful counsel is required. I do expect her to find her way to the Coro. Her father is a working musician."

The Prioress dismissed them to Vespers, and Elena followed the others in quiet to the chapel. As she walked in and headed to her assigned place in the first four rows, she scanned the littles and looked for Agata. She spotted her sitting at the back among a group of sweet girls in red and white. Her distress stood out among them.

She took the obligatory genuflection and made a sign of the cross before sitting down. But in her heart, she began a prayer with Agata in mind.

Baruch Atah Hashem, Elokeinu Melech haolam...

14
AGATA

The sky held onto its last hour of darkness, and the stars were exercising their last twinkle when a high-pitched bell sounded throughout the *figlie di commun dormitorios*. The girls of the *commun* were housed on the outer wall. Though the bedroom windows were not large, the March morning air that had found its way through them was dank. The girls rustled under their covers, hoping one last toss might extend their dream. Their feet found the cold stone floor and with it, their morning song:

"Lord, open my lips, and my mouth will proclaim your praise."

Agata yawned, desperately wanting quiet. Was it morning already with this dark? Her fellow sleepy inmate sang sweetly and quietly in a round, passing the tune throughout the room as they dressed, growing a little more awake each time it came back to them. The verse was sung by girls from every *dormotorio* as they met in the morning. It served as a reminder that idle chatter was not accepted, and they should focus their desires on the dependable rhythm of a new day at the Pietà.

Agata dressed and made her bed, following the quiet procession out the door. Their walk, though still in rhythm, hit the stone like a soft slipper as if their shoes were not awake yet either. The song spilled out into the hallway, joining the girls from other rooms, merging into a beautiful braid of vocal clarity and innocence—announcing their arrival into a new day.

As they made their way down the corridor, the older girls of the *figlie del Coro* joined the filed lines from their rooms in the inner part of the building. Together, they made their way down the circular staircase, their song and symmetry in perfect balance. The choir of delicate voices amplified, filling the building. Agata peeked down to see the ideal curve of red and white that wound down in a corkscrew, not knowing whether she enjoyed the visual beauty or the audible beauty more. It was so beautiful she was tempted to join in but instead mouthed the words to give the appearance of complicity. It had been two months, and she still refused to sing. Though Discrete Margarita had told her she'd never see her again, she hadn't given up holding out for her Nonna. She carried this longing with her every step she took. It filled her body with a dull ache she wasn't willing to surrender.

The gathering of girls sang their way to the Pietà Chapel for morning mass. The movement of the line dragged as they approached the chapel interior, stopping to dip their fingers in the well of holy water and genuflecting before taking their positions in the pews. Agata had grown to like watching the order of white and red filing in, rhythmic and predictable. The folds of skirts moving in and out of aisles reminded her of the water moving through the canals. She thought of how she used to sit and watch the gondolas pulling up and the water hitting the dock's side walls with Gabriele on weekends. The view and memory were calming and subtle.

The Prioress and more senior teachers took their seats at the church's front right, and the older girls, Sotto Maestras, not unlike Signora Elena in their small lace collars, took their places in the first few rows at the upper left. Down and down, the pews filled, laden with girls getting younger and smaller as they moved to the back of the chapel, to the girls with two braids. That was where Agata found herself. She was proud of the nimble way her fingers had memorized the motions needed to weave her two low braids in the dark of morning. Every day, she challenged herself to make the weave tighter than the day before. Her mammina used to comb her hair into a single braid. Nonna had been too busy and let her sometimes stringy hair run free.

Agata sat squished closely to Candida for morning mass. The two girls had quickly become inseparable. Agata thought Candida seemed to enjoy her job as Agata's guide. She always offered helpful commentary, expressing her insights on the Pietà's staff and inmates' personalities with much detail. Don Giambattista Bollani was the parish priest of the Pietà and had baptized Agata when she entered. Candida had explained to her very early on that:

"We call him 'the nose' because of his pinched voice. We listen to him every day for Mass. And then, after he bores us, we have to go to him in the afternoon for confession." Candida rolled her head back to mimic falling asleep.

He greeted the room of girls—the only man within it—that morning as usual.

"The Lord be with you," he spoke in his well-observed pinched voice.

"And also, with you," the throng of girls replied.

"Let us lift up our hearts."

"We lift them up to the Lord."

"Let us give thanks to the Lord our God," Candida joined in, holding her nose to imitate his sound.

The entire row of braided girls giggled.

Maestra Prudenza, in the constant habit of catching slight misbehaviors, whipped her head around and squinted in Candida's direction. The girls squeezed each other's hands to work their faces blank again.

They got through Mass and then filed back out the door to begin their day with breakfast. Agata had learned to acclimate by taking careful note of the girls' actions around her so as not to stick out: sit, stand, sit, kneel, stand, sit, stand. She would have done the same if Nonna were by her side. She followed her in everything she did. She was, in fact, a good follower and had never considered herself ready to take any steps on her own, with or without Nonna, especially after her mother's death. Thank goodness her new friend Candida was so vocal and brave. Sometimes, just being next to someone confident could make a person feel like the brave one. It was as though Candida's extra assuredness existed to make up for what she'd lacked. Agata had barely spoken aloud since her arrival at the Pietà. There seemed to be so many unspoken rules and steps; she was afraid to break them.

But she had grown more than she'd imagined she was capable of. She had learned to navigate the hallways, classrooms, and the circular schedule. The furthest she'd ever ventured in San Canciano was the Sellas' house, which was only a few paces away and much like an extension of her home. Behind the Pietà's walls, Agata had learned to govern the steps of her schedule. The bells cued the end of class, and her Maestra closed with a short prayer before they were released to a tempo of white, red, white, and red, weaving in and out like her long braids with dexterity before settling again. The pattern repeated throughout the day: bells, prayers, and study; bells, prayers, and study; and she moved along in the same way, woven into the existing pattern, her body surrendering to the rhythm of it without much thought anymore. With so many girls like her, in their youth and white dresses, she hoped she could keep her head down, follow their lines, and keep dreaming of going home to be a bigger help to Nonna with her new skills. If she stopped dreaming about Canciano and the bakery house where she last held her mother, how would she find her again? It could all disappear forever. She followed the line and Candida's thick braids with the image of her mother's face in her mind.

The girls took their quiet march to breakfast. Maestra Prudenza enthusiastically led the Bible reading while simultaneously eyeing them as they walked in.

"Stop," Prudenza commanded, interrupting herself. "I am quite sure I heard unnecessary noise at the back of the church this morning, but only you can unburden your hearts in confession. We will start confession early today, and this group here can lead the way without breakfast."

"Maestra Prudenza!" The Prioress stood up. Her chair screeched back in submission.

"You have your hands full with the reading. We will proceed as normal. Girls, should you require confession, your conscience will advise you, and you can go at your scheduled time." The Prioress sat back down.

The quiet reasserted itself with an air of discomfort.

The braided girls moved in silence to retrieve their bowls and sit at their assigned table. They were spared. Candida was a reminder to her that it wasn't all dread when she took her seat next to Agata and risked turning her face toward hers with enlarged eyes. Agata responded by letting a nervous sigh escape.

In the past two months since her arrival, now eleven-year-old Agata had learned that the foundlings communicated in gestures and expressions. Candida knew how to glimmer without a sound coming out. But this same "Talking" was happening all over the lunchroom. Giulia, the blond-haired girl who always acted bothered by Agata, averted her droopy eyes sideways when she made eye contact. Lorenza, her roommate, caught her eye and flattened her lower lip to feign fear; the Prioress sat as poetic and regal as ever. This was the secret language of the foundlings. It was a language carefully spoken with a keen eye and awareness of those who weren't talking as much as those who were. With the room full of quiet conversation, Agata had to wonder how anyone could listen to the words read by the great Maestra Prudenza? *Maybe this is why she is so angry all the time.*

Whenever Prudenza moved near, Agata felt the need to double-check herself for something she might have done wrong, a rule she might have overlooked, or a response that was expected in return. A small bead of sweat traveled down the back of her hairline to her neck. She wiped it away quickly and found the side of her skirt, feigning to dry it. She calmed herself by rubbing her index finger.

The bell ringer sounded the high-pitched ring, indicating a close of prayer and a walk to class.

"This is the Word of the Lord."

The girls stood and said, "Thanks be to God."

While Agata would not sing out loud, she projected the responsorial in sync with the other students. The girls cleared their bowls and walked out silently. There was still morning classes left and movement to follow, including midday supper, more of Prudenza and her reading, and more rice to be consumed. That didn't include rest or chores. It was the start of a long day. After the surprise calling out by Prudenza, and the outward conflict it created with the Prioress, Agata decided she needed to pay better attention. It would horrify her to be caught in one of the Maestra's outbursts and made an example of that tended to penance. She grabbed the side of her skirt as she walked, moving her finger back and forth against the fabric.

Thank God she had a music fundamentals class with Sotto Maestra Cristina for the first hour. Agata let the Sotto Maestra's calm voice and the practice of learning the names of each little black dot that found its home in the lines and spaces soothe her. She unraveled her hands from her skirt and let them sit openly in her lap. Her math and Latin classes didn't come with the excitement of music classes, but Agata was determined to try, and the noise in her mind quieted enough to let her. After a quiet lunch hour with no verbal outbursts, Agata looked forward to her last class of the day: *Piccolo Regazza Choir* with Sotto Maestra Elena.

The hallway was a blur of motion as white dresses traveled to their final classes. She interrupted the flow as she stepped into the line and stopped. Was that a man's voice? A tall girl behind her breathed into her hair and stepped onto the back of her shoes.

"Sorry. I mean..." Agata stumbled over her words. *Not supposed to talk. Put your head down.*

The line in front of her was disrupted at the same time. Buongiorno after Buongiorno rung out in a low voice. Agata caught a glimpse of a black pant leg. It was a man. Her heart pulsated. Besides Don Bollani, she understood men weren't allowed in these halls of women. There was talk that the Coro girls were instructed by male teachers from the outside. Maybe he had come for her. Was Nonna okay? Had she sent a letter? All her nerves were on edge, increasing the pace of her heart as she cranked her neck, trying to get a look at him.

Throughout her life, Agata hadn't talked to many men: Signor Betranozzi, with his presence as the neighborhood grandfather, with his inky hands and twinkling eyes; and strong and kind Signor Sellas, Gabriele's father, the mysterious but dependable man in the red coat. Her father's presence never made Agata feel safe. All the others never touched her.

The thick walls of the Pietà were to keep men out. The thought of one of them inside troubled her. The man greeted all the inmates by name with his hands clutching each other firmly behind his lower back as if someone had tied them there. Why was he allowed to talk so loudly in the halls? The rules for men and women were never the same, even here.

The loud man spun on his shoe, exposing a large, fuzzy black mustache that seemed to cover his whole face. "Ahh, you must be Agata. Tomasso Sovarizo, the governor of the Pietà." His sharp hazel eyes twinkled when he spoke.

Agata took a small step back, his exuberance a little too close for her liking.

"By your face, I can only guess you are surprised at seeing a man in your gleaming hallways of white. But I am quite as out of the way as I can be. You will find me checking on things here and again. I do hope you meet Signora Sovarizo soon. She is here more often than I and will be less harsh on the eyes. Nice to meet you, Agata. I don't want to be accused of making you late."

She picked up her pace in tandem with her thoughts. But it was an ease that welcomed her into her *Piccolo Choir* class.

"*Bondi* Agata," sung out Sotto Maestra Elena.

"*Bondi*, Sotto Maestra," echoed Agata.

It had all become familiar.

While she had learned the notes' names from Sotto Maestra Cristina, she learned how to sing their pitches with Sotto Maestra Elena. Elena taught them a new word called solfeggio, giving them a visual wizpresentation of the pitch by moving her arms up and down with an assigned syllable each time and then asking the girls to move their arms in sync with hers, thus matching the corresponding pitch. Agata didn't sing in group times, but she found this practice irresistible. Up and down her arms went, mirroring her teacher and committing the sounds to memory.

She recalled her father grabbing her finger and moving it up and down the page that day long ago in her Nonna's apartment. He was so gruff compared to her new Maestra. She never wanted to see him again, and what was more important, she didn't want him to see her. Maybe it would be a good idea to hide a little while longer in the Pietà so she could grow up a little and then run her Nonna's bakery. She would never let him back in the door.

The bell rang for the close of class. She was antsy to escape to her bed for a nap. It was the only time when she was alone. All she had to do was close her eyes, and she'd be back home, her Nonna kneading dough at her counter, her mother singing again. Her papa's voice was shut out of these dreams. He wasn't allowed. She followed the line in front of her, ready to escape and spend time with them.

"Agata, while it is the rest hour," urged Sotto Maestra Elena, "I thought we could take advantage of the quiet in the room for you to let me hear your voice." She brushed Agata's arm and led her back to the harpsichord.

Agata followed but shook her head. "No. No, grazie."

"I know it is overwhelming, all this newness, this busyness, but I assure you we have all stood where you do before. We are just little girls at heart who knew no talent until the Pietà gave us the realization that we had the capacity to learn it. This is your chance to learn from your imperfections and grow along with the girls next to you."

Agata, again, shook her head several times in timid defiance.

"And no one else can hear you but me," she teased and smiled. "How about we sing something together then? Let's try," Sotto Maestra Elena kindly persuaded and began to sing:

"*Adeste Fidelis.*"

Agata could no longer see; the tears came in a rush and blurred her vision. "Not that song. I cannot sing. I cannot sing." A heat spread across her chest, pulsating and expanding until she thought it might explode inside of her. Feeling a sudden urgency to flee, she ran outside the choir room, not knowing where to go. Her instincts told her to hide. She couldn't return to her bed; the room would be full of her bedmates tucked in for the afternoon rest hour. They'd stare if she walked in with a face full of tears. She ran down the stairs and through the chapel doors. She rushed in until reaching a few rows from the back and then crawled onto the floor. She made her body as small as she could, a little ball, and then found the knee rest from the pew pushed against it with her back. She folded her dress until a wrinkle lifted and rubbed her finger over the fabric. She closed her eyes. The pulsing eased. She could hear her breath again.

In her mind, Agata was right back at the well, in the fog of morning, the women singing and the gray clouds covering them. Her memories blurred into one. She recalled how heavy the bucket had been as she came around the bakery corner and into the back hall. She had never carried it alone. Nonna had gone to the *fornari* to drop off the *bivolo*. That was when Agata saw her mother's gray skirt splayed at the bottom of the stairs, her blonde curls spread on the floor, baby bump face down.

"Mama?" Agata dropped the bucket and put her mother's head in her lap.

Her curls were so soft despite being out of place. Agata had smoothed them behind her mother's ears, running her hand up and down the curve of her still face. A giant puddle of liquid formed beneath them. Had she kicked the bucket over? All that work—Nonna would be upset.

"I'm sorry, I'm sorry. I was just trying to help," Agata blustered. She looked around, hoping for help to walk in the door. The water became tinged with pink.

"The baby, Mama. Where is it?"

"My sweet, sweet Agata. You're my baby," her mama had said, looking up at her. "You will always be my baby, and you will be stronger than I ever could." Her mama's hand reached to touch Agata's face but then slumped back before reaching her.

Agata could feel the thick, warm ooze beneath her legs, the blood sprawling in all directions, carrying the life of her mother away. Mammina's eyes closed, and with that came her last breath.

"Mama, no. Come back, Mama. Come back. Help! Help me. Someone? Nonna?"

Agata cried out for her mother in the chapel, overtaken by the memory, all alone again on the floor. How could she tell them that if she sang, she'd only hear her voice? If she sang, she would drown out her mammina's voice. She couldn't lose the only thing she had left of her.

15
MARGARITA

Margarita closed the door to her bedroom and entered the hall with some of her spunk back in her step. She needed those afternoon naps more than she had in all her years in the Pietà. Every day, when early afternoon came, she'd feel her shoulders slumping and her patience waning, ready to shut out the worries around her and blow her bedside candle out. She would never admit that to anyone. It would make her sound old, and then there would be all their fussing. While her schedule no longer consisted of classes, private lessons, or choral rehearsals, it was as full as the girls in new lace collars. She still had hers, that lacy shawl, a little more cream than stark white- one could never stop the cycle of aging. She would wear it when special occasions called for it: a full choir for a dignified guest or a celebration, but mostly, it hung in her closet, a trophy of her femininity, not the public image of virginal and ethereal but the honest image: persevering, unruffled and wise.

The Pietà took careful measures in recording the names, titles, entrances, and exits of every woman who spent any time behind its protective walls. Some listings were short, poor, sick babes that only lasted a night or diseased women who spent their final days cared for with the dignity society did not give them—others, like herself, whose decades were sub-marked by all her different roles in the Pietà. The path was different for everyone. Some women did not possess the musical predisposition to train for the Coro, which is why they tested every foundling's aptitude by the age of eight. The less musically inclined girls trained in textile arts or medicine, with the potential of working in the Pietà's ground-floor ventures in their later years. The hospital administered vaccines and cared for the unwanted, while the textiles area had a successful laundering and hat-making business.

In her current assignment, she was listed as Discrete, a nice way of inferring: a retiree with no more obligations to the Coro—and as Margarita internally joked, whom they decided to keep around a bit longer instead of shipping off to a convent. Indeed, she was worth more than the average old woman slippering around.

"Discrete," a loud yet hushed voice called out to her.

Margarita turned to see Elena rushing over, her eyes scrunched with panic. "I pushed her too hard. I thought I could coax her. She ran out. I haven't been able to find her," Elena exclaimed in spurts between breaths.

Before Margarita could ask, she said out loud in sync with Elena, who clarified: "Agata."

"The child is tender, but you did what you were asked to. And there will be time to ask again. For now, we can't have her lost when there is no way she could be behind these walls," Margarita affirmed. "You start from the top, and I'll start from the main floor. I doubt she has managed to get across the walking bridge into the Church," Margarita encouraged. "Breathe."

Margarita watched Elena circle up the stairwell while she walked down it. She decided to start by inquiring about Don Giambattista Bollani in the Pietà chapel. She walked into the space, the smell of holy water filling the air, and caught sight of her old friend, the priest, who looked to be talking to the knee of a pew. She knew it was his daily practice, ambling up and down the pews, praying for each little girl who would claim her spot. He'd confided in Margarita that he felt awkward socially outside the church walls; he desired to lead the young inmates with conviction and provide the physical space they needed.

"Oh, oh, my child. Have you come for your confession? We always schedule those with one of your, ahem, Discrete present," Don Bollani bumbled. "That's it. Perhaps you should catch your breath for a moment and sit on the pew just there. It's okay. I will be backing up to and moving to the row in front of you so you can get your bearings."

Agata sat up, speaking in a whisper of clarity, "Agata. My name is Agata, and I miss my Nonna, my mammina." She half-cried, half-sighed, and then confessed, "And I'm afraid to sing."

"Oh, Don Giambattista, you have found her," Margarita exclaimed and crossed herself.

The priest let out an exhale. "I have found Agata. Well, she found me in the middle of my prayers." He continued, "She was hidden here under God's protection, and like us, He is not going anywhere. As you know, Discrete, we are all quite locked up in here together. We can't escape His protection even when we run and hide from Him." Margarita thought she saw a subtle wink twitch in her direction before he went on, "Agata has been brought here by God because Agata needs to find her voice."

Margarita held back her impatience. "I am quite sure, in the full peace of God, Agata will find her voice. Moreover…" She looked down at Agata. "…we will teach you how to use it."

Margarita spoke to the priest, "I thank you for watching out for our Agata and the reminder that God is indeed with us. I am sure you will see Agata again properly before the week is out for a confession. It seems we all require it." She gazed down at the young girl. "Agata, tell Don Giambattista thank you and apologize for the intrusion."

"Grazie, Padre," Agata mumbled.

"It is a good instinct already to seek protection under the shadow of His wing." His steps scurried toward the safety of the altar.

Margarita took Agata's hand and spoke to her calmly and with intent. "Agata, I understand your heart is heavy still with home, but this is your home now. In our home, we follow our reliable schedules, and the women put in place to guide us. In doing so, we ourselves become reliable. You need to apologize to Sotto Maestra Elena for running off." She paused and sought Agata's receipt of her words.

The girl's brow hadn't unfurrowed since her arrival; her cheeks were stained pink with leftover tears. But she finally mustered the courage to speak: "If I sing, how will I hear my mammina's voice? If I sing, I will cover it up."

Margarita placed her hands over the top of Agata's and held them together like a clam. "You will learn the value of your voice here and the appropriateness of measuring it. God grants all of us a voice unique to us. No one can ever replicate or dampen it—it is our signature from our Creator."

"Like Nonna's 'G,'" Agata responded decidedly. "Nonna said that once you write something down with your signature, it will be written down for generations to see."

"Your Nonna was a smart woman," Margarita admitted.

"Was?" Agata inquired.

"There is a strong girl inside you and a strong voice behind it waiting to come out. I am eager to hear it when she does." She patted the girl's small, clammy hand beneath hers.

"I had a special class in mind for you to finish your day. I see it is very timely. We must leave now so as not to be an interruption," Margarita advised.

They stood up together. Margarita walked Agata to a very large classroom on the main floor. A room of girls sat with their heads down, focused on the cloths in their laps.

"I'm sorry, Poeta, to interrupt. This is Agata," Margarita implored.

"Yes, I know Agata. We met her first night," Poeta said. Margarita appreciated the familiar tinge of liveliness in her eyes.

"Agata, your seat is just there. Please take a seat, and I will catch you up," Poeta directed.

Poeta brought a big white cloth to her and set it on Agata's lap.

"I took the liberty of stripping these from your bed. We all weave an insignia on our sheets to keep track of them when we wash them. Have you ever used a needle before?"

Agata shook her head.

"I see you still aren't much for words. Maybe we need to start with a practice fabric first, then. While I fetch that, I want you to think of something special, a mark that is just for you that you can embroider on your pillowcase and top sheet. Maddalena has a cursive 'M,' and Giulia has a bird. Do you have something special you would like to be yours?"

"A flower," Agata said decisively.

"A flower. That is a lovely idea. Let's see. There are roses and daisies, and we could start with a round shape…"

Agata interrupted, "I'd like to learn to make a Camelia for my mother. That was her name."

"I knew someone stubborn enough not to talk must have lots of meaningful things building up. Camelia, that's perfect. What a way to honor your mother and have her close to you every time you lie down your head. We will start with short lines and then move to loops."

"You see, you are in good hands, my dear," Margarita encouraged. "I have another errand to run. I will find you later."

Margarita walked into the main entrance, where a verbal scene was at play between the shy Innocentia and a brambly older woman.

"I have written to her three times, in fact, and I have never received a reply." The older woman's deep voice echoed throughout the entry.

Goodness, she was a loud one. Innocentia had likely never interacted with such vocal girth.

"Excuse me, madam. If I could have you come with me, I will see to your request." Margarita put her hand up to the loud woman's shoulder blade, removing her from the echo of the entry.

"My name is Discrete Margarita. We talk at a level proportionate to our peaceful surroundings. I would ask that you do the same so as not to disrupt the quiet here. Please tell me your name and how I may help you."

"Oh, I'm sorry, of course. It is just that I am upset. Let me begin again. My name is Benedetta Betranozzi. I have recently lost a very dear friend who placed her granddaughter here for safekeeping as she was unable to care for her. And I thought I could come to check on Agata and let her know we are still thinking of her, maybe offer some of her Nonna's belongings for comfort."

Margarita pulled Signora Betranozzi behind the first closed door, which happened to be Prudenza's office. Prudenza looked up at the intrusion, looking ready for battle, but Margarita disarmed her with a request.

"I am so sorry for the interruption, Prudenza, but it seems we have a great need for Madonna. Could you please?"

Prudenza got up without remark. It was mere seconds before Madonna pushed through the door.

"I am Benedetta Betranozzi, and I am a very dear family friend to Agata Farusi. I have written three letters…"

The Prioress pushed her palm in the woman's direction. Benedetta stopped mid-sentence.

"Signora Betranozzi, I know who you are, and I thank you for taking the time to come today. I note your concern for Agata and offer my condolences regarding Guilelma. This is a sad time for your community. I understand you were good friends."

"Life-long friends."

The Prioress held her hand out, inviting her guest to sit in a chair directly in front of her as she took Prudenza's seat behind her desk. Margarita remained standing near the door.

"Life-long friends, which mean family to you," said Madonna.

"Yes." Benedetta obeyed and sat down as instructed. Guilelma observed Benedetta, clearly dumbstruck by Madonna's assertiveness and calm.

"You are right. I consider myself Agata's family. It has been one month since her grandmother died, two months she's been away from us, and I had hoped to bring her home and know she has support and a home when she is ready."

The Prioress remained still, but her words moved proficiently. "Agata's home is here now. This is the wish of her grandmother, who herself sent us a notarized note directing any funds from her estate to Agata's future. I have full knowledge and documents on every inmate here. If there is news to be had, a background or name to know, it is in their files," the Prioress continued designly. "I know Pietro Farusi. He is part of the extended music community in our Serrenissima. As the head of this musical institution and one who hires teachers from that very community, I also know he is not in a position to raise a child."

Benedetta softened. "I don't want her to feel abandoned. I love that girl like my own. That man has already made another appearance in our neighborhood, and I am not sure of the extent of damage he will cause with his lies and dramatizations. I want Aggi to hear the truth of her Nonna's words and wishes from us." She spoke not as the fighting soldier who had gone in but as a weakened, loving aunt.

"It is true. The lies of one man can wreak havoc. But the truth of a healed life once broken speaks for itself." Madonna paused. "We are fighting the same opponent, you and me. The sins of the Serrenissima are carried on the backs of the infants laid at the *scafetta*. The retribution comes as we heal them. I believe wholeheartedly in this. I spend every waking minute thinking of these girls, believing in these girls, and standing up for these girls. I maintain firmly that Agata will flourish most fully in her future here."

Benedetta lowered her head in defeat. "Can you at least give her this?" She laid a long item wrapped in cloth on the Prioress' desk.

"I can assure you she will see it when she is supposed to." She laid her hand on top of the bundle, meeting the fingers of Benedetta, who didn't quite let go of it.

In one swift movement, Signora Betranozzi nodded, stood, and pulled her hand away.

The Prioress walked Benedetta toward her office door. "I assure you, Signora Betranozzi, Agata will grow and be taken care of here. I wouldn't see it any other way. In time, I trust you will be able to witness her maturation and healing from the audience seats of the Chiesa della Pietà."

A grim Signora Betranozzi walked out the door with her chin held high as if she wouldn't dare show defeat. Margarita recognized the doggedness in her spirit; if they had been on the same side of the scafetta green door, they could have likely been friends. Margarita softened when she saw the tears pool in the woman's eyes. She placed her hand low at her back, barely skimming the fabric.

"I'll walk you out, Signora," Margarita said. "I still have someone I need to check on."

Margarita looked back at the Prioress to see whether she understood who her someone was. After concluding her business there, Margarita moved as fast as she could back to the sewing room and found Agata completely caught up, with the bedsheet pooling in her lap and the pink string clutched in her hand. Margarita released a breath. It was apparent she was utterly unaware of anything but the moment she was in.

"Let me see your progress, Agata," Margarita said and crouched close to view Agata's work.

"My Camelia." Agata beamed. Her smile was soft and her brown eyes radiant. It was the first time Margarita had the pleasure of seeing such an expression on the girl's face.

"Oh, dear, it really is beautiful. A perfect tribute."

"If I finish my last petal, I can sleep on them tonight." Agata, for once, had more to say. "Discrete? I'm going to try. I'm going to try to be happy here and learn. I know my Nonna would want that." It was the second time today Margarita had heard her speak with such clarity.

"Oh, child, I have every faith you will find your way in here," Margarita responded.

The child's disparity was acute, and her youth could not absorb that her current circumstance was not temporary. But Margarita had just walked Agata's old life out the door, knowing it would be the only way for her to find her new one.

16

AGATA

A year passed quickly in the time signature of the Pietà.

The morning bells sang, releasing the foundlings from their sleep. Agata opened her eyes. It was dark. Only the candle-bearers' flames moving up and down the halls cast dashes of light off the walls and sheets of dreaming girls. She slipped off her nightgown and folded it back under her pillow. She pulled her white dress over her head. Her hands moved dexterously, plaiting two braids as she sang alongside her sleepy roommates:

"Lord, open my lips, and my mouth will proclaim your praise."

Agata stood and made her bed, flattening the sheet with her palm.

She broke away from the song, leaned down, kissed the flower on her pillowcase, and whispered, "I'm off, Mama."

She walked the same routine she had a year ago, but now with the nimbleness of her braid-making—practiced and anticipative. Agata sang her way to mass, moving in cadence with her fellow foundlings to breakfast, then moved on to her busy schedule: Latin, arithmetic, and beginner violin ensemble. Her teacher, Maestra Maria, was known in the Coro as Maria del Viola, her primary string instrument, though she could play all string instruments proficiently. Maestra Maria had been a part of the performing Coro for ten years and was as prized for her teaching as she was for her playing. In keeping with the expected instrumental differentiation, she taught the beginner's violin three days a week; during the other two, she switched to the theorbo, an instrument held across the lap instead of under the chin. Maestra Maria was brash but brave and honest. She had black hair wrapped in a high bun, dark brown eyes that looked right through you when she spoke and a wide waist. Agata wasn't threatened by her directness; instead, she was inspired to please her.

Agata warmed up her violin along with the others and felt the familiar buzz of warmth at the end of her hand. She stopped to inspect her fingers, admiring the tiny pink calluses that had grown. During the first few months at the Pietà, her hands throbbed and ached. During mass or lessons, she'd pick at the new skin, soft and tender to the touch, clenching her fists to hide the sores. But the skin had darkened, a sign of the more experienced musicians she roomed with in her *dormotorio*. She was a year or two older than her classmates since entering the Pietà after they had started their education. She hesitated when the larger group departed the *caffeterria,* aware of Candida and her other roommates walking off to their shared classes. At the same time, she was clumped with the beginners to learn on her own. It had sparked a gnawing feeling she had not experienced before. She hadn't decided yet what to name it.

"Good morning, class," said Maestra Maria. "We will spend the next hour on our *Te Lucis* piece. Let's pull our music out and begin by reciting the count verbally while patting the rhythm rests on our knees. We will count through two verses at tempo without stopping."

The Maestra raised her hands, counted, "One, two, three," and then mouthed *four.*

The counting patterns came easily to Agata, but she found an anticipatory joy in saying them with her peers sitting around her. She imagined the tones and pitches of their individual speaking voices as if they were talking. The only other times she heard the other foundlings was when they sang in the choir or responsorial in mass. She didn't count their hallway or bedtime whispers. Though Agata was not much of a talker, she missed the sounds of banter and conversation around her. How long would it take, she wondered, to get used to the quiet?

The scales and pitches she spent time with daily became her friends. They were reliable and unchanging. She knew whether she read the letter on the staff or placed her fingers on the fingerboard, the same note would come out every time. It was up to her to know the pitch and placement.

"Pasqua, you need to stay on the beat, not behind it," Maestra said. "Rosanna, sit up tall, please, no slouching. We will try again."

As new as Agata still felt, she saw many girls in her music classes struggling. It was easily detectable when a look of embarrassment followed an extra clap thrown in. She watched as Pasqua bit her lip, and Rosanna frowned in her eyes as they were scolded. Maestra left no room for imperfection, which Agata had quickly learned was not acceptable in any classroom at the Pietà, but Maestra Maria let you know it.

"Agata, child, I would like you to switch seats with Pasqua, right there next to Michelina."

Agata moved her music over to the music stand furthest from the right, along with the other first violin, and tried not to show her excitement. Pasqua brushed her shoulder and sat down firmly in Agata's old spot. Competition played with the balance of making friends and securing enemies. Agata sighed quietly in relief as she heard the bell chime through the halls, marking the end of class and the tension that filled it.

Agata jumped up to meet her roommates at their table during lunch hour. She couldn't wait to share the news that she got bumped up to first violin, that was, until she heard Maestra Prudenza's grave voice. Agata stiffened. She would have to walk past Prudenza to get to her table. Prudenza remained the one person in the Pietà who struck fear in Agata. She clenched her tray and set her feet and eyes forward.

"Don't ever make eye contact. She could turn you to stone!" Candida's earlier warnings whirled through Agata's mind. She was only joking, she told herself, but Agata's fear made her uncertain.

"Agata!" Prudenza commanded.

Agata snapped her shoulders up to her ears and froze. Scary Prudenza had stopped reading. All eyes were now on her.

"You have been here long enough to know that we walk toward the tables, not in front of someone speaking."

In her nervousness, Agata hadn't realized she was as close as Prudenza claimed. Or was she?

"Sorry, Maestra, I will watch my steps more carefully," Agata apologized.

The admission must have satisfied her enough. Prudenza continued reading as if there hadn't been an intrusion.

Agata placed her tray between Candida and Lorenza, a dark-voiced, black-haired bass player. Candida searched for her hand under the table and gave it a *You're okay* squeeze. Prudenza stared at their table as if awaiting an opportunity to pounce. She undoubtedly had the entire bible memorized and was holding it for show.

Annetta, a thin-cheeked, cheerful violin player, sat across from her, her back to Prudenza. Annetta fluttered her eyes in hello. It calmed the nervous flutter in Agata's heart. The group of friends greeted one another with smiles in their eyes and under-the-table hand squeezes. Agata had become a part of them. The revelry and companionship gave a kind of joy she had not experienced before. It was never long enough to sit in their company and always too long to listen to Prudenza read the scripture, yet Agata was still too far from home. While on the outside, some of her smiles were restored; inside, she could not completely sever Canciano.

While the strict rule against chatter could result in a missed meal or time mopping a floor somewhere between the *caffeterria* doorframe and the hall on the way to their next class, a few whispers still snuck out between the foundlings.

"That woman! She looks for things to make an example of us, and how is it possible not to expect us to talk? It is, in fact, impossible for me." Candida spoke emphatically.

"Oh, that we know. It's a good thing for the rest of us, or you'd never shut up!" Lorenza said.

Giulia, whom Agata had learned made a regular habit of keeping everyone in order, gave a "Shhh!" sound with her mouth in a neutral position so she wouldn't get blamed for noise if she got caught.

The warmth of friendship helped to fade the newness of grief that still clung to her. Agata walked, feeling hopeful, into her favorite class alongside her friends.

"Attention, *Piccola Regazza Choir.* I have a special announcement," Sotto Maestra Elena said. Their normally calm teacher had a tremor of excitement in her voice.

"Our beloved Madonna is allowing both the Coro and Commun beginner choirs to watch the debut of Maestro Vivaldi's new work, *Gloria in D.* This is a rarity, but both the Prioress and I agree that hearing what you can be will make some of you understand the purpose of being here. In turn, you will see how your hard work can dictate your future."

Agata had learned there were two distinct sides to the Pietà. The *figlie di commun,* where she currently found herself, was housed on the outer wall and comprised of girls from ages six to eighteen. By six years of age, all the girls were introduced to instruments in addition to their other classes: Latin, arithmetic, religious studies, and introductory textile arts. If their aptitude proved worthy, they would be tested to be a part of *figlie del Coro,* the side of the Pietà housed in the warmer interior. This was the pathway to the performing Coro, 'The Poinsettia Girls'. It took fifteen to twenty years of training and auditions to get to the top level, where the performing Coro played for the public, primarily in the connected *Chiesa di Pietà*. Agata had never heard any of her Maestras perform outside of their instruction times, nor was she permitted to pass the locked door to the hall of the Chiesa. It was as mysterious as the green door itself.

She looked from Lorenza to Candida; all of them were grinning. Finally, they had been awarded the chance to be a small part of it. Lorenza grabbed her hand.

"*Te Lucis Ante Terminum* is the name of the piece we will sing as we enter. All of you should have been playing this in your instrumental classes this week, so the rhythm and tune itself should already be sealed in your memory. We will sing with music to solidify the text." Sotto Maestra Elena continued, "The most important thing we can do in any concert is to remain quiet. Not a sigh, giggle, or cough can be heard while the Coro performs. This is a privilege Madonna rarely grants here to girls your age. This said, we will practice our quiet as we practice the music. We are weeks away from its debut, but we need to know it like we know our path to the *caffeterria*."

For months after arriving at the Pietà, Agata had struggled with opening her mouth to sing. She'd longed to shut out all the newness: the stark white walls and countless women whose alabaster skirts scuffed against the floors—and in her dreams, she could. The hours of the Pietà took over, boldly marking the predictability of her time. As her days busied, her thoughts did too. She found she'd fallen asleep exhausted, and her mammina's voice became distant, buried behind Latin phrases, numbers, notes, and whispers all stirred up. She prayed to her every morning at mass as she'd promised herself on that dark day on the gondola. She didn't tell anyone. Prayers were meant for God or the Virgin or to express her iniquities at confession to Don Bollani. She tried to talk to her Nonna too, but every time she started, she'd convince herself, *Nonna knows I love her, whether I speak to her or not*. She liked to picture her with Benedetta and Alba playing cards in her bed. She couldn't bear to consider the possibility of anything else.

"You need to pretend you are singing with your mom instead of without her," Candida told her.

Agata didn't know how to do that on her own, but when Sotto Maestra lifted her arms, and the familiar voices of Candida, Annetta, Lorenza, and the others surrounded hers, it gave Agata the permission she needed to let the notes come out.

Sotto Maestra counted the choir's entry. Agata felt something unlatch like a heavy door she could not lift on her own. Inside the door were fragments of memories of her Mammina: the warmth of her hand wrapped around hers as they ventured to market, the sky full of clouds and movement. She pictured the back of her, the small blonde curls that never stayed off her neck, and the sound of her light voice humming alongside her. Agata wrapped her fingers around a piece of her skirt, rubbing the top of it, and sang with her.

Te lucis ante terminum

Rerum creator poseimus
Ut solita clementia sis presaul ad custodian
Te corda nostra somnient
Te per soporem sentient
Tu amque semper gloriam vicina lucie cocinant
Vitam sa lubren trubue
Nostrom calorem refice
Taetrom noctis caliginem tu a calustret claritas
Praestra Pater omnipotens
Per Iesum Christum Dominum
Qui tecum in perpetuum, regnant cum Sancto Spiritu.
Amen

The music opened the door to that secret place where the dream meetups faded. And so, she sang, quietly and mostly to herself so she could hear her mammina's soft soprano voice next to hers.

17
ELENA

When one spent a lifetime inhabiting quiet and nurturing it through dogged discipline, freedom of thought was akin to sin. Elena stared at the ivory wooden keys of the harpsichord, lost in her sentiments. While she needed time in the practice room to rehearse her music, the enclosed space had a way of inviting secrets from her mind's hidden corners. She had found it indulgent as of late to fall upon a thought or feeling and then chase it down, one after another. It was the recall of small moments in her day, like walking out of mass and noticing the younger braided girls, their pale faces concentrated to mind the quiet, but their small feet swinging as they dangled inches off the floor. Those feet would be running and bare if they lived outside of the Pietà.

Sometimes, it was the empathy she felt when a child seemed frustrated as she tried to understand a new concept and was not allowed to verbalize her feelings. No matter where they spiraled from, it struck her that she wanted children of her own and the calm of her own home to raise them in.

She went as far as to imagine the details of her house: a small kitchen, a stove to warm them, and what was more, a husband. She wasn't exposed to many men besides a few outside teachers who came in, though none sparked her interest in them, unlike her fellow Coro members, who ogled over this teacher or that or even the conductor himself. To Elena, those were men to take direction from, only a means to an end to help her improve musically. The Pietà encouraged a spirit of personal growth and finding gratitude within the solidarity and with the women they lived with. Was this discontentment or mere desire? She bore the weight of it in her mind, grappling with it, trying to remove the thoughts one minute and then completely immersed in them the next.

Bang, bang, bang. Someone pounded at the door behind her.

"Your hour is up! Is anyone in there?" an irritated voice asked.

"Yes, I'm here." Elena jostled. "I am gathering my music now."

Elena scrambled to gather her things and opened the door, coming eye to eye with a second-year student. Embarrassed as if the girl knew the thoughts she entertained, Elena pushed past her with a muffled, "Sorry."

While she mentally punished herself for the oversight, she countered the feeling with swift steps down the hall, remembering what was next on her schedule. A body pushed into her shoulder.

"We have that staff meeting with the board. I wonder what they want to tell us. It can't be for nothing." Slight Cristina knocked into her with a surprising jolt of force. Elena looked around to make sure they were alone.

"Don't worry, I wouldn't have done that." Cristina moved back to the appropriate distance and swung her blond braid over her shoulder. "You seem distracted. Are you doing alright?"

Elena wasn't ready to share, even with her closest friend. "Just busy, trying to fit that practice time in."

Cristina looked skeptical. "I am sure whatever this meeting is about will get that worry out of your mind. You know, Elena, I do not doubt that you will be one of the next major soloists to step on that balcony stage. You only have to get through one more audition."

Elena took the compliment to heart; she admired Cristina's musical abilities. What she couldn't decipher was whether a lifetime in the performing Coro was what she really wanted anymore. After all the years she had put in, though she wouldn't admit that to anyone, she couldn't believe she was still asking it of herself. Could she really give up the dream of finally becoming a Poinsettia Girl?

The two young women walked with purpose into the chapel. Usually, the Sotto Maestras and Maestras met with Madonna weekly in her large meeting room and office. The governor and the board also met with Madonna weekly, but the two groups never met together.

"Good afternoon, Sotto Maestras, Maestras, our esteemed board members, and our governor himself, Signor Sovarizo," Madonna spoke from the front. "I will let the governor begin."

The perky governor popped up. "Good afternoon, ladies, young Sotto Maestras, and honored Maestras. First, I'd like to thank you for the tireless work you put in to keep the Pietà's revolution moving forward. And it is a revolution of sorts, isn't it?" He interrupted his speech with a wink. "A government that supports the less fortunate around us and lifts them up to sing and perform on what is arguably Venice's greatest stage."

Elena glanced at Cristina with the intent of measuring the sensationalized fluff that came from the governor's mouth. He was well-intended. But to constantly be referred to as a derelict Venice *lifted up* was tiresome. Every woman there had fought for and earned their coveted position in the Coro.

"I wanted to make a staff change announcement to all of us in one place, so we present it as a singular message with no other addenda. Our beloved Assistant Prioress Signora Clara has left our coveted walls of the Pietà. We approved an offer of marriage from a respected member of our Serrenissima who apparently couldn't take his eyes off her." The governor chuckled. "While it is sudden, we wish her the best in her new life. We have had several considerations and delegates who wanted their chance next in line." He took a dramatic breath. "After much deliberation, we are pleased to announce Maestra Prudenza as the new assistant prioress."

Elena and all the Sotto Maestras in her row exchanged glances, unable to contain their shock. Elena looked at Madonna in the front row. She sat poised with a calm smile glued to her face, then turned her head toward Prudenza and offered a congratulatory nod in her direction. Elena hoped this would not cause problems; Signora Clara was such a delight.

With her head so full, Elena was grateful to get the last announcement.

"Remember, our alms walk is next week. Sotto Maestra Elena? We look forward to seeing the 'literal' profits of your hard work."

Elena nodded to show her gratitude, though what she felt was, stuck.

Elena hurried down the spiral staircase from her orchestra rehearsal, fussing with the right side of her hair. It had fallen out of her low bun, and she had no time to return to her room and fix it. Because rehearsal ran over, she was barely going to make the set meeting time to warm up her choir of littles for the alms walk. She was aggravated; it was bad luck to start any performance tussled. It was also unfortunate that the first person she locked eyes with was the newly appointed Assistant Prioress Prudenza, pacing in the entry hall. It seemed she felt obligated to be at all the places Madonna might be, whether she had a specific duty or not. Prudenza called out to her.

"We wondered if you would make it, Sotto Maestra. I thought I might have to warm them up myself," said Prudenza.

Thankfully, Madonna and the governor's wife, Signora Sovarizo, were less concerned with her schedule management. They had organized the girls together in two lines.

"I did not wonder, Sotto Maestra. Take a breath." Madonna turned toward her, "Did Signor Gasparini get inspired today?" and permitted a rare, playful smile.

"I think so, Madonna. Thank you for asking," replied Elena.

"Have you met our governor's wife?" asked Madonna.

"Marcella Sovarizo," a dark-haired woman in a burgundy coat with an unusually confidant air, interrupted them. "And you are Elena, the up-and-coming soprano, I hear. Nice to meet you. My husband says the future is bright. The crowds will be lined up when it's your turn to sing solos in the Coro."

Her generous comments and forward demeanor took Elena aback. *That must be a lively home,* she thought, reflecting on the governor's earlier presumptuous commentary. She returned a smile. "You are so kind to say so. If you'll excuse me, I need to get these girls warmed up for our outing."

"Here, let's give you a hand," replied the governor's wife and reached for her hair to fix her bun before Elena could accept or refuse her.

"Thank you." She stood there awkwardly, unused to anyone fussing over her. She was more than anxious to get away from her hands and get to her class. She stood before the girls, took a breath, and began.

"Good afternoon, girls. Eyes on me," Elena directed as the girls' eyes lifted to hers. Elena warmed them up as Madonna and Signora Sovarizo negotiated who would be at the front and how the best singers would blend into the group so that the sound resonated evenly throughout the line, swapping one girl for the next until they were satisfied. Prudenza circled them like a bird of prey.

Discrete Margarita and Discrete Orsa joined the group to aid Madonna and Signora Sovarizo in the outing.

"Assistant Prioress, thank you for seeing us out. I trust you will keep things in order during the short time I am away." Madonna did not wait for a response. She picked up her collection vessel—the cue that it was time to go.

Elena counted the girls in, and they began their first song. She felt the fresh outdoor air fill her as the doors opened behind her. They walked out slowly in song. As soon as they were visible, it would become a deliberate show to the community.

The Prioress walked ahead of them, making an intentional slow entrance to the passersby on the large waterfront walkway, the Riva degli Schiavoni. Elena squinted at the cloud-covered sunlight that hit her eyes, careful not to let her focus detract from the eighteen small girls who stared back at her. Some looked nervous and frail, precisely what the board intended—to invoke the public's pity. The point of it all was to collect money. For Elena, it was one of many "First times outside" of the Pietà she had overseen. She thought specifically of Agata, who had joined them a year ago and couldn't help but question whether it was a good idea to expose her so quickly to the outside elements. She had arrived so affected by her former life. Agata stood in the middle of some of her favorite young singers and leaders: Candida, Lorenza, Annetta…those who would take Elena's place in the Coro long after she retired herself—a cycle unchanged for many generations.

Elena was struck by the cold, salty air against the water and the Lido perfectly displayed in the distance. She let the shoreline sky cleanse her, wading her conducting arms through the damp air. They sang a simple chant as they walked and made a half-circle with their backs to the water, close to the Prioress. A group of listeners stopped their errands as the rarely seen foundling girls alerted them with their song. It was uncommon for the public to interact with the young girls, their donations a luxury for those to later afford tickets when the gifted ones would perform in the Coro. Heads bent to whisper and fingers pointed in their direction. Elena hated that they were such a spectacle.

The young choir completed two songs as the Prioress led them west on the Riva Degli Schiavoni, nodding in thanks at those who put money in the small vessel she held. After singing several rounds of their first song, they came to the great columns of St. Mark's Square. The crowds in the already busy square began to thicken. Elena kept her arms moving but was aware of the strangers encircling them. Groups of men huddled and stopped their chatting at the sight of the virginal foundlings from the Pietà. Elena noticed the girls averting their eyes from the attention. She stood firm in front of them, motioning the girls to gather close, and directed them through another two songs in a simple two-part harmony. Quite hastily, a gaunt man with long black hair pushed back by a white carnival mask on top of his head moved up to the front of the crowd. He had a strange familiarity about him, but something seemed off. Had she met this man before? Her eyes locked with Discrete Margarita, who offhandedly stepped in front of him. The other women, Discrete Orsa, Marcella Sovarizo, and

Madonna, formed a square around the girls, all while exchanging glances. It was time to move.

Madonna initiated, leading them away from the square, forcing an escape path with her mere presence. People parted for the serious woman in a white headdress with the alms vessel. Elena had the girls sing as they proceeded toward a quiet calle away from the large square to prevent the stares from overwhelming them. Madonna stopped in front of the Chiesa di San Giorgio; a Greek church tucked into a quiet corner and steps away from the Pietà's back door.

There was a breath of calm once the girls were tucked in, followed by a breath of panic after one misstep. Out of the corner of her eye, Elena saw a man's body step into her view of Annetta, who stood at the corner of the front row. Before she could think of what to do, Discrete Margarita again placed herself between Annetta and the man, her head a whole length shorter at his chest. She looked up at him as if in challenge.

This irritated the man who yelled out, "Aggi! It's my Aggi! It's me, your papa!"

The man pushed his mask further back, revealing his face to the choir of girls. He had a look of desperation framed by black, intense eyebrows. Elena scanned the choir to locate Agata, safely placed at the center of the group. But Agata had stopped singing. Elena watched a look of fear sweep across her sweet face like a dark shadow. The unmasked man stared directly at Agata with those familiar sad eyes—just like hers. A wash of cold air poured over Elena. She shifted her weight as if to fight the instability of the moment, keeping her conducting arms in motion. Agata's eyes fell back into her head as she sank into the shroud of white dresses and to the ground. Elena lowered her arms. She couldn't move. The young, ethereal voices screamed for their friend and tightened around her. Madonna joined Discrete Margarita, and the unmasked man shrank back away from the crowd.

Signora Marcella pushed everyone out of the way to jump in and assist the unconscious foundling. Elena knew the governor's wife had spent a lot of time volunteering in Pietà's lower-level hospital and rushed to Agata immediately, demonstrating she was as knowledgeable as she was expeditious.

"We need to give her space and make her comfortable," Signora Marcella exclaimed.

In the chaos, a gentleman in a dark blue jacket with a short black beard approached Elena, speaking softly. "Excuse me, Signora, I am Lodovico Rossi, a friend to the Pietà. How can I help?"

Elena, quite in shock, took in the scene and the gentleman's calm, steady countenance. His thick hair fell at his temples in a wave bordering his clear, almond eyes. She stumbled on her words. "Thank you…Signor." Elena turned back toward Agata, unsure of how to respond to him.

"It's not a long walk, but long enough. I could at least carry the girl while we get the others in," Signor Rossi suggested.

"Yes, of course." Elena snapped herself alert by walking him over to where the governor's wife sat with Agata's head in her lap.

Signora Marcella administered maternal shushes while smoothing the sides of Agata's hair. Lodovico Rossi bent down, recognizing the governor's wife, a long-time family friend.

"Hello, Signora Sovarizo. Please let me be of assistance and carry the girl back."

"Oh, Buongiorno, Signor Rossi, a saint in your timing! I will take you up on your offer. Please be careful with her."

Signor Rossi lifted Agata in one swoop. Elena was awed at the gentleness with which the man held the small child.

Discrete Margarita appeared to assist Discrete Orsa, who had already begun guiding the choir girls toward the Pietà's back gate. Elena looked back for the unmasked man. The quiet corner remained empty as if it had never been anything else. She looked down at her hands. They were trembling.

Lorenza ran past Margarita to hold the back garden gate open.

"Stand back and let her through!" Signora Marcella kept pace with Signor Rossi.

"Agata, you are going to be okay. Can you hear me? We are getting you back to your safe, warm bed in the Pietà," said Signora Marcella.

Elena helped round up the girls and stood next to Discrete. Madonna joined them.

"Girls, remain calm and go straight to the dining hall. We have missed the lunch hour. Not to worry, we will get you all fed," Margarita directed the others.

Margarita's voice went straight to a whisper. "Was it him?" she asked Madonna.

"I'm afraid so," she whispered back, "But I let him know in uncertain terms that all the children present belong to the Pietà. He is misinformed if he believes otherwise."

"Hopefully, this isn't too much of a setback for Agata," Elena said, uneasy as they made their way through the courtyard. "Feelings tend to ripple through every room of the Pietà."

"Our job is to make sure they don't. She will be fine. An unexpected day, but nothing we won't get through," said Madonna, as resolute as always, which Elena needed after a day like today.

"And it's nothing you won't either," she said, turning to face Elena." Go and take a minute alone, splash some water on your face, and say a prayer. Rejoin us when you're ready. I will aid Discrete with the girls." Madonna walked off.

Elena wanted nothing more than to get back to the quiet, but she didn't want to be alone.

18
AGATA

The wind pushed the edge of the black cape toward Agata's bed. If she tucked her face into the sheets, maybe she'd avoid it seeing her. She peered back out. Was it still there? She recognized the large square window in the corner. She wasn't in her bed on Papa's apartment floor; she was in her Nonna's bed. The black mourning fabric blew and danced from the window like water in the sea. Dark had made her imagination the truth-teller. Her panic eased, and she drifted into deeper sleep, safe. She found herself walking all alone down Venice's cobbled streets.

In this congested city of people, no crowds gawked; it was just her alone. Instinctively, she shaded her brow with her arm and then realized the black lace mask already offered her protection. The bright sun wove itself in and out of clouds, highlighting her course. The *calle* wound tighter and tighter before her until she was face to face with the fabric that had grown from a black strip into a dark mass. There was nowhere to go. The street behind her had shut her in. She reached out to grab the taunting fabric. It was silky and slipped between her fingers as if something was sucking it up from the other side. The billowy fabric became a tiny black dot evaporating between the walls. She awoke and sat straight up, taking in her surroundings. She sucked in her breath, relieved. She was in her *dormotorio*, with her roommates' quiet hums and snores.

Giulia woke to see who was sitting up in the darkness and then flopped back over, facing away from Agata.

Candida whispered through a yawn, "Another nightmare?"

Agata nodded, thankful for a companion in the dark.

"He can't get you in here, you know," Candida encouraged. "And by the way, he backed down from Madonna and our little Discrete as if they were giants..." Candida stopped to giggle.

"Ugh, what time is it?" complained Lorenza in the bed next to Candida.

Agata shrugged. "Early."

Lorenza rubbed her eyes and sat up.

"You shouldn't worry about your papa, Agata. Madonna would never let a man like that through the doors. Even if he is a musician," said Lorenza through a long yawn.

"You know he's a musician?" questioned Agata.

"We all know. Why else would you be in here?" said a voice in the corner. "Now, would you be quiet? I'm trying to sleep," grumped Giulia.

Agata looked back at her two friends, perplexed, but they had already lain back down. For the first time, Agata knew with assurance that she was glad to be under the Pietà's protection and not flung out into the big world with only her father to lean on. Something was very different about him than she remembered. She had thought him to be a respected musician in their Serrenissima. But he looked like something wild she had no word for, lost and frightened. When his mouth opened, she could no longer hear his voice. It was only his pained face that she saw. Not the one she lived with, that was haughty and forceful one minute, reticent and dark the next. As she thought about it, her mind could no longer recall the sound of his voice either.

Agata went through the next day tucked inward, her body and mind working as separate entities as if not of the same person. It was hard to concentrate on her music with her thoughts stomping around so loudly. She played the same warmups she had day after day in Maestra Maria's class. Her bow seemed to move on its own while she rehashed the previous day's encounter. The world outside these walls wasn't free like she remembered. It was chaotic. In the crowds full of gray faces stood her papa, a faded version of himself. If it hadn't been for Madonna praying over Agata as she lay in her little bed later that same evening, she would have convinced herself she hadn't seen him, that it was only fear chasing her in memory as it had for months.

"Agata, where are you? Let me hear you play the first two lines," Maestra Maria directed.

Agata awoke from her thoughts and hastily played the lines without flaw. Her playing had improved tenfold over the last six months. In time, class was released, but the fog she was in wasn't. She spent the entire thirty minutes of nap hour staring at the ceiling. She knew Candida couldn't stand it when Agata was quiet, which, comparatively speaking, was all the time. But her friend knew her now, and Agata was conscious that she hadn't stepped out of her thoughts since the alms walk. She didn't feel like talking about it. She needed to work it out herself.

"Agata, cheer up. The *Gloria in D* concert is just a few weeks away. And we get to hear the Coro perform finally!" Candida implored over nap hour.

The bell ringer clanked the bell. Time for afternoon *la tasca*. It saved Agata from having to be cheerful when she wasn't ready to be. Agata marched with the girls out the door, happy to veer separately from most of them as she headed downstairs to work in the laundry room.

"*Bondi*, Agata," Poeta greeted her. "You can get started folding here with me." Poeta stood behind a large table mounded with sheets that resembled puffy clouds.

Agata had forgotten how much she liked clouds until she saw them on the alms walk. Looking up at them, knowing they had been floating over her family's bakery just minutes before, made her feel connected to her old life and shielded in her new one.

"*Bondi*," replied Agata and approached the table. She placed her hands in the middle of the pile of sheets, which were stiff and dry, not really feeling like clouds should be to Agata. But she had a sudden urge to lie in the middle of them. She pictured moving the white fabric all around her and then tucking into the clean silence. Around her, the whir of working hands and water sloshing released something inside her.

Poeta cocked her head at Agata. "Everything alright?"

"Po—ettaa," someone called out. Poeta was transitioning in as the head of laundry while they eased the former one, Claudia, out to retirement.

"I can see you've got this. I need to check on the others," Poeta said, patting the top of Agata's hand before scurrying away.

Agata bent over the table and moved through the white fabric, letting it come up to her shoulders. She felt around for a corner, folded it over, and rubbed her finger over the neat square she'd created. It felt good to choose what movements to make with her body. She recalled the former freedom of skipping her way out of the bakery to visit Benedetta or running through the square with Gabriele to watch the gondolas. But yesterday, while outside of the Pietà, all she wanted was to be back in it. Freedom meant she was unprotected, vulnerable to attack.

She reveled in the noise of work. Something about being bound up behind the walls with a bunch of working women reminded her of being indoors with her Nonna and the neighborhood ladies warming up the space with their gossip. Upstairs, her new movements were counted and calm. Here in the workspace, she could be less controlled. The whispers required by the Pietà, even for the women, were not whispers at all downstairs. They were belly laughs, teasing jokes, and thrashing about to call for help with this or that. There were heaving buckets and sweating brows. The women often raised their voices at each other because sometimes that was what hard work called for.

"Who has the next load for the water? I can't wait here all day. It will go cold," Fiametta, a full-cheeked, heavy-set woman, shouted with her hands on her broad hips.

A much younger woman, her hair wrapped so well that Agata couldn't see the end of it, came around the corner with a basket piled high above her forehead. "I'm here, Fiametta. This last load was just dropped off," Simona replied and breathed heavily.

"Well, I'll need another fresh bucket of hot water now. You sure took long enough," Fiametta replied.

Fiametta must have felt Agata watching her. She looked up, raised her brows at Agata, and then began humming loudly, turning the stick and swaying her hips while she stirred the fabric.

Although the environment differed from the bakery house, Agata felt a familiar playfulness in it. She let her thoughts wander, and her body moved with exertion instead of forced rigidness: sheets meeting one corner with the next, sides smoothed and creased with her hands. The noise and the movement made her lighter. It would have been easy and not an unhappy way to spend her days, downstairs with women such as these, as she got older. Maybe she should settle on that, staying safe, working with her hands and avoiding the competitiveness and heartache of the musically driven upstairs.

The surprise of the lower-level workrooms came in the subtle interactions with the outside world. The couriers who retrieved the silks from grander houses came to chatter and tell, as well as carry and deliver. They brought the complaints of those customers who wanted their silks done a day earlier than their neighbors and their opinions of them back to the laundry room. The laundry front door, so named by everyone because of its location, which opened right to the laundry room, was a side door on the canal used for all Pietà deliveries, including dry supplies and food. The couriers used small boats to retrieve and drop off their laundry, as did the delivery man, who brought the *sapone* and other household supplies used in the laundry room, hospital, kitchen, and for bathing. Each time he arrived, he insisted on coming in and carrying the heavy supplies to the storage room.

"Poooooeta!" he called that day from the gondola. It echoed through the open door like the song's chorus he had been humming on the water minutes before. Agata snuck around the corner to watch the interaction. She could tell he liked to say her name. Poeta giggled, then recovered. Their eyes spoke to each other in a glimmer.

After the man was back on his way, the women downstairs teased Poeta openly as she smoothed her unruly curls against her head.

"He never carries the supplies in for me when you're not around, Poooeta," sang another laundress.

Agata heard stories of the women at all levels getting married and wondered how marriage could even be possible when they were closed in. As far as she knew, the women in the laundry room were stuck inside like the foundlings were. Clearly, she still had much to learn about this place, which dictated futures she could not foresee. She saw the flirtatious man walk into the laundry, but did anyone ever walk out of it?

Sneak out of it? Poeta walked back to Agata, interrupting her thoughts; Poeta's face was flushed.

"Okay, sweet girl, it's time. Why don't you take these up to the new guest bedroom and then get back on your schedule?" Poeta pushed the basket of folded sheets toward her. "I don't need to be on the bad side of any of the Maestras, especially the already grumpy ones." Poeta had a way of delivering her instructions with a punch and a smile.

Agata walked out of the basement lighter, disarmed. She made her way back up three flights of stairs, humming loudly with the sheets piled in her arms. A contented smile hung on her face, and without thinking, she began to sing. It wasn't as if that was an unusual act in the Pietà; in fact, the girls were instructed to sing hymns when the desire to talk became strong. But for Agata, it was quite out of the ordinary to open her mouth without fear or the need to worry about who might be listening. With such quiet, there was always someone listening in the Pietà, whether one saw them or not.

Agata stopped abruptly when she arrived at the upstairs guest room. It was a blank, small space with four unmade beds, where she had stayed her first lonely night in the Pietà. Poeta hit her foot firmly against the last floor behind her with a forgotten pile of pillowcases.

"Agata, you have no business being down there any longer outside of work hours. With a voice like that, you need to get into the scarf-wearing, lace-collar side of the Pietà."

Agata turned to face her, struck.

"When you make it into the *figlie del Coro*, I will knit that red scarf for you myself." Poeta squeezed her forearms. "And later, when you are a successful soloist, and you've worked all that quiet out of you, I will crochet the most beautiful lace performance collar for all of Venice to see." She released her arms.

Agata felt the heat radiate off her skin where the woman had touched her. It was the closest thing to a hug she'd had in over a year.

Agata made up the beds, picturing her violin tucked under her arm and a lace collar hugging her shoulders. She twisted her braids behind her, holding them against the back of her head. What would she look like when she was twenty years old? Would her hair be wrapped in gray rags like Simona's, or would it be twisted up behind her head like her mother's, forgetful pieces artfully dangling down her neck?

She walked away from the little room and into the rest of her day with that hum on her lips.

19
AGATA

At the sound of the bell, Agata's stomach did a little dance of excitement. She jumped up with her roommates, and they all tied their red aprons into perfect bows and smoothed out each other's normally braided hair with brushes. Discrete Margarita and Discrete Orsa appeared like chubby, joyful fairies.

"My Piccolos, we have a surprise for you!" said Margarita.

The Discrete each pulled out a handful of deep red ribbons, shiny and satin, held behind their backs.

"Ooohhh," the room sang.

"A special adornment today for our backstage debut," Discrete Margarita teased, as if as excited as they were.

Agata reached to touch the bow. Discrete Orsa tightened at the top. She felt as if her whole head gleamed from the beautiful thing in it.

The Discrete led the girls quietly to the choir room, but the joy in the air was loud among them. Even Giulia exchanged giddy smiles with the rest of the girls. Maestra Elena's dark hair was pulled back tighter than usual, and she stood with her shoulders back and her small, thin hands held in front of her. Agata thought she had never seen anyone so beautiful.

"Ladies, you look lovely," she said with a calm smile. "Let's begin with our warmups."

In the day's excitement, Agata opened her mouth wide and let herself sing.

Sotto Maestra Elena lowered her arms. "My job is to compel you to want to work hard enough to sing and play in the future Coro. I hope tonight, in all the excitement of lace collars and poinsettias, you hear how extraordinary these women sound. Their music represents years of practice and a tireless goal of perfection. They are women worth aspiring to, and you will be closer to them than the audience. So, hold your heads high, keep your lips tight when not singing, and listen like you have never listened before," Sotto Maestra Elena instructed.

"Discrete?" Sotto Maestra looked back at Margarita and Orsa at the door. "If one of you could lead and the other follow behind?"

Sotto Maestra turned to the choir. "Let us begin."

The girls of the *Piccolo Choir* stood with their shoulders back and necks long. Sotto Maestra Elena counted them in silently and moved her arms fluidly as if stirring them in a pond of water.

Te lucis ante terminum
Rerum creator poseimus
Ut solita clementia sis presaul ad custodian

Agata walked in gentle cadence with her fellow Piccolos in red bows. The girls from the *figlie di commun* not in the choir lined the hallway, gazing wistfully. Agata had wanted to get away from anyone hearing her voice for so long; she could never have fathomed that when she finally did sing, she would experience such pride in the act. The sound of her voice, blending in with the other girls, rushed through her like a powerful sea wave. She surrendered to it, becoming part of something that her voice alone could not produce. Though each voice was frail and young, their combined sound filled the hallway. She pictured a wake of awe on the faces left behind them.

They made their way down the main hallway to what were normally the *Chiesa della Pietà*'s locked doors. The doors were propped open, framing a corridor that crossed what would be on the outside a small *calle* below them. The corridor was dimly lit with only a few tall candles; there could be no outstanding lights to distract the upper stage from seeing the audience below them. Agata stood tall, attempting to peer down into the church interior as they walked out of the corridor's darkness and to the light of the balcony stage—the same strong white walls as the spiral staircase gleamed back at her in a wink.

Te corda nostra somnient
Te per soporem sentient
Tu amque semper gloriam vicina lucie cocinant

Suddenly, they were before them: the Poinsettia Girls. The women sat elegantly, focused and tall, instruments perched, ready to play. Their skirts were a deep velvety red contrasted by crisp white shirts, and their infamous large lace collars draped their shoulders. Each had a fresh red poinsettia behind their ear. They faced the audience seats below, sheltered by a low metal grille. But their focus was on someone else. Between the grille and the orchestra stood a man on a step with a red curly ponytail and a red jacket. It was him! The man who had awaited them after the funeral gondola ride, who sat at the back of the church during her mammina's funeral, who escorted her to the Pietà on that cold, dark night. And now she stood face to face with the man in the red jacket —a teacher in the Pietà?

Sotto Maestra Elena cued the girls to pause and finish their song.

Vitam sa lubren trubue
Nostrom calorem refice
Taetrom noctis caliginem tu a calustret claritas
Qui tecum in perpetuum, regnant cum Sancto Spiritu.
Amen

"Bravo, our beloved Piccolo choir. Let me introduce our *maestro di violin* and the composer of tonight's anticipated concert piece, Maestro Vivaldi," Madonna announced.

Agata stood gazing, caught in the space's aura. It was her first experience savoring the backstage moments before a concert, and it was spiritual. The moment was so different than her times at mass with Nonna, which had always been safe but predictable. With the reveal of Vivaldi, the striking women in red, and the open space in the church balcony, something inside told her she had been invited to become part of something bigger than she understood. And she also knew, somehow, it was just the beginning.

Maestro Vivaldi spoke. "Thank you, young ones." She remembered his shy voice and unassuming nature but felt instantly connected to home. The women in red poinsettias acknowledged the girls with nods and smiles.

"If we could go back to the second line in the third movement. I want to hear the oboes there," said Maestro Vivaldi.

The performing Coro turned around and went right back to their rehearsal. Elena moved the girls out of the way and to the sanctuary's far end. After a few minutes, the church bells rang, indicating it was time to let the public join them. One, two, three bells echoed throughout the ample space. Quiet unfurled from the Coro's music stands to the back hall where the Piccolo choir sat still and cross-legged. Silence. The doors opened with a creak below them, and the sounds of footsteps and shuffles made their way across the church's rust-colored stone floors, cut in diamond shapes like her home church in San Canciano.

It wasn't hard for Agata to imagine who awaited them there, considering the many rumors of the guests who often filled the pews. The girls had spent weeks describing them to Agata. Most assuredly, noblemen and their wives dressed more elegantly than anything the girls would have been exposed to. Agata pictured rich-colored skirts and jackets, hair pinned and in place. And young men. Often, their oldest sons accompanied their parents in hopes of glimpsing a maiden worth making a bride offer on. There could be opera singers on their off days, traveling dignitaries, or even the doge himself. Seated on the floor above, Agata and her friends only saw the arched windows that brought in light near the nave ceiling. It made her feel as close to God as she'd ever been.

There were whispers, a throat clearing or two. Then movement. A banner of white-and-red skirts lined the balcony as the Coro choir women stepped up to the smaller grilles so their sound could be heard in circumference. This would be the only opportunity for the crowd below to catch the top of a head, a feminine profile, a neckline. Would it be enough to talk about later? They stood back far enough for the light to hit their crowns while keeping their faces in shadow. It was most assuredly a tease to the restless crowd below.

Maestro Vivaldi stepped up to the broad grille in front of the orchestra and bowed to the audience below.

"I present to you *Gloria in D*."

Agata thought her heart might leap from her chest.

The low strings entered with a strong, syncopated eighth note, laying down their intention. Then, the higher strings, the violas, answered in sixteenth-note response. The music built in this tandem play and came to full power with the singers joining in:

"Glo-ri-a! Glo-ri-a. In ex-celsios de-o…"

The notes swirled around the top of the room, the intensity pressing externally around Agata: the high strings, the low ones, the low voices all bartering to deliver the same message. It was nothing her mind could create words for.

The Coro moved through twelve movements; some were slower, others darker, and others brighter. Agata's favorite was the third movement. It started with a cheery invite from the strings and was answered by a clear soprano who stood before the seated girls at the back balcony.

She looked up quickly at the other girls when she heard the talk about the soprano.

They all mouthed simultaneously, "Apollonia!"

Another darker-voiced soprano echoed her line back to her from across the other balcony.

The two sopranos met above the crowd, their voices tangling in and out of each other and pulling apart again. Candida gave her an elbow shove when another soprano started singing and mouthed: *Anna Maria.*

Though her view was limited, her imagination filled in the details from her place on the floor. Agata looked at her friends, who had to be thinking as she did: *Maybe one day I can be like her.*

Laudamus te, benedicmus te, adoremus te, glorifcamus te

When it was all done, a feeling stirred in the air, but no response came from the audience below. There was no clapping or cheering. Agata thought she heard a sniffle. Was someone crying? Vivaldi bowed. The women of the Coro stood and filed back off on through the mysterious dark hall from which they entered. Then she heard the shuffling again, feet moving out the door. The girls of the *Piccolo Choir* sat noiseless, unable to move until the exhilaration in the air and the Poinsettia Girls cleared the room.

That night, as they dressed for bed, the room was abuzz with more whispers than they knew were allowed. It seemed like a stricter rule when they all had something they wanted to say. But one could never be sure who was on hall duty, listening for their silence.

Lorenza teased Candida, "Did you see the way they just floated in and seemed at ease in their quiet? Your face is too loud for Coro talk, Candida. You're going to have to learn to turn it down if you're ever going to make it in," she scolded playfully.

Quiet snickering floated around the room as the girls took off their white day dresses and put their nightgowns on.

"I can't help it! Sometimes, I just need to get things out," Candida protested in response, pulling off her socks and falling into her bed.

"Candida, what's that on the bottom of your foot?" Agata asked.

Candida looked down at her foot and made a face. "Agata!" she responded with a raw incredulity.

"Shhhh!" The room full of girls shushed.

"You mean in all this time, you haven't seen it yet?" asked Candida in disbelief.

Agata looked around the room, hoping someone would explain. No one had a word to say—or didn't want to.

"Look closely at it, Agata. What does it say?"

Agata bent close to her foot and crinkled up her nose. "P?" She didn't understand.

"Those of us who came as infants came through the green door just like you. Clementina weighed us and measured us. Nurse Laura bathed us. Then the Prioress baptized and named us. Then, they branded us with the letter 'P' for Pietà. No one could slip in who wasn't supposed to be here. The Pietà owns us, Agata. We all have them."

In pure Pietà form, the girls in the room gathered around the bed without prompting and flipped their feet over to reveal their brands. Agata's brown eyes filled with tears. It was the quietest the room had been all evening.

The stark quiet was interrupted by a defiant ask:

"What's going on here?" An angry-looking Prudenza stood inside the doorframe, her hands fisted on her wide hips.

On cue, Giulia started singing, "*Te lucis ante terminum.*" She moved away slowly, following the flow of the chant.

All the girls responded in song as if they had been directed to: "*Rerum creator poseimus.*"

They moved intuitively in a slow walk around the beds, each making their way back to their own as they finished the verse. Satisfied, Prudenza watched them with a raised brow. She blew out the candlelight in her lantern with a large huff.

Once the woman had departed, Candida turned to face Agata in bed.

"Agata, it didn't hurt us. We were too young to remember it. We have all lost something. We just lost it earlier than you. But we can gain something no one else can. We can be like the women in the Coro, and I plan to do just that."

"Me too," said Lorenza.

"Me too," whispered Annetta.

"I am the only one in our audition group who plays organ and has private lessons with Madonna. Of course, I'll make it in," added Giulia.

"You know when I make it into the Coro, I won't be sleeping next to you anymore," Candida whispered.

Agata looked concerned. "Where will you go?"

"I will be with the other girls in the Coro. Their rooms are in the inner part of the building."

"Will I ever see you again?" Agata demanded.

"Yes, but not like it is now. All my classes will be with the Coro girls. I may see you at meals, but I will be sitting at their table. I will sit at the back of their performances instead of going to mass with the girls of the commun on Saturday nights. Agata, this is why you must start singing and trying to learn the violin well, like your father."

"Would you two go to sleep? I saved you once today, Candida. You're going to get us all in trouble. I am not going to have my meals taken away from me because you can't be quiet," Giulia whispered loudly.

"Fine," Candida responded to Giulia. She stretched out her hand for Agata to grab. Agata took it in hers and squeezed it tight.

Agata closed her eyes, picturing herself behind the grille, a large poinsettia tucked behind her ear. She thought of her Nonna smiling at her proudly from the Pietà church pew. She thought of her father banging on the green door, but no one could hear him. It wouldn't be enough to watch them all go by as she was stuck in the basement laundry. She had to try. *Oh, Mammina, help me to be brave like you said I would.*

20
MARGARITA

Margarita walked through the halls, soaking up the energy from the practice rooms. Audition week had arrived at the Pietà. Voices ascended in *oohs*, strings tuned with long strokes and fast-fingered through short ones, and wind instruments glided through fast-circling arpeggios, preparing their embouchures. The auditions began with the youngest of students, mostly eight to ten years of age, whose desire was to move from the Commun to the Coro, and ended with the oldest, those twenty-five years old who had finished all the levels of Coro schooling with the hope of making their dream of the performing Coro a reality. There would be as many yeses as no's handed out to hopeful musicians. Anxiety loomed with the anticipation—the two went hand in hand.

Margarita coveted the freedom to roam from one place to the next; she felt a little like a truant student. She liked that too. On a day like this one, older staff members made their rounds with their faces entirely on display, offering a show of togetherness and support for the process. Often, an encouraging look or a pass-by to a Maestra or student who needed bravery came from little old women like herself.

She had a little time before her next assignment, which she intended to fill with prayer not only for the girls who were auditioning but also for the Maestras who decided their fates.

She patrolled her way to the chapel, passing, peeking in whenever she felt the urge, into the Commun's classrooms. Their excitement spilled out into the hall. It was a big day for everyone in the building. The girls in the Commun who did not audition kept a modified schedule. Most of their classes were filled with substitutes or assigned longer stretches working in the hospital or textile facilities on the bottom level.

Two young women walked by hurriedly, their instruments in hand.

"Good morning, Discrete," they said in unison.

They were in the final stages of auditioning for the performing Coro. Their long red skirts distinguished them.

"Best of luck to you, young ladies," Margarita replied. She paused at the sight of them—their youth in contrast with her present appearance.

Some might have considered her earlier days slightly more illustrious than her current stage. She had once been a contralto, something special and different for composers to write for and crowds to be awed by. She pictured herself standing at the front of the balcony behind the metal cutout, remembering what it felt like to be seen. She ran her hands over her hips, feeling the smoothness of the deep red skirt over her narrow hips, and then moved them up to touch the heavy drape of her lace collar, forcing her shoulders back. Her thick raven hair was brushed back in a woven bun, and the poinsettia behind her ear was striking in contrast. And now, she was a spry (well, she thought so) sixty-two-year-old, young enough that her widened hips still moved nimbly, and old enough that when her gray hair was unwound from its head covering, she could find not one of her former black strands left. She was known as the old woman in the hall, called by the name Discrete, which meant separate. That little skip flipped in her heart like it did occasionally, and she moved her hand from her gray hair to her chest. *I just push myself on some days. I can take it easier tomorrow.*

The Pietà chapel was a simple one, with the same white walls she had walked past for years, throughout the building. It was not even blessed with a small stained glass like the *Virgin with Child* that gleamed in the private, two-pewed Infants Chapel. Only a simple crucifix and a table to handle the communion chalice and plate stood at its front. That and several rows of wooden pews to accommodate all the foundlings for morning mass. While Governor Sovarizo would have had it adorned with paintings and other such relics that depicted service, Madonna insisted it remain unaffected by such preoccupations of wealth. Any monies brought in from the Coro's public concerts went to pay its members and were deposited into their personal accounts for their future dowries. The Venetian government and some dependable benefactors paid a sum to cover the operational costs of the facility and its staff. Margarita had quite a dowry of her own saved, and she had no plans to use any of it. She had already asked Madonna to put in writing that her life earnings be poured back into the Pietà with Don Bollani as her witness. Her life was the Pietà, and she had no regrets.

She knelt in the front row and prayed one by one for everyone she could think of, students and teachers alike. When she was satisfied with her requests and offerings, she made the sign of the cross and stood up to exit the aisle as Don Bollani was making his way up it.

"Good morning, Padre," Margarita greeted.

"Hello, my child," Don Bollani replied. The sentiment almost made her blush. He was at least ten years her junior.

"We find ourselves in a day of prayer. It's all we can give them today," Margarita said.

"It's all we can give them most days," he replied.

"It is enough, isn't it?" Margarita stated more than she asked.

"I do believe it is the purest form of love we can give them," he replied.

"You're right in reminding me of it." She bowed her head toward the altar. "Good day, Padre. It's time for me to check in on Madonna."

"Good day to you, Discrete," answered Don Bollani.

Margarita dabbed her two fingers in the holy water stoup in the doorway wall and almost walked right into Madonna.

"Ooph," rang Margarita. "I was coming over to find you, Madonna. Is everything…?"

"No, yes. Thank you for asking. Signor Papafonda is here for his weekly organ tuning, and of course, Giulia is set to audition for it. I can't be anywhere near her. It would appear to be a show of favoritism. But I need to address him myself. I have another matter to discuss with him."

"I have a moment. Let's see if I can catch up to Giulia to avoid any impropriety. I am sure she is coming from the practice rooms."

"Thank you, Discrete. I'll meet with him now, then. Of all the women I've run into, I'm thankful it was you," Madonna said.

Just then, a shadow of white walked across the hallway away from them.

"Something else is bothering you," suggested Margarita.

She immediately recognized the silent shape. "Assistant Prioress Prudenza? Can I help you find something?"

"Oh, no. I'm finding everything I need today, thank you," Prudenza replied. She dipped toward them in a subtle bow and walked away slowly.

"That's your worry," said Margarita and turned back to Madonna.

"She seems to be everywhere I am," Madonna expressed. "At the beginning of her appointment as Assistant Prioress, it was more discreet. She would appear out in the open wherever I was. But lately, she seems to be more secretive, hiding in the shadows, sneaking around. I'm quite agitated by it."

"You know, we've always," Margarita replied.

"*Bondi*, Madonna!" rang out a new tenor voice.

"Signor Papafonda. Thank you for coming today." The Prioress smiled.

The two women locked eyes and affirmed in Pietà talk that she would check on Giulia. But as she turned to walk away, she got an internal catch that reminded her Madonna wasn't supposed to be left alone. Prudenza was up to something. She would respect her openly, but she didn't trust her. She had witnessed the long history of Prudenza's jealousy of Madonna. Margarita had reached the height of her Coro career just as

Madonna, formerly called Sotto Maestra Marietta, and Sotto Maestra Prudenza were auditioning for the performing Coro. Both were multi-instrument talents. And both excelled at the organ. As Madonna was a year older, she had the opportunity to audition for the organ before Prudenza could. Prudenza would have understood that the instrument gave unique advantages. Only one person could play it at a time and would be as visible as the organ player was in the Coro. Ever since Margarita had known her, Prudenza tended to make decisions that put herself forward. But despite those efforts, like her current role as Assistant Prioress, she remained just the backup, never at the center of the limelight.

Prudenza had never forgiven Madonna for auditioning for the organ position, though the choice hadn't entirely been up to Madonna. Her abilities and the timing of the current organ player's retirement worked in her favor. She made it in and excelled at it. Prudenza was a better cellist than she was an organist, but Margarita had learned that Prudenza held grudges against her. And everything Prudenza had wanted, she fell short of, while Madonna was recognized for what Prudenza sought, including the appointment of Prioress.

It was a well-known rivalry. Unfortunately, in a competitive environment such as the Pietà, rivalries, though frowned upon, were inevitable. What new webs would be spun with this new group? The interactions and favoritism showed early. She was happy to leave those thoughts behind and go to her next assignment as a substitute for Sotto Maestra Elena's *Piccolo Choir*. What a treat that would be. These girls were in a formative, moldable stage. It brought her deep satisfaction to explain their next steps and let them relax in the joy of song. She spotted Giulia before she made it into the chapel and asked her to take a fifteen-minute walk of prayer for her audition and the others she felt compelled to pray for. Discrete Orsa arrived soon after at the chapel door.

Satisfied with her interception, Margarita floated into choir class and took her spot behind a small lectern. She looked through the music left for her, tapped it together on the stand, and then laid it back down—no need for all that. The foundlings walked in twinkly and bright when they saw her. Just as she'd hoped.

"Discrete, are you, our teacher?" Agata asked.

"I didn't know you could conduct," said another.

"I've had my fair share of experience," chuckled Margarita.

Margarita warmed them up, embracing the power of song between her hands. She put her arms down, and the mouths of the girls closed in suit. *I'll give them a little something of me.* She closed her eyes and opened her mouth, taking in a gulp of air. As she released it, her resonant, deep voice swirled through the room in a short aria. When she was done, she looked at the foundlings. They were speechless.

"Nothing is comparable to the instrument of your voice. The sound and the texture are unique to each of us. A true gift from God. It is His design—and not for us to decide whether it's good enough." She paused to ensure she had their attention. Some nodded in understanding; others stood captivated.

"When your voice pairs with those around you, equally singing with all your gifting and training, there is no more remarkable place to be to feel the music as it was intended. The crowd will seek it out, but the best seat will always be the one you are sitting in as a choir member," Margarita continued. "Now, we will take the first phrase of one of the pieces you are working on, and we will pass that phrase from one to the next. I want each of you to hear the beauty of the voice next to you. To know of your potential to use it," she said.

Margarita looked around the room as she spoke, and her gaze landed on Agata as she emphasized that last instruction. Agata bravely eked out the notes as they were passed to her. They were a meek but tuned melodic line. Margarita knew she had more in her. Poeta was not the only one who'd heard Agata's voice floating up the stairs that day months ago after the alms walk. Margarita herself stood in the shadows. Hearing Agata sing buoyed her with eager hope. The thought of this particular orphan girl from a family she knew, who fought her pain with quiet and stubbornness, could have the potential to be one of the shining stars on the balcony, the literal dream of the Pietà. She must make sure she gets there.

21
AGATA

The Adriatic churned its dark waters, blending seamlessly with the low clouds above. A light wind at its back blew, and together, they produced the *caligo*, the dependable Venetian mist that sprinkled the island that early February morning. Although the Acqua Alta had been quiet, the full moon meant St. Mark's Square would experience a gentle covering of the sea's long fingers at high tide. Morning revealed itself in an alluring pink and gray fog that wound its way through the Giudecca, across the Canale di San Marco, and onto the main island, enveloping her buildings and squares, and producing a palpable pensiveness across the city. It landed at the Pietà's doorstep, where its front walls faced the sea.

In the Serene City, no matter where one sat, water was the constant. Everyone was tucked between its boundaries, some affected by its sloshing and others by its stillness.

Inside the Pietà, though their movements were quiet, the girls had risen from their beds. Agata looked up at the lack of skylight as she subconsciously sang her way from her nightgown to her day dress. She forced her cold fingers to put tight plaits into her hair, ignoring the shiver that tightened across her chest and into her shoulders. Though the walls were high and the windows small, the turmoil of winter found its way into the Pietà.

Agata looked over at the bed next to her, where Candida used to lie. A small child lay in her place.

"Chiaretta," urged Agata. "It's time to wake up. Everyone is almost dressed."

Fall auditions played a significant role in propelling the Pietà's cycle forward. The girls' move from the *figlie di commun* gave room for a new, younger set to filter in. Chiaretta had entered the Pietà as an infant foundling, left inside the green door like hundreds of girls before her. She was paid by the Pietà to be nursed by her mother (a common practice) and then spent her formative years on dedicated grounds in the Veneto, along with the other babies and toddlers left to the Pietà. She was taken care of there until age six, when she and other foundlings were considered old enough to begin their educational path in the Pietà's *figlie del Coro*.

Agata learned all this from the new occupant of Lorenza's bed, Elisabetta, who slept on her other side. Agata could not understand a mom giving up her baby so easily when she still felt so close to hers. Was it because she talked to her every day? Chiaretta had said she had never seen her mother to remember what she'd looked like.

The change in verse hinted they were ready to walk to mass. Agata looked down at Chiaretta, this slight little girl with thin brown hair who already felt like her responsibility. Agata grabbed her hand and moved Chiaretta in front of her, gently pushing her thumbs into the upper center of the girl's back to train her shoulders straight. She took each braid that had fallen to the front of her dress and placed it behind her. It was only shy of two years ago when Agata came in alone and lost in the Pietà's quiet structure.

"There, let's go."

Agata sang her way in morning chorus to mass and dipped her fingers in holy water, making the sign of the cross—the cue to stop singing and inhale quietly. She stepped into the white-walled chapel, which was already two-thirds full. The only sound outside of her small finger in the stoup was the shuffle of steps walking in front and behind her. Chiaretta peeled off in front of her to the row of six- and seven-year-olds. Agata walked three rows up and genuflected before taking her place next to Elisabetta, already kneeling in prayer, her dark red braids unlike anyone else's in the building. Agata joined her, lowering to her knees. They smiled at one another —a quiet Pietà, good morning.

In all the shuffling of auditions to balance small children and the older ones in the *figlie del Coro*, Elisabetta was moved to Agata's room. As the older girls, they were expected to watch over the younger foundlings, just as the teenage girls in the next hall were expected to watch over them. This watchful caretaking trickled down throughout the Pietà. Agata and Elisabetta, a year apart in age, had become fast friends. They were a quiet duo who whispered more than they laughed. They both played the violin and sang soprano. Agata liked that Elisabetta's calm presence made her feel that in all the newness, she was doing things right. She also enjoyed the dark freckles across Elisabetta's cheeks, a tinge red to match her hair. Agata had never heard of freckles. But then again, neither had she thought that so many girls without parents to care for them all could all exist in one building.

Agata turned her gaze to the altar, her posture tall, her thoughts in prayer.

"Good morning, Mammina. How are you? I miss my old friends, but I do have Elisabetta. I hope you are proud of me. I play two instruments now, but I still have a long way to go to improve my skills. Please watch over Nonna. I can't see her from in here, but I am sure you can. I miss you most of all. I imagine you walking with me, to the violin and choir and everywhere I go."

Agata sat back in the wooden pew, braver than she had been three months ago, stronger than she was six months ago, and more capable of being on her own than a year ago when she paced into this chapel, clutching the Discrete Margarita's arm. But the loss of her mother, she was sure, she could never get over. How was it that she could be proud of herself and sad all at once? She wiped her cheek to rub off the tear that snuck away. She might never have the answer.

She scanned the girls from the Coro filing into the center aisle as if checking off a list. She first spotted Giulia with her familiar pout, and then Candida, Lorenza, and Annetta, all of whom were like her in their white dresses. Their hair was worn in the first-level Coro style, half pulled up and half brushed out behind them. They wore red scarves woven by the *figlie del Coro* sewing class to keep their necks warm in the dank winter air. It made their necks appear long and elegant. They already seemed much older than her in her plain white dress. Her glance met Candida's, whose lips turned down in a pout before she turned off into her new place across the aisle and a row ahead. In this brief exchange, she knew her friend missed her just as much as she missed her friend. Agata had so much she wanted to tell her about this new child, Chiaretta, who always occupied the spot next to her, and her new friend Elisabetta. If Candida could meet her, Agata knew she would like her, and they could all be friends. But her whispers would never be heard with such distance between them. At least not without significant cost or punishment. It was very much like another kind of punishment to leave it all stuffed inside.

Mass began, and the sanctuary of girls repeated after Don Bollani:

"God, come to my assistance. Make haste to help me."

The new students of the Coro experienced a complete change from their life in the Commun. Their classes no longer focused on arithmetic, Latin, and sewing; instead, they taught sight-singing, solmization, ear training, and lessons on all the Coro's instruments, as well as private lessons to specialize in at least two of them. Their chores were reduced to two hours a week, primarily light housekeeping. Gone were the hours spent mopping, doing laundry, and assisting in the hospital or nursery on the bottom floor. With their new schedules, they rarely went below the second story or toward the front of the building. They slept in smaller dormitorios of six girls, in the back part of the building and away from the windows that faced the sea. Most of their classes were tucked into these back halls as well. To Agata, they felt a world away.

The chapel emptied, and the girls in white walked to the cafeteria for breakfast. Even for meals, Agata was separated from her friends. She looked at the table of red scarves and back at little Chiaretta, who sat in front of her, greedily spooning her rice in. Though just steps down the hall and weaving in and out of their schedules, their lives and hers only intersected with plaintive glances. Or maybe for her, plain mopey ones. She felt a tug on her sleeve. Elisabetta gave her a knowing smile. She was thankful for her. A true equal in demeanor and a kind-hearted presence—a reminder that she wasn't alone.

Like the tumultuous sea outside, the wave of hard work swept in and filled the halls. It was impossible not to get caught up in it. Though she missed the camaraderie she had had in her first year, in her second, Agata had much more to occupy her time. She advanced from the Beginning Strings to the Level One string class. Though frail-looking and small on the exterior, Chiaretta was a force on the violin. A prodigy, they called her. Her fingers were nimble and her spirit driven. She and Agata played next to one another. It took everything for Agata not to get ruffled at the young girl's skill.

Agata discovered a greater peace in playing the harpsichord; something about visually seeing each of her fingers produce a chord rang a satisfaction. It was something entirely new to feel her longing and uncertainties absorbed in those keys. The violin was more of an eking out and direct comparison with others, like Chiaretta, who's gifting only exposed everyone else's weaknesses. The harpsichord was a solo instrument taught by now Maestra Elena. The opportunity gave Agata time away from the buzz of girls circling the building. Agata finished the song and enjoyed how it reverberated around the room.

"Agata, you are progressing beautifully on this instrument. I am going to give you some more challenging pieces, which means you will have to practice more consistently outside of class. I will arrange three thirty-minute time slots in the practice rooms. You must be prompt. These Coro girls are covetous of their schedules and their practice times," Maestra Elena explained.

"I will be with the Coro girls?" asked Agata.

"In the practice rooms on the Coro side of the building." Elena smiled. "The next thing will be to increase your vocal work outside of choir, but we will think on that."

At first, just walking down the hall toward the Coro was daunting. Agata was sure she had no business being there. Older girls and women moved in and out of rooms with their instruments dangling, their focus intact, and their red scarves and vests hugging their bodices.

Agata was bare in all white. She stepped into the little room. Alone yet empowered. She hadn't been left alone since she had entered the building a year ago. And here, she oversaw herself for a full half hour. She plucked a few keys. Could others hear her play? Would they laugh at the beginner in their midst? She lay on the floor next to the legged instrument and looked up at the blank ceiling. It felt good to be by herself. The cello's low rumble in the room next door, followed by a flute playing arpeggios across the hall, entered her little practice space—she had better get started.

Mammina, it's time for me to be brave.

She went through the two new songs several times and noticed the cello stopped playing next to her. She heard the door open. Thirty minutes already?

She opened her door just as Candida was closing hers.

"Agata! What are you doing here?" Candida asked in an excitable whisper.

"Maestra Elena scheduled practice times for me so I can improve on the harpsichord," she replied.

"That's amazing!" Candida pulled her back into her practice room and threw her arms around Agata. "I've missed you so much!" she rattled on. "I love being in the Coro, but it is a lot of work. Well, more stressful. Everyone is so serious all the time. And that Prudenza, would you believe, of all people, she is my private instructor for cello? Blahhh."

Agata laughed through her bantering. "I've missed you, too."

Someone knocked on the door. "Your session is up. It's my turn."

They opened the door, about to apologize when they recognized Giulia, holding a viola in her hand, annoyed.

"I should have known it was you," she said, facing Candida. "You are the only girl who persists in talking when literally no one else is." Giulia sighed loudly.

"Hi, Giulia, nice to see you," whispered Agata.

"Hi, Agata. Now get out, you two," commanded Giulia.

Agata and Candida pushed themselves through the doorway at the same time, giggling as quietly as they could. They doubled over into a half-run to distance themselves from their minor crime. Just then, Discrete Margarita crossed by them with another student at the junction of the main hall.

She raised her eyebrows at them. "Ladies?" asked Discrete Margarita.

They were caught.

"You're finding your way then?"

Agata spoke up first. "Yes...Discrete. Good afternoon."

"Good afternoon, Discrete." Candida gave the old woman a little curtsy.

"Agata."

The two girls were forced to split at the hall. Candida turned to walk away. When the Discrete was out of view, she turned back to Agata and mouthed: *Next time.* Candida gave Agata one of those smiles and then scrambled back toward the hall of red.

Agata turned in the opposite direction to walk to her hall of white. *I'm tired of being left behind.*

She furrowed her brow, keeping up her quick pace, her feet directing her as her mind reeled. She looked up and saw Innocentia sitting next to the green door entrance. No one decided whether to come in that door. But every girl had the opportunity to decide what they'd do once inside it. If they took a chance, she came to an abrupt stop at the bottom of the curved stairwell. An excitability flickered inside of her. She felt something ready to flip. The Pietà and its pulse were becoming part of her.

Perhaps it is I who is ready to join with it.

She stomped up the circular stairwell. *I'm going to do it. I'm going to audition for the Coro in the next round. It will be me walking the halls with my scarf and sitting in the special section with my friends. It will be me playing better all the time.* She was determined she'd see her Nonna again, sitting in the front row, pointing her out to Alba and Benedetta while she sat at the harpsichord. *It will be me who makes my Nonna proud. Me that she goes to see, her own Poinsettia Girl when she breaks outside of her bakery door.*

22
ELENA

Maestro Gasparini tapped the top of his stand with his baton to stop the orchestra. "I need to hear the bass line on its own. There is someone slightly behind the beat that isn't connecting with the cello line. Let's start at measure twenty-two."

The performing Coro was deep into the precision of their work. They sat on the upper balcony of the *Chiesa de la Pietà*, where they did so three times a week for full orchestra rehearsals. Though Elena's primary instrument was her soprano voice, she was needed that week on the violin, her first chance to perform as a Poinsettia Girl. They were to play a large-scale piece for an unnamed dignitary arriving in Venice that week. She sat between two experienced Coro members trailing the end of the second violin section.

While Gasparini worked with the basses, Sylvia leaned over to Elena and said, "I hear something out of tune on the accidental in measure eighteen. Is that you?" The intense first-chair violinist Sylvia was known for her perfection. She had played her part in the performing Coro for eight years.

"I apologize. I'll keep my eye on it," said Elena. She tried not to reveal how Sylvia's comment had embarrassed her.

"Be sure you do. I pride myself on Gasparani never calling on my section to rework their flaws in front of the entire orchestra," Sylvia pressed. "That's what the practice rooms are for."

Elena swallowed back her emotion. She had made it into the performing Coro, but it hadn't made all her weaknesses vanish. In reality, she had to work harder than before to keep up with the demands of their weekly performance schedules and her added teaching responsibilities. While she was proud of her achievement, surviving this final stage of the Coro process was physically and emotionally exhausting. Technically, she was starting all over again. In the pecking order of the performers, she was just a beginner. The pressure was taking a toll on her confidence.

She looked over her shoulder and met a hidden smile from Cristina in the woodwind section. Rehearsal ended and the two friends met up in the hallway to put their instruments away in their *dormotorio*. Elena thanked God that was one thing that hadn't changed after the auditions. Rooming together gave them each a confidant when they needed someone to talk to; other days, someone who knew how to give the other their space. Today, they'd take those ten minutes of freedom to shake out their grumblings, enabling them to button their composure back up for their next lesson.

Cristina spoke as soon as the door shut. "I saw that look on your face, Elena, when Sylvia was obviously scolding you. Look, I don't think she meant it as an attack. She's just..."

"Intense." Elena stole the end of her sentence and huffed. "I know. You are right. Thank you."

"It's a lot, Elena. We are doing things that a small percentage of women get the chance to do. The rehearsals, multiple lessons, and meetings… Not to mention all this added teaching time. The men that come over from St. Marks are only here to teach two or three classes a week, and then they are free to go to their own homes, roam the city if they want!"

"I needed to hear that. We are under certain pressure. Not just for our growth but also for the ones coming behind us." Elena continued. "I've got this new choral ensemble, and they are so sweet to be around, but I'm struggling with their inexperience and lack of confidence. How do I teach drive, or better yet, how do I teach them not to fear their own voices?"

"You are getting very philosophical for eleven o'clock in the morning," Cristina teased. "I think we do what was done for us. We remain patient as teachers and let time mature and practice mold us. It got us here and several others before us."

Cristina changed the subject. "So, I have heard that the 'secret dignitary' is a Frenchman with a high opinion of Italian music over his own France and…he's unmarried."

"Oh, I don't know about what we hear. Things get spun up in a hurry," Elena said.

"Well, I would certainly not turn down any offers to get out and make my own life with a Frenchman or otherwise."

"But you're so talented, Cristina. Don't you want more time on the stage after all the work you've put in?"

"And don't you want to fall in love after all the time we've been hidden behind these walls?" Cristina responded.

Elena didn't confess that she, too, had waffled between her desire to stay and her desire to have her own family as they walked out the door and back to the obligatory quiet of the hall. They brushed shoulders—their way of saying goodbye. *I'm here till next time. I'm always here.*

Cristina's question dangled in the air and followed Elena all the way to class. She did tempt imagination, dreaming of a kind, decent man waiting for her below the grilles, intoxicated by her voice. But he always looked the same. He had the bearded face and kind eyes of handsome Ludovico Rossi, whom she met that day outside the Pietà. It was a vain, girlish thought. She heard later, as that day's circled amongst the staff, that he was a longstanding benefactor of the Pietà, and he and his wife attended the Coro concerts every Saturday. It didn't make her as glum as it did dreamy. He was generous and a musical supporter, too? She couldn't shake the way he'd looked at her. But her work took precedence, and she focused on her next task. Each step propelled her concentration away from fantasy till it was tucked beneath her ruminations on her students.

The halls were empty except for an older Discrete who crossed a side passageway; the foundlings were still in lesson. Elena swirled in heavy contemplation. The Pietà, despite all its attempts at structure, program, and calm, contended with something of a strong wind. Did they underestimate the power and vitality of hundreds of maturing girls all confined to one space? The Prioress's focus and direct instruction were for all of them to leave their pasts at the green door. But some of those pasts clung to their minds in choppy memories. It was impossible to leave those beginnings, faint as they were, untouched. They were their roots after all, roots that produced saplings that never had a chance to grow past their barren surface. The desire to know where we come from persists in all conditions. Even if a sapling is pulled and replanted, somewhere in that original place, a weak tendril fights to come back. In her darkest days, Elena still heard the dark, raspy voice of her mother, healed and sound, whispering instructions. She would give anything to have her mother's arms around her with her long raven hair draped around her shoulders in protection like she had as a girl. But she was no longer a girl.

The foundlings of the Pietà had experienced viable losses; others, abuses; and many like her, the ghost feeling of a missing mother's arms around their being. What would it have been like to grow up in a home, with family, with freedom—*with sound*? In the Pietà, though, the attempt was to provide such a home with individual beds and linens, family in the form of sisters of every age, and sound in the call and prayers to God through music. It fell short in terms of longing. Elena understood this as she grappled with hers. *How do I contend with longing? Can my unmet dreams of the past find their way to my future?* Those young girls had nothing tangible to rely on, but still had a secure timetable to answer their questions.

Elena had to press into the constant, be the constant. It was her turn to offer protection. She knew no other way. It was harder now as one of these elite women than ever. Her turmoil intensified with each step toward the Coro. As she walked, she noticed the atmospheric shift from the Coro side of the building to the Commun one. The aura of hard work floated on a high wave of air, joining a much simpler—and childlike—execution of sound.

She arrived at her classroom. A small group of basses hummed through the space between the wooden door and the stone floor. Discrete Evangelica, a decisively short woman, moved to the hallway's center. She held the bell with two hands in front of her and proceeded to rock her sturdy frame to produce three loud clangs. Her prominent nose was framed by cheeks that puffed out around it, her smile surprising and making her whole face gleam. And just as her thoughts spun her worry around moments before, that simple, happy face calmed her.

Door by door swung open, and the twists of white streamed out in perfect lines. Braids stilled by their postures, milky skirts swishing quietly. She stepped into the classroom, ready to greet her vocal ensemble. These girls had been tagged for a future in the Coro but were still without approved resources from the board for private lessons. Among them were Elisabetta, Agata, and Chiaretta, a young violin prodigy who had everyone earnestly anticipating her future.

They stood in their places, polite and eager. Elena wondered how Agata had grown right before her eyes, standing at the height of the middle spot in the small line. Was it that she was taller? Or perhaps she stood taller.

"We are going to spend our time today on a simple chant. I want you to sing it while listening to the girl on either side of you pushing enough to meet her voice, pulling back enough so as not to override it." She raised her arms; eyes locked with theirs.

"Caaahn- ta- ah-ah-teee Doooo-mii-nuuuum," the small voices repeated in a round.

The further she directed their song, the more their sweet voices filled the holes of her insecurity—measure by measure, the spinning questions that buzzed loudly moments before stilled to a stabilized whir. Only the notes' vibrations stood between them, weaving an indescribable connection. She looked at Agata in the middle of them, her brown eyes focused on her director. The clarity of her voice traveled straight to Elena's ears. While everyone praised her singing, Elena knew her time was for these girls. In these moments, she poured out her knowledge and received the gift of their voices back. She could see Agata's growth, Elisabetta's steadiness, and Chiaretta's fire. *How could I be so foolish, Lord? It's always been these girls.*

"What does it mean, Maestra Elena? Cantate Dominum?" asked Chiaretta.

"It means sing to the Lord a new song," she replied.

The chant stuck with her all week, and she made it her prayer. It folded into her violin as she performed her third month with the Coro tucked into the orchestra, the top of her head and movement of her bow exposed to the audience below.

Sing to the Lord a new song.

My new song will be to hold my desires close, to let my lips praise yours, to let my arms teach them, and to wait. It's not time yet for anything else.

23
AGATA

Agata danced her right hand down the harpsichord, letting eighth notes descend playfully in a 3/4 pattern toward the middle of the keys. She punctuated a chord with both hands and sat back. "Hahhh," she exhaled. For three months, she'd faithfully spent hours willing her fingers to memorize what her ears heard so easily. It was what it would take. To be accepted into the Coro education process, she needed to demonstrate proficiency on two instruments, in addition to a vocal audition, where she would showcase a prepared piece on each. She was also expected to sight-read short passages on all three instruments she auditioned with and demonstrate proficiency on four scales without fumbling. Her stomach grumbled. She had rehearsed her audition song so many times in the last thirty minutes that she didn't want to hear it anymore. All she could think about now was dinner. What she wouldn't give for Nonna's sopa de spessati on this cold day, instead she'd have to be contented with a reliable bowl of rice.

A knock came at the door. "Psssp, it's me."

Agata opened the door, and Candida forced her way in. "I'm tired. I finished a lesson with Prudenza before my solo practice time, and I couldn't focus. I needed someone normal to talk to. You sound good, by the way," Candida offered. "Prudenza-cghh gets meaner every time I see her."

"I hope, if I do make it, I get to keep Elena for harpsichord as my private teacher," Agata replied.

"You audition with three instruments, but they choose what your focus instrument will be and assign a teacher with that specialty who they think will work best to progress you," Candida explained.

"I think the harpsichord is my strongest instrument. Chiaretta is far better on the violin than the voice. Well, you know how I feel about that."

"I wouldn't get too attached to what you'll do. Anyway, I like your voice. Who knows what they think? We don't really make any decisions in here. I've got to start practicing again before we get caught. Prudenza booked me an entire hour today, and she will know if I didn't employ it." Candida scurried back out to the small room next to hers, turning and waving furiously on her way out.

Agata had thirty minutes left before dinner hour. Every foundling was allotted an extra half hour at their day's end to be utilized for additional practice, time volunteering beyond their scheduled times, or confession. Agata knew she needed prayer more than anything else. She still had two weeks until auditions and already, she was a nervous wreck. She desperately needed to talk to her mammina.

The building buzzed with the upcoming auditions. It was all anyone could whisper or think about. Chiaretta made a habit of whispering to Agata at night, just as Candida used to. She was what could best be described as a confident girl. She had become quite vocal about her abilities. *Ironic in this order of enforced quiet,* Agata pondered. But admittedly, she was exceptional.

"Agata, I've liked being paired with you in our current arrangement, but this could very well be our last week sleeping next to each other. I know I will make it into the Coro, and I want to tell you that if you don't, I am sure you will next time."

Chiaretta lay on her side, facing Agata, genuinely excited. "Just think, in two Fridays, I could be eating dessert!"

Agata rolled over and shut her out.

"Good night, Chiaretta," Agata responded.

Was it evident to everyone else that she wouldn't get in? Agata wasn't sure she could take another whole year of being separated from her friends. She knew Elisabetta would get in. Elisabetta was pretty to look at and dependable on the violin, with excellent pitch and finger placement. Although they said looks didn't matter, it was a known fact that fathers brought their sons looking for a pretty wife behind the grilles. On top of that, Maestra Elena placed Elisabetta in the back row for the others to tune off her when she sang. Not making it in would put Agata back a whole year behind them musically, and as a twelve-year-old, she would have to move to a new room where most of the girls were fated for a lifetime in the Commun. The best teachers were in the Coro; it was her only chance to improve. Agata's mind ran amok with what-ifs. What if she were only destined for the laundry? What if her Nonna would never see her on the stage?

Two weeks passed. It was the day before auditions. She greeted the morning restless but determined. One day was all she had to sharpen her practice. Tomorrow, she'd have to prove herself ready. Agata intended to get through her morning classes focused and ignore any conversation. It could only lead to more unwanted comments that would make her question herself. Finally, lunch was done, and it was time to rehearse.

The practice hall was full of sound—voices, wind instruments, and strings alike. Every small room was reserved for aspiring Coro members, including those who had previously been selected and wanted to advance to the next level. Before that moment, Agata could never have grasped the concept of pushing her body in such a way as to compel her mind and fingers to align, and here she was doing it amongst all this talent.

Agata had already planned to start with the violin and end with singing. She would run each scale and song five times to give them equal attention—a practice trick Maestra Elena had taught her to manage her time. It was going as she had hoped; her fingers were cooperating, and her spirits were high. It was time for her vocal piece. Singing was more complex work than she'd ever expected it to be. It used to be something she didn't have to concentrate on. Now, her focus was on her breath and the shape of her mouth. It left her feeling tired and vulnerable.

The practice hall quieted, with only a single cello playing the same phrase over and over. Agata smiled at the thought of being closer to her punchy friend again; she was tempted to check on her. But so as not to be distracted, she sang through a few warm-ups softly—she still wasn't comfortable being heard.

"Again," a harsh tone pronounced. It was followed by a cello phrase.

Is that another voice?

"Again."

The same cello part followed.

"Again."

The voice was angry. The cello part played.

"Again!" said the voice.

"Pleeease, Maestra Prudenza, the blister on my finger is bleeding," Candida cried out.

Agata snapped her mouth shut and clasped her hands together, twisting and shaking her fingers in and out of knots as she listened.

"I don't think you have what it takes, Candida. You might have made it into the Coro, but it doesn't guarantee you will ever be in the performing Coro. It takes work over pride. All you care about is your frippery. Sometimes hard work hurts." A pause. "What is this frivolous thing on your head?"

Agata heard a smack.

"I've had enough of your self-indulgence! You will miss dinner tonight and stay here until you get this piece right." There was a pause. Agata could only hear heavy breathing.

"I will be back to deal with that later," Prudenza said.

Agata heard her footsteps march away. And then crying.

Agata jumped to open her door and shook the handle of Candida's. "Candida. It's me. It's Agata."

The door opened to reveal her red-faced friend, her hair half pulled apart. Candida fell straight into Agata's arms, sobbing. It was the first time she'd had nothing to say.

"Why is your hair like this? What did she do?"

"She saw my ribbon," Candida barely managed to say. "It was just a thick thread of my scarf. I wanted to see what it would be like to wear that big red flower in my hair."

The dinner bell rang through the outer hall.

"Maybe we can go now," Agata said.

"I can't. She'll be back to check. I know her."

"They'll have to wonder where we are if our seats are empty. They'll look for us!"

Candida didn't answer; she just tugged on Agata's sleeve, so she'd look up.

Agata turned her shoulder, her arms still wrapped around her friend.

Prudenza stood with her hands on her hips. "What is going on here? It is not enough to have one misfit, but a follower of one?" She pointed at Agata. "You are nothing but a follower. You are wasting your time, thinking you'd make it to the Coro. You are weak, and everyone knows you are not ready."

Agata squeezed her mouth to hold back a sob.

"You are a follower because you have no family and not enough talent to be guided out of your reality. You should sleep well tonight to save your strength for the laundry room because that's where you are headed," Prudenza managed to shout in a whisper.

At this, Agata's heart pounded from the inside, and a silent courage thrust her off her feet.

"You are wrong!" she stood and shouted back." I have my Nonna, and she would be proud of me."

Candida looked up at her like she didn't recognize her.

"Your Nonna is dead," Prudenza seethed.

Agata shook her head and moaned, "No, no, you're lying."

Prudenza reached over her to get to Candida. "Perhaps you can think more clearly and hence, play more proficiently when we have removed the temptation to be frivolous, especially when the frivolity is so near your mind."

At that, Prudenza grabbed onto Candida's ponytail, pulling it tight in one hand while vigorously sawing it off with a small knife in the other.

"No, please don't." The normally willful girl retreated.

"Practice, Candida, practice. It is your penance to God." Prudenza looked down at Agata. "And you. Go to dinner. You are late."

"And so are you." Madonna stood tall behind her.

Prudenza moved to walk away.

"Prudenza, you stay with me. Maestra Maria has taken over the reading for tonight."

Prudenza pulled her shoulders back to face the Prioress.

Discrete Margarita, who stood beside her, broke the rules of touching and grabbed each girl by the hand. "I will take care of them." Agata couldn't help but listen in as Margarita pulled them away.

"Signora, Prudenza. What were you thinking?"

Prudenza did not answer.

"I understand that it is often necessary to encourage the girls in discipline, and sometimes that takes imparting a certain discipline ourselves. We have an obligation here to protect the girls and ourselves. This should have been brought to my attention and addressed together in our staff meeting."

Signora Prudenza responded, "The girl is impudent and self-absorbed."

"You are not her priest! Don Bollani issues atonement as God leads him to. If the board hears of this, you could be sent off to a nunnery. I know this is not the first time you have acted harshly toward a foundling."

Agata gave one quick turn of the head as Discrete gave her a tug around the next hall corner. "We will deal with this between you and me this one time. The next time, I can't save you."

Agata lay heavily on the back of the wooden pew, with Candida on the further side of her, and Discrete Margarita tight between them. Discrete dabbed the tears off Candida's face. Agata didn't need such attention. She was too hollowed out to cry anymore. Only a few stray tears made their final exit from her chin. She was, in fact, more aware of her inner self than she had ever been.

"I knew she was gone," Agata said. "I couldn't feel her anymore. I haven't felt her for most of the time I've been here. But I couldn't face even the thought of it."

Discrete Margarita spoke, "Do you remember how I told you Nonna would live right in your heart? That's how you'd keep her with you? I'm sorry. Prudenza was out of line to speak to you in that manner. She will, as you saw, be dealt with."

"I could have stayed with Nonna! Why didn't she let me stay?"

"There would be no one left to look after you." Discrete patted her leg as if to dampen the truth.

"I miss her bivolo. She was a really good Nonna," Agata blubbered. "The best Nonna. If I could walk through the door and smell her bakery one more time…"

Margarita responded, "Of course, she was."

Candida welled up again and rolled into Discrete. "I can picture how good it smelled, Agata. It makes me miss your Nonna, too."

"Both of you will be okay. This is just a blip."

"My hair," Candida whimpered. She took the wrap off, and the chopped ends stuck straight out of the side of her head. They all had a good and hearty laugh.

"Oh, my dears," Margarita said through a sigh. "Just a blip. There are better days ahead for you." She kissed the tops of their heads. "You'll see."

A reality washed over Agata with Discrete's words. In the days ahead, she would discover if her fate was to be stuck behind these walls indefinitely. Would she ever see Canciano again?

24
AGATA

It should have been a night without sleep. Instead, something steady and steely ran through her, and Agata slept hard and dreamless. That is, until the cool of morning waved across her sheets, and the smell of fresh bivolo tickled the underside of her nose. A warm pressure clutched her arm, and she heard her Nonna whisper, "It's time."

At the sound of her grandmother's voice, Agata woke instantly. She raised her hand to touch the blanket, but the warmth of Nonna's hand dissipated. The clang of the morning gong cleared out the dreams in the room. The *dormotorio* responded in mumbled harmonies of the morning song's foundlings. Agata's thoughts churned, her self-consciousness speaking to her with a new understanding, as if she had aged overnight, with the realization that her future was designed for something far more unexpected than she could have planned. This thought brought Agata to her feet. Braids tight. Dress smoothed—heart beating, anticipative, quiet.

Every student must have hoped for mass and even breakfast to pass quickly as she did. Maestra Maria read the scriptures from the front of the *caffeterria*. Prudenza was noticeably absent. The room should have felt more relaxed, but it was stifled with anxiety. Agata had learned to recognize that days like today showed up, and no one could separate the orphan from her fear of rejection. It was like trying to separate salt from the sea. In this, they were all the same.

Agata headed toward the choir practice room to meet Maestra Elena with the other fifty auditionees. The halls were louder with the shuffle of stress in their shoes as they exited the breakfast room to face their fates. She was focused on the bobbing heads in front of her when one whipped around, and she saw the white mask she had seen in her papa's apartment.

She stopped, causing the girl behind her to run into her. Agata blinked, and the mask was gone. She looked down and saw her fingers white in a tight grip on her instrument. *He can't get me in here.*

Maestra Elena led the girls through twenty minutes of their regular vocal exercises to prepare them and calm their nerves. It was so good to see her, especially in light of her recent understanding of her Nonna's life and death. If she had followed her instincts, she would have run up to her in an embrace. Instead, she remained in the cue behind Chiaretta and got as close as she could as she passed by.

"Agata, good morning," Maestra Elena greeted. She gave Agata a large smile.

"Good morning, Maestra." *I'm nervous,* she wanted to say.

"You will do great today," she responded as if she heard Agata's thoughts. "I won't be in the room, but I will be near enough and thinking of all of you." Elena then announced to the entire room, "You will wait here while the auditionees are called out. Discrete will call three names at a time. The second and third will wait in the hall to keep the process moving as succinctly as possible. You can keep your instruments warmed up but consider your neighbors' needs and play softly. Good luck to all of you. I'm very proud of each of you."

When Elisabetta was called up with the first group, she looked toward Agata with a creased forehead, her arm stiff and her violin dangling at her neck. Agata tried to offer a smile in return, but it wouldn't come. She raised her crossed fingers to her lips for good luck instead. She began instinctively tapping them on her skirt. She had to keep her fingers busy. She moved through slow scales and small phrases on her violin to pass the time.

"Solaria, Chiaretta, Agata. Please wait in the hall," Discrete Orsa called.

Agata's stomach lurched ahead of her as she stood. She walked to the front of the class and looked past Orsa. Was that a white mask lurking in the dark hall behind her?

"Join me," Discrete Orsa whispered.

Agata focused back on Orsa, whose cheer glowed, illuminating her covered head and white dress in a bright light. Orsa clutched her rosary beads and held them against her round middle.

"Our father, who art in heaven…"

Agata must have recited the Lord's prayer ten times. She looked up, and the mask was gone. Solaria walked out of the audition room; Agata couldn't read her. Chiaretta gave a little skip-in. Her confidence made Agata's heartbeat faster. She looked past the Discrete in search of the mask.

"Again," instructed Discrete Orsa. "Hail Mary, Full of Grace…"

Chiaretta sounded perfect. Agata's breath quickened.

Slowww, Discrete Orsa mouthed.

"Blessed is the fruit of thy womb, Jesus. Holy Mary, Mother of God."

Chiaretta emerged with a smile on her face.

"Pray for us sinners now and at the hour of our death."

"Amen," Discrete Orsa joined her. It was Agata's turn.

Agata walked to the center of the room. Four women sat before her. Some were teachers she knew; others she had heard of but never spoken to before.

"Good morning. Just there in the middle, Agata," Maestra Maria della Viola directed her. "We will start with your vocals. I will play your starting note, and you can begin when you are ready."

Agata heard the note and stared. She was so overcome with worry that the note came out in an airy breath.

"Stop, please. Agata, we know what you are capable of. Please project the note so we can hear it."

Maestra Apollonia, a well-respected Coro soprano and the soloist from the Gloria in D debut, stepped in. "I will join, and we can sing it together."

Agata took a deep breath and sang along with Appollonia —her voice sounded so much better with hers behind her. Agata felt held by this unintentional duet, and she sang for two measures on her own, enjoying the beauty of it before she realized Apollonia had dropped out and she was singing alone. She did it.

The violin and the harpsichord seemed to go much quicker. And like that, it was done.

"Thank you. We will let you know on Monday."

Agata walked out of the room into the light-filled hall. She felt herself smiling, and little Orsa returned the expression. "You did it, child. I expected nothing less."

"I did, didn't I?" asked Agata, feeling such ease that she couldn't stop smiling. The white mask in the hall was nowhere to be found.

The weekend came and went, slower for some than for others in the *figlie del Coro*. It was marked by excitement and a lot more whisper-chatter than would have usually been allowed, especially without Signora Prudenza roaming the halls, whom the girls knew was solely on the hunt for talkers. Suspiciously, no one had seen Prudenza for the entire week. Agata did not reveal anything she knew about her disappearance when questions swirled, such as, "Weren't *you late for dinner that night, Agata?"* With Candida distanced at the *figlie del Coro* table, there wasn't a chance to get caught discussing it together. Thankfully, everyone was focused on the announcement of Monday's audition results.

Agata thought her nerves at breakfast were worse than on audition day.

Madonna stood to make the announcement: "*Bondi*, ladies. As you are aware, we have some audition news to share with you today. I was not in these meetings. These decisions were discussed and hashed out by the Coro's senior members until they reached a unanimous agreement. I won't waste any more of your breakfast reading them here. Postings for the new

Coro members will be up in the choir room after our meal this morning, and postings for returning Coro members will be posted on the door to the *Chiesa della Pietà*. Once read, those of you who made it will go promptly to your beds and gather your belongings for moving day. The rest of you will line the halls as a formal send-off and congratulations. We will return to our second-hour normal schedules after that."

Agata walked in pace in the long line of girls toward the choir room. She held an extra-large mass of her skirt between her fingers and ran her index finger over the top double-time. She exchanged glances with Elisabetta in the line next to hers and watched Chiaretta bounce in front of her. Her heart raced. She pictured breaking into a run, pushing the non-auditionees out of the way in delicious mayhem, but she steadied, or her feet did for her. The results were read one by one in line order, so each could read her fate privately before moving on. Chiaretta made a little jump and faced her with a big grin. No surprise. Agata walked up and put her finger on the list. The "A" names were at the top. She sucked in her breath.

Agata, primary instrument, soprano voice, private tutor, Elena.

She did it. She was no longer a plain Commun girl, but a Coro girl with an uncharted future to explore.

Agata felt a hum well up in her as she removed the sheets from her bed, folding them into a tight, pressed square, as she had been taught. She kissed the camelia on the corner edge of her pillowcase.

I'm moving again, Mammina, but this time with my own two feet leading me.

She got in line with Chiaretta, Elisabetta, and seven other girls who filed into a singular line from nearby rooms. They walked proudly down the hall with their only two possessions: their personally embroidered sheets clutched in their arms and their voices.

As they entered the hall, they began singing a new chant, announcing their acceptance to the Coro.

Ave Maris Stella	*: Hail, star of the sea,*
Dei Mater alma	*: blessed Mother of God,*
Atque semper Virgo:	*: and ever Virgin,*
Felix Caeli porta	*: happy gate of heaven.*
Sumuns illud Ave	*: Receiving that awe*
Gabrielis ore	*: from the mouth of Gabriel*
Funda nos in pace:	*: establish us in peace,*
Mutans Heavae nomen	*: changing the name of Eve.*
Solva vincla reis	*: Loosen the chains of sinners*
Profer Lumen caecis	*: give light to the blind,*
Mala nostra pelle	*: drive away our ills,*
Bona cuncta posce	*: Obtain for us all good things.*

The girls of the Commun lined the main hallway to watch the newly accepted girls walk away from their former lives. Agata couldn't help but feel bad for those who hadn't made it; they stood solemnly, tears of cupidity filling their eyes. Others with no intention of pursuing the Coro appeared wonderstruck. They walked past the circular staircase, where the cooks from the kitchen came out to watch the procession. Their chorus amplified as the Coro students and teachers left their classrooms and sleeping quarters to join them in singing the Coro's song, welcoming them to their side of the building. Elena sang loudly and with a proud smile. Discrete Margarita and Discrete Orsa sang louder than all of them as they passed.

Agata walked into her new room of just six beds and squeezed Elisabetta's hand once they recognized the red scarves dappling both their necks. Chiaretta ran past Agata, seeing her name on her new bed, grabbed at hers, and threw it around herself. Agata picked up her scarf, ceremoniously unfolded it, and noticed a small white thread tucked in the middle of all the red loops. She looked closely and recognized the hidden camelia sewn in just for her to keep hidden right by her heart. Tears pooled at the corners of her eyes. Poeta had kept her promise.

Her face was damp with pride as she squeezed the scarf to her chest, catching the stray tears that rolled off her chin, the sad ones absorbed into its strong weave. This was her new life, and as far as she knew, goodbye to Canciano and all whom she loved there forever.

In all the celebrations, no one seemed to notice a prominent figure missing. At the back of the basement sat a solitary cell intended for confinement and punishment when deemed necessary by the board, but it wasn't the board that had sent Prudenza there. She could hear nothing of the singing upstairs, nothing of the laundry room workers or the hospital on her floor. All she could hear was the sound of her anger building as she hatched a plan to ensure the Prioress' removal—so she could stand in her place.

ACT THREE
FIGLIE DEL CORO

25
AGATA

The young Sotto Maestra walked with purpose down the long, central hall of the Pietà. Her steps were quick, her shoes marking the cadence of her day. Though it was gray and damp outside, the Pietà's white walls gleamed back at her in a sunny wink at how she needed their approval. Agata hardly believed this day had come. She stepped away from Discrete Margarita's office, feeling comforted but still anxious.

Discrete offered her blessing with a short prayer. "Firsts always make us nervous, child. But you will be more confident next time, and the time after that and the time after that..."

Discrete Margarita wore her confidence in every gesture she made. Agata tended to be insecure. She stopped in the foyer and looked up, recalling her first view of the spiral staircase on that dark night years ago, and the mask she had worn that hindered her vision. The fear she wore as they took her cloak.

She walked away from the memory, no longer held by it, her vision no longer protected. She knew exactly where she was headed, with her red full skirt swooshing at her ankles and her white shirt tucked into it firmly. Her hair was pulled back into a low bun; its hue darkened to a deep chestnut from her years spent indoors. The braids of her youth were a yesterday she could not return to.

She rubbed her fingers together, that reliable nervous tic still strong. The hard, callous circles were rough yet delicate, making a small announcement with their sound. Their subtle scrape soothed her. It had taken them years to work. She habitually fingered a line of Psalm 139 when she found herself in any distress. She spoke the words repeatedly while playing the line with her left hand as she would on her violin, in its absence, on the side of her skirt:

"You hem me in behind and before; you have laid your hand upon me."

She moved her fingers away from her side and patted the small lace collar that lined the neck of her shirt, pressing her hand into it as if it might release some good luck for the day.

She saw the small feet first and the white dresses above them. She raised her head to meet the gaze of her familiar teacher and friend, Maestra Elena. Elena's eyes twinkled at the sight of her. Her Maestra had grown into a beautiful woman and an esteemed member of the performing Coro, and the years had given her small crinkles at the corners of her gentle eyes. She was admired as she had been for years by her students and respected by her musical peers.

Maestra Elena made an introduction to the class: "Children, you've had the chance to hear from her as a student teacher in class. You should know that she is a gifted vocalist, violinist, and detailed copyist—a favorite, really, among the composers for her precision. I give you Sotto Maestra Agata.

You are lucky to be learning your music fundamentals from her."

Agata had earned her new title by advancing in a competitive audition and via the majority board's approval. Sotto Maestra had been appointed a master teacher to assist the lower-level classes for a two-year commitment. Agata noted the pride in her mentor's voice. She inhaled in a breath for courage:

"I thank you for your vote of confidence, Maestra. Now, class," Agata exhaled. "Can you tell me what this is?" She scanned the room, focusing on her calm presence and vivacious tone, memorizing the young faces that peered back at her.

"Yes, you are right. It is a circle, but in music, we know it as a whole note."

She heard her voice quiver; Elena would have detected it, too, no doubt. They had worked together so long that each other's habits and physical tendencies were confessions of their inward lives, and on some days, in this building of enforced quiet, they were the only way to communicate. In another world, she would have loved the chance to discuss her misgivings. But the Pietà protected anything from exiting its rigid walls.

Agata gave a thank-you nod, permitting Maestra Elena to leave the room. Agata understood it was not Elena's job to coddle her but to propel her forward, even while she shouted with fear on the inside.

After ten years in the Coro, Agata recognized her growth as a musician. But it was the fear of performing before a crowd that made her learning seem obsolete the second she opened her mouth. An unfortunate result of an unresolved past that clung to her twenty-two-year-old self. The loss that had never left her side. How could she complain when most girls hadn't enjoyed family life as long as she had? She kept the remembrances of her mammina, her Nonna, and Canciano tucked away in this quiet place inside, visiting it whenever her loneliness tried to take over. A flicker of the contrasting image of her papa, Pietro, still roaming the *fondamente* in search of her haunted her. He stuck close in a quiet fold of her mind, a dark, inaudible ghost who could appear at any time. She sought reprieve by visiting her happier memories locked away.

In her safe inner place, such as the practice room or her bedroom, her voice projected her confidence. She could do anything. But outside of that safe space, she struggled to find the gumption to sing out or audition for solos. She was not comfortable with being so exposed. What if they saw the darkness she'd tucked away as neatly as her white shirt tucked into her red skirt? She stopped and rubbed her palms flat over the seam at her waist.

Agata was relieved when her two classes ended, and she managed to complete the rest of her schedule. Finally, she'd be in the same room with her friends for orchestra rehearsal. She sat heavily in her chair as if to give it the day's stress and looked across the orchestra to the cello section. Candida sat in the second row waiting for her, her face purposely twisted—her cello propped between her knees. Agata chuckled and shook her head. Although her day had not gone perfectly,

Candida's antics reminded her she had sisters who understood her.

Chiaretta sat to the right of her at first chair and interjected her daily wind-down: "Rough first day?" Chiaretta was still a tiny, small-boned girl; her thin hair had fluffy wisps that encircled her diamond-shaped face. It was as if all her body's efforts to grow had been directed to her playing, which had advanced exponentially—as had her confidence. She loved to share her great musical wisdom and strong opinions.

Chiaretta continued, "I remember when I started student teaching, I had a hard time finding time for all I had in me to educate and make them understand. That's when they put me with the more advanced students. It's been going well ever since. Don't worry, Agata, it will just take you more time, but you'll get there."

Agata gave Chiaretta a weak smile. "Thanks, Chiaretta."

She meant well, Agata told herself. Agata had developed the habit of extracting the good from what could seem like sour commentary; it was how she managed to survive the pressure and competitiveness of the Coro environment. In this, Chiaretta had a point: she would get better at teaching as she had with playing. She sat in a room with some of the top musicians of the Coro. The ones left had made it through the first stage of training, known as *Piccolo*, and auditioned to reach the second level and longest stage of education, called *Mezzane*, which, on its own, took six years to complete. The girls present at the afternoon orchestra rehearsal represented the third and final level of Coro training known as the *Grandi*. It wasn't until they graduated from the *Grandi* program that they were eligible to audition for the weekly performing Coro, or, as was affectionately referred to inside, a Poinsettia Girl.

Tap, tap, tap. Maestro Scarpari used the small baton to bring order to the room. He was a gentle soul with a mass of dark curly hair that rose high on his head. The hair tended to dance as if emotionally connected to his work. The third-level Coro girls regularly giggled at him.

"Ahem, ladies, we all seem a bit energetic. Let's put that into our practice. We will work on our piece for this Sunday's mass." Maestro raised his arms, and rehearsal began.

Agata clicked her violin case closed and hopped up, hoping to avoid any more inspiring conversation with Chiaretta. She was tired after all the emotional propping up for her first lesson, and if she beat her roommate to rest hour, she could get a start on her nap. Candida asked her a hands-up question, and Agata replied with her hand over her open mouth in a simulated yawn. No matter what, Candida would find her.

Agata sped from the practice room, past Coro classrooms to the *Grandi* dormotorio wing. Finally.

The wood door required her shoulder to open it; it tended to catch after it sat closed for several hours. As it creaked open, the force created a small gust of air, which caused several papers to whoosh up at her entrance. They rocked slowly, descending one by one all over her floor. *Oh, that.* She gathered the music sheets that danced around her, capturing the few that floated under either bed. As she went to place them on the shared desk, she saw the piles with new eyes that might be a bother to her roommate. Admittedly, she employed the entire desk's surface; her sheets of music were always strewn across the top of it. She needed to straighten it up.

Agata had discovered a new gift quite unintentionally during her studies as a musician. Her theory classes provided the opportunity to use her detailed propensity to write the note patterns she studied. So much so that it had earned her a part-time job of sorts. Most of the work was designated by the professional teachers (male musicians) from St. Mark's who instructed the higher-level Coro classes. Several copyists were required to keep the pace of practice and production. They rewrote exercises and practice pieces, simplifying them for the Coro's lower levels. Needless to say, a fair share of music always needed duplication.

Agata was proficient and enjoyed the work. She couldn't resist taking a generous pile from the music storage room, where a stack was left for music to be copied, as well as a finished pile for the ones that were. Some had notes on the front of the scores, requesting that Agata personally rewrite them.

She found solace in sitting between the notes, relishing the excitement of reading what hadn't been heard yet, the new melodies playing loudly in her mind. Those moments alone, with the notes singing in her head, led her to fashion some additions and musical phrases. Several of which she dared write on scraps of paper with mistakes or ink bleeds, undoubtedly unacceptable to any conductor's score or musicians' music. She thought of them as little gifts just for her.

Her thoughts were interrupted when Candida and Elisabetta gave their secret knock and pushed their way in.

"That Scarpari, what an odd man," Candida said and flopped on her roommate's bed.

The three friends had a habit of meeting together during rest hour once a week and changing the day to throw anyone off who might be watching.

"Candida, I was hoping actually to rest today. I'm exhausted after my first day of teaching," Agata replied.

"That's right, Agata. How did it go?" Elisabetta asked, her brown eyes fluttering. Her childhood freckles still dotted her now high cheekbones that complemented her dark auburn hair.

"Pretty well for my first day. I am just tired. I came back and saw all my music and thought I should pick this up before —"

"What now?" Giulia, Agata's roommate, interrupted the chatty trio as she barged into their room. Giulia squeezed her forehead as she took inventory of her room, finding it quite full of not only papers but also people. "I am a Grandi-level Sotto Maestra! I am only supposed to have to deal with one roommate, but it seems with you, I am still living with three, like I was a third-year Coro student!" Giulia looked directly at Agata, disgusted.

Candida tried to slip over to Agata's bed as Giulia walked over to her own.

"And this mess. Agata! Ugh, I am going to the practice room, where at least I can find some quiet."

Agata felt the same. Giulia tried to slam the heavy door, and once she was out of the room, her friends giggled at the drama. Agata returned a tired smile—so much for that nap.

26
MARGARITA

Margarita felt a warmth pull around her bent knees. After the commotion of morning bells and song, mass, and breakfast, she felt she had earned her quiet. It was but a thirty-minute pause before the urgencies and tasks came calling. Prayer grounded her. It gave her life, a sense of reprieve. She could unburden all that she picked up from the halls and relieve herself from them. Her gaze lifted to the simple crucifix hanging in the Pietà chapel. She moved her right hand tenderly from her forehead to her heart in the sign of the cross in response. *Now, if I could get up off these stiff knees,* she heard movement behind her and anticipated her friend Don Bollani tending to some of the same needs in prayer.

"Back at it, huh?" Don Bollani let out a chummy whisper as he approached her pew.

"Yes, Padre, the most reliable thing in my day. It is easy to return to," she replied. She moved to rise, ignoring a weakness that made it easier to stay kneeling.

"Is there anything I can pray for you? Even something small? An ailment or the like?"

"My knees get tired, and my hip gets creaky, but yes, as long as you are only sharing with our Father, we can't have everyone in a rumple about the old lady in their midst." She pretended to be annoyed. She wasn't.

"I will add that, in quiet, to the other things I pray for you," Don Bollani confided. "You are one of the Pietà's greatest assets. God sees your work, and we are all better because of it."

"Well," she said, pushing herself up with no great show of force. "Thank you, Don Bollani, but don't spend too much time on me. My days are numbered, and the needs of all these girls should take precedence," she replied. "Off to a new day."

"I hope it's a good one, Discrete."

She hoped so, too; it was Friday, which meant she'd attend the weekly board meeting with the governor and his staff of appointed volunteers. The men would walk in their brocade jackets and clickety shoes from their illustrious homes and step inside the unadorned white lobby to chatter. Margarita circled them like a little rowboat, guiding the ship's occupants to calmer waters as a reminder for them to whisper.

Once they all arrived, they would be paraded to the meeting room adjacent to Madonna's personal office, where they gathered at a round table. Margarita didn't love the men congregating or the sense of power and pride they brought. It wasn't as though she didn't like them personally or respect them (some more than others). The Pietà women in senior roles didn't *need* them to perform their duties, as the men seemed to think inherently. They just needed their money. Ultimately, Margarita had to pray before she went every week to ensure she walked in less annoyed than she would be when she walked out.

Her primary reason for attending these meetings was to support Madonna. Margarita was particularly protective of her after they spent years working alongside each other. She noted the way Madonna's shoulders tensed when the board members filled up what was, every other day, her working room. Margarita knew Madonna had to mentally prepare herself to respond graciously to the agendas and ideas brought in from the outside when her list from the inside should take precedence. It was a bit of a fight. But Margarita was proud of how she consistently navigated the heady men who were well-intended but often unaware.

"What will it be today, Discrete?" Madonna muttered as the men took their places.

"God has named you in charge. Don't forget that when they get insistent," snapped Margarita back in a whisper.

Among the many topics addressed in the meetings, which weighed heavily on approvals for staff and their pay, as well as offers of marriage, were suggested outings that provided opportunities for both additional income and exposure. The Pietà received numerous requests and invitations for musicians, particularly singers, to entertain at private events. Most often, it was a noble's birthday celebration or a son's coming-of-age party. They were circumstantial excuses to see the young, renowned Coro singers up close and show them off to curious friends who were also anxious for a peek. These parties played out as a game of approvals and denials, of bargaining and flirtations.

In return for this show and backhanded bargaining, the girls were paid well for their musical displays. They were allowed to keep the money they earned to add to their growing dowries, maintained by the Pietà. It was generally known, but only spoken of by the board, that these families provided the perfect excuse to shop for an eligible wife and the bragging rights to say she was once part of the esteemed Coro. In exchange, unless specifically requested, the board voted to send those of a pleasant demeanor and promising talent, who also possessed unforeseen gifts, as only a young woman could, with the understanding that once she was married, she would never be allowed to use her musical talents again.

It wasn't appropriate for Madonna to attend these outings, and Margarita was happy to accompany the young innocents. Her mission started here, right in Madonna's little boardroom, and Margarita would take note of all of it.

After greetings and formalities, the black-mustached and excitable Governor Sovarizo began. "A certain celebration requested a string ensemble and ten singers for musical entertainment to enjoy an afternoon in the garden of a grand estate for a May affair."

"I believe Elisabetta has the softness of voice to ease the wits of man," interjected Signor Troy, a vocal board member from a notable Venetian family. Signor Troy had a large frame for a Venetian man, and an equally big voice that stemmed from it. He liked to discuss how the girls fit into the choir's look; he was conscious of public perceptions.

"You mean to say she has a known disadvantage, and it's time we find a place for her," interjected Signor Mocenigo. He came from one of Venice's wealthiest families, and every comment he made steered back to finances. He was alternately a thin man, with a long face and a sour voice. "She is easy on the eyes, so as long as we can avoid an incident that can be overlooked in negotiations, should we have one."

Madonna cut in, "Elisabetta has dealt with an infrequent showing of epilepsy. But she has not had a seizure for months. I agree, though she has been a prodigious student, I don't see her future in performance. It wouldn't be right to place that stress on her with all of Venice watching." She continued, "I see Candida as another good proponent for the outing. She plays with such vigor and expression."

Signor Troy took a deep breath and pursed his lips. "It may sound objectionable, but should we consider allowing some of our lead musicians to find their path out? We have a talented batch of Sotto Maestras who will need to find their place in the future performing Coro. I see Maestra Elena as one of those. Maybe Appollonia herself." His volume increased with every opinion.

"Now hold on. Let's not get carried away." Signor Mocenigo huffed, trying to gain control. "These performing Coro lead ladies are our bread and butter. Cycle, yes, of course, but not all at once. Appollonia still draws in the crowds. Elena, fine. She is talented, but not one they come to see. I vote for that little shy one."

The Prioress poised and interjected, "I believe you are referring to our new Sotto Maestra, Agata. She needs time to gain her footing to be a future soloist, but her musicianship is not in question. And she is another soprano. I think it is time to make a firm list. We must consider voice parts and balance."

Another board member, perhaps the only quiet one at the table, was Andrea Foscarini, acting secretary. He was generally responsible for legacies as he provided a substantial one to the Pietà himself. He was quite skilled at keeping track of board records. He could often be seen rubbing his thin, brown beard instead of talking.

"I've already started one, Madonna," Foscarini confirmed.

Margarita heard a knock at the door, though it wasn't heard over the names and musicians verbally thrown across the table. The hardwood door's bottom edge then scraped the floor, and the banter stopped. Heads turned toward the intrusion.

Assistant Prioress Prudenza stood next to the door, easing it closed with her foot while remaining upright in stature.

What in God's good name does she want? Margarita thought. She may have let an eye roll slip.

"I am sorry for the interruption," remarked Prudenza. "I wonder if I might bring a suggestion to the table." She stepped closer to the group of men.

Margarita was suspicious of Prudenza's atypical subservient tone. But she couldn't have anyone outside the board listening in. She shuffled over to close the door behind her.

"Assistant Prioress, we would gladly hear your request," the Prioress said. Margarita noted her forced joviality and planned to commend her for it later. "If you would, follow protocol and provide a written request to the board that we might discuss it at our next meeting. We follow a tight agenda."

Governor Sovarizo, sensing the tension, looked from Prudenza to Madonna. The situation lured his naturally curious flair for more play. "Good afternoon, Assistant Prioress. I am sure the board doesn't mind a short departure from our conversation."

"That is if our board can offer their opinions," fought back loud Signor Troy.

"I'm intrigued," responded Governor Sovarizo. "How can we help you, Prudenza?"

Madonna and Margarita locked eyes.

"As Assistant Prioress, I should be granted access to these weekly meetings. What if something should happen to our beloved Madonna? We should have someone capable in the wings so that the detailed work of the Pietà never risks slipping."

"An interesting observation, Assistant Prioress. Let's vote to move on it, gentlemen," responded Governor Sovarizo. "What do you say?"

A vote was taken. The meeting continued despite the interruption by Prudenza, who was granted permission to stay until the end and be included in future meetings.

"I'm happy to help walk the gentlemen out, Discrete," Prudenza suggested. Her tone was cheerful.

Margarita hmphed. She didn't need her to grasp her job, too. Margarita walked away more ruffled than usual, deciding to march straight back to the pew to get herself together. She could offer better support to Madonna after that. But before she could make her way toward the stoup, Elena intercepted her.

"*Bondi*, Discrete. Sorry to interrupt," Elena explained. "I had hoped I could discuss something with you."

"It's never an interruption, child. Let's sit in the chapel so we can have more privacy." The two women genuflected and sat in a pew a few rows up from the back.

"It's Agata," Elena sighed as if releasing something.

"I figured as much."

"Oh, how?" Elena seemed surprised.

"You have a certain look of tenderness on your face when you speak of her," Margarita responded gently.

"She has become like a younger sister to me. It's just that I have poured into her for many years. And I'd like to think the fruition of that relationship had something to do with her growth. But I am finding I am at a stalemate with her vocal training. While I do believe she is capable of more, I don't believe she can grow past where she is with me." Elena spoke with a hint of sadness, as if she were fearful that she had let the young woman down by asking for a reprieve.

Margarita was quick to respond. "She has stayed with you longer than we normally advise a pairing. But I believe her loss of family was so close to her, she wouldn't have been able to survive without a replacement one. You offered her that." After a brief pause, she added, "You have served her and the Pietà well. Our life comes in seasons, Elena. And God uses those seasons to twist and release the people he intended for our greatest growth. Are you sensing a new season in your life, Elena?"

"Funny you should say it that way." Elena let out a small laugh. "But yes, I think I am. I just can't interpret what that means right now."

"Spring is coming and, like always, new opportunities with it. I am sure it will reveal why."

"Thank you, Discrete. Your words are always such a comfort."

Margarita patted the top of Elena's hand that grasped the pew. Margarita felt the winds of change swirling within her, her impatience, and dared to admit her tiredness. What would those winds bring her way?

11
AGATA

A sliver of midday light dispersed in strands across the lunch table of the *Grandi* Coro. It reflected off the spoons and bowls as they clattered and clinked, echoing their conversation across the broad *caffeteria*. Agata was feeling particularly warmed by the runny polenta in her dish and the presence of her friends around her. Although she had only the sky view from the windows and the small courtyard to see it, spring had finally arrived. She had adapted to the challenges of her new schedule, and although she couldn't claim it had become easy, on most days, she walked away energized from accomplishing another lesson taught.

Not all was sunny in the Pietà *caffeterria*. The reason for the quiet was the absence of a mealtime scripture reading. A tradition Agata didn't mind a break from. It didn't last long. Assistant Prioress Prudenza glided in and stood directly in front of the Prioress, fiddling through the pages in her hands. She was never late. Agata and Elisabetta shared a quizzical look, which they passed from one to another and around their table.

Madonna cleared her throat. "What scripture are we enjoying the pleasure of, Assistant Prioress Prudenza?"

"We are starting at Ecclesiastes three, if that pleases you, Madonna," Prudenza sniggered.

"Thank you for reading at your usual spot to the left of the head table," Madonna replied stoically.

Agata's head shot left at Candida, who sat across from her, a few students down. Between them, Elisabetta put her head down to hide her giggle. The icy interaction between the two Pietà heads was not new. It had been that way for years, ever since Agata's and Candida's terrible practice room interaction with Prudenza, who consequently went mysteriously missing for a week after that. Since that time, it seemed Prudenza had come out fighting. Not with Agata, who fortunately never had reason to interact with her; she played entirely different instruments. She got the feeling Prudenza avoided her as well. Good riddance; Agata was just fine with that. The tension between Madonna and Prudenza was often masked by formality and decorum. On this particular day, the outward expression of their mutual dislike was readily on display.

The ending gong was a welcome interrupter. The *caffeterria* emptied quickly, and Agata maneuvered away from the weave of girls with her head down before she could be lured into any whispers or Pietà talk. She rushed over to the music copy room to see whether any work had been left for her. After she let herself in, she stood with her back to the door, breathing heavily for a second as if the disquiet from the masses were chasing her down. In the room of scrolls and stacks, her breath steadied, and her consciousness wakened.

The room was dark and less spring-like than the rest of the building, with only one small window at the top that filtered dust beams of golden light. Agata didn't feel afraid but hidden in its duskiness—like a crab under a rock. In this room, she was privy to the music staff's creations and communications, while the musty air hid the imperfections she fought so hard to hide. She stepped up to the to-do basket and began greedily combing through it. It wasn't only the Pietà teachers who left music to be copied. Notable musicians and composers who passed through Venice also made significant musical contributions. They wanted to boast to their countrymen that the mysterious virgins of the Pietà would perform their works.

Elena had explained to Agata that the audiences who loyally came to the Pietà were eager to hear new music, so they could boast to their neighbors who had missed Sunday Vespers or the weekly Saturday concert about how glorious Apollonia sounded or how the violins played with more ecstasy than the week before. The board complied with their audience's desires and voted in a standing rule that nothing could be played twice. In fact, the compositions were never to be performed anywhere before the Pietà played them for the first time. This placed significant pressure on the current Maestro di Coro, Scarpari, whose responsibilities included producing new music for the weekly concerts and conducting rehearsals. He was likely grateful for the external contributors, especially those with a well-known reputation. But to Agata, it was destined to be a basketful of projects and their melodies to discover.

Agata thumbed through the stack of music. Exercises for the introductory string class. A new orchestration on a melody meant to feature a mezzo voice. Her fingers stopped when she spotted a handwritten note: *for Agata*. She glanced at the top right to see who the composer was and drew a breath of humble disbelief when she saw the name *A. Vivaldi,* whom she formerly referred to as the man in the red jacket. Agata had learned that though he was the fastest-producing composer, Maestro Vivaldi was awkward and skittish to deal with. She also heard that the board had a complicated relationship with him. He scored a vast amount of the Pietà's music and served as a violin teacher, but the board never invited him to be Maestri do Coro. While he had produced sweeping pieces like *Gloria in D* and *Juditha triumphans,* most of Vivaldi's compositions were smaller-scale songs, many written for Anna Maria, whom he had composed over twenty concertos, and even a few lately were for Chiaretta. Agata took a closer look at the page with her name on it. It was a short vocal piece intended for a soprano voice, consisting of three verses. There was no orchestration included with it. But he evidently meant for her to see that it had been written for her.

Agata's thoughts churned. Could he have known how she struggled to find the courage to sing? Clearly, her voice was good enough as she was a permanent fixture in the choir. She never auditioned for solos. Although the official performing Coro could only audition for them in public, the girls still went through the process of auditioning and performing for the other choirs to prepare them. It was pretty standard for the solo parts to be written with a particular singer in mind, someone with a specific timbre and sound that was desired, and until now, none had been written explicitly for her.

Oh, mammina, give me courage. What is this meant for?

She hastily scanned the lines of music, tracing the melody with her finger—impatient to sight-read and read it out loud. As she whispered the melody, a quick knock and a shove of the door startled her before she had the chance to answer.

"I thought I might find you here," teased Discrete Margarita. "How are you getting along, my dear? I understand you've had lots of transcribing to do."

Margarita personified a gentleness that Agata had learned to find comfort in. She spoke with a natural candor when she was with her.

"Yes, I have had my hands full. I really enjoy it. In fact, I get lost in it. I have a new request in my pile here that surprised me."

"What is that?" Margarita asked.

"It is a new short vocal piece without orchestration, written by Maestro Vivaldi in the strong part of my range. Look here: In the right corner, it reads *'for Agata.'* Could he really mean me?"

"Agata, of course, that's what it means. You see yourself differently than we do. In our eyes, you are capable and talented. Maestro Vivaldi had a special hand in getting you here. He has witnessed your growth and felt he played a small part in it."

"I am not sure what I am supposed to use it for. He didn't include his intentions."

"He is not, as you recall, a man of many words. But I think...it would be a great question for your new voice teacher." Margarita turned to face her.

Agata stopped and looked back at her. "What about Elena? I've always had Elena."

"Elena has been integral to your growth, Agata, but you are ready for someone who will challenge you in new ways. You aren't just supposed to hunker down and copy others' music. You have a voice that needs to be heard. And I understand Elena is facing her own time of change. You will now train with Apollonia. It will be a challenge for you. She is more direct, but you are ready."

Agata shook her head, taking it all in. "I need to get back to my desk and get started on some of this."

"You do that and let it absorb. You've overcome many things, Agata. You will with this challenge as well."

Agata tried to smile at her before turning back to the hall, but she was frustrated. She *knew* Discrete was right. But she was so comfortable with Elena! Agata did not like being exposed. It had taken her years to trust her voice teacher, and now she'd have to start all over again. She gave her stress to her heavy bedroom door with a hearty push before stopping in the threshold to see a full room of people.

"Welcome to your room," exclaimed Candida, sprawled out on Agata's bed like it was her own.

Elisabetta leaned against the wall with her hands pressed together in excitement. "Hello, Agata." Elisabetta continued the girls' spicy conversation, which had started before Agata's entry, "It's not a secret they don't like one another. If you ask me, Prudenza is really pushing her boundaries."

"I heard that she barged into the boardroom and insisted on being part of the weekly meetings," taunted Giulia from her bed as she swung her legs off the edge of it.

"Where do you get your information?" Candida demanded.

"I am privileged to overhear conversations the Prioress has during our private lessons. Many seek her out because the organ is so far away from other ears, and they forget I am sitting there."

"Unbelievable," Candida swore. "But as an organist, you don't get invited to garden events."

"I am so excited," fluttered Elisabetta.

Agata was serious as she spoke, "Candida, you don't need a husband. I thought your dream was to get into the performing Coro, to become a Poinsettia Girl."

"I did. I do. I want whatever gives me the most freedom, and if they think I am not fit for performing… I would never have to listen to or be pushed around by Prudenza again. Then that's what I want."

"What about you, Agata? Are you okay with not getting invited?" Elisabetta asked meekly.

"It's fine. I'm not pining for a husband. I'm happy with my music copying and with you, my friends." She moved her hand across the desk to her pile of work, and the inkpot tipped and got the edge of her skirt before she saved it.

"Ugh, I've got to take care of this before it sets. We have an orchestra rehearsal in half an hour."

Still flustered, Agata made a soft run-walk down the Coro *dormitorios* to the main hall, preoccupied with the mess on her skirt. All this talk of marriage and performing. Maybe she desired neither. Why couldn't she be left alone with a quill in her hand, copying lines of music? That way, she could hide from the pressure of it all.

With her head down and her focus on her agitation, she didn't see the young man standing with his back to her. She proceeded to walk right into him.

"Oh. I'm so sorry. I wasn't paying attention," Agata said, out of breath.

The young man turned around and stared at her, not moving. "Aggi?"

She stared back at him, and for a second, the quiet in the round entry hall let their minds reel and remember.

"Aggi, it's me, Gabriele."

Agata looked at his face, confused. But then she recognized the curl near his ear that had darkened with age. She took the rest of him in, looking down at the three lute cases in his hands.

"I've wondered so long about you," he said. "Where you disappeared to and whether you were okay." He stepped toward her with the ease of familiarity to give an embrace that was not unnatural.

Agata stepped back and smiled, overwhelmed. "It's good to see you, too, Gabriele. I'm well."

"So much has taken place in San Canciano. My father—he's been sick, and I'm practically running the lute shop for him now. Benedetta said she wrote to you several times. Can I write to you? Maybe now that time has passed..."

"Good afternoon! How can I help you?" A voice ran out behind them. It was Poeta.

"I have this stain. I was coming down to see if you could help," explained Agata.

Poeta forced her brows together.

Do I appear as flustered as I am? Agata asked Poeta from the inside, her heart skipping like a stone on water.

"Why don't you head over to the laundry room, and I'll help this young man," Poeta instructed.

"Gabriele. His name is Gabriele. He is from my old neighborhood." Agata's voice quivered when saying his name out loud.

"Ciao, Gabriele. It is a busy place here, but I see you have managed to get in. Do you have an appointment?" Poeta knew how to be forceful and friendly simultaneously.

Agata moved away from them unhurriedly, knowing she could get in trouble for loitering but finding herself not ready to leave.

"I'm from *Sellas Lutes*, here to deliver these," he said, holding the cases up but craning his neck to watch Agata.

She looked back at him. He grinned back at her. A mirthful exhale was released from her mouth. She turned back toward the laundry room and sauntered away quickly; a silly smile stuck to her face. Her mind, like her steps, was all a flutter.

28
ELENA

E lena watched the chordal wave blow back onto the standing Maestro di Cori, Pietro D'all'Oglio Scarpari. He held his arms up, seemingly caught in the intensity, leaving the note and his tall black curls to dangle in the air. Elena tampered with a giggle back at the sight of him. His physical expressions were as theatrical as his name. She was singing with several of the younger Coro girls, whom she knew regularly teased about the eccentric Maestro, and she was cognizant of her example.

"Bravissimo, ladies. Just like that. I will be but a wallflower as you shine for the nobility," Maestro Scarpari said.

"It's time," Francesca whispered, standing outside the choir room door.

Francesca, a retired theorbist and former Poinsettia Girl, had taken a post as record keeper and general event liaison. The girls had gotten used to seeing her on both sides of the Pietà. She carried a kindness and was readily liked. It wasn't hard for anyone to do what she asked. Elena was thankful for a dependable presence to accompany them on their much-anticipated garden party outing, as they could only take one Discrete away from the busy Pietà.

"Ahem, of course. Ladies." Maestro Scarpari arced his arm elegantly toward the door, signaling them to take their exit.

The girls walked to the back hall, lining up at the locked door that led into the courtyard. Elena noticed how the younger girls, like Candida and Elisabetta, squirmed in their shoes with anticipation. She felt a little nervous, knowing some of what to expect during an outing like this one. There would be plenty of gawking young men, whispering mothers, and small talk. Elena also knew that, at thirty-two years old, she would not be the target or the subject of anyone's intentions. She felt it was her responsibility to watch over her young counterparts, where the young women would learn quickly that behaviors at these private parties were not as they were in the quiet Pietà. In such an environment, expressions would not be repressed but would be outwardly displayed through gestures and speech.

Francesca walked ahead of the line and opened the back door, revealing Governor Sovarizo, who looked quite pleased. He stood under a lone tree, waiting to escort them to his friend and Pietà supporter, the effervescent and loud Signor Capello. The governor opened his arms in an energetic greeting.

"Good morning, young ladies!"

His wife, Marietta, who had been chatting with Discrete Margarita, smiled broadly at the girls passing from the Pietà's closed halls to its humble courtyard. Marietta handed each of them a straw hat, constructed by the weaving class in the *Commun*. Every hat displayed a different variety and hue of flowers.

"Thanks to my wife, Marietta, who oversaw the hat-making. You, like the flowers on your hats, will be unique and distinctive, allowing our new friends to identify you easily. I will escort you directly to Signor Capello's back garden for your spring musical display. It's a glorious day for an outing. Marietta? Will you follow at the back?"

Governor Sovarizo guided them through the Pietà's back gate into the quiet alleyway, where their actions would make less of a scene than they would have had they all exited the front door onto the busy Riva Degli Schiavoni. Elena mentally recalled that, many years ago, when she entered through the back gate, Agata had passed out after seeing her father on the alms walk; it was nothing less than a dramatic scene for the public. It was when she first met Ludovico Rossi face-to-face. She had heard from some of the other girls that the generous benefactor was a recent widower. She shook off the thought before her mind could travel with it further.

As it was a rarity to see a wave of white feminine youths passing through the cobbled streets, it was hard not to be a spectacle. Word got out, and onlookers gathered on their path. Elena felt their stares following them, curtains falling back into place as they walked by. Some shopkeepers stepped out from their work and nodded at them, while others scanned the procession from their shop counters.

Like a curtain rising on the stage, Signor Capello's servants opened the back heavy gate to his property as soon as Governor Sovarizo rounded the corner, the flowered hats and dark-haired conductor, Scarpari, following tightly behind him. All eyes were on them as they entered the garden, where it appeared the guests had been given an earlier invitation time. This appeared to fluster Maestro Scarpari. After eyeing how the chairs had been incorrectly set up for the string ensemble, he set right to work rearranging the setup and forgetting the choir behind him.

"Thought we'd have a few minutes to ascertain the function of the performing space," the Maestro mumbled.

"Here, let me help you, Maestro. I can gather a few girls to assist," Elena responded, turning to grab a few hands.

The new girls stood in a clump, hiding behind one another, looking shy and exposed. A similar clump of men stood nearer the house and returned their stares, their faces greedy and searching. Those who had experience performing outside the Pietà broke off quickly from the group and approached the ogling nobles with confident familiarity. Some even cozied up to those they knew on a first-name basis.

"Well, thus it begins," said Elena to Discrete Margarita as the group dispersed.

The two women stood beside each other, taking it all in. It didn't take long for a young man with a swift step and apparent generosity of spirit to head toward Elisabetta, who appeared to be hiding under her hat's shade. He soared over to his innocent prey with two glasses of wine clutched in his hands.

"We need more chairs!" exclaimed Maestro Scarpari behind them.

"Go. I will help the Maestro," urged Discrete.

Elena rushed over to Elisabetta, interjecting herself in the conversation by handing back the cup of wine the young man had already given Elisabetta.

"Our throats mustn't be parched before song, Signor..." Elena responded.

"And a lovely throat it is," he replied, still staring at Elisabetta. "I am Vincenzo Capello, your host. And you are…?" Elena was aware that he was addressing the young, pretty face before him, not hers.

"Elisabetta," Elisabetta said shyly.

"Elisabetta," he repeated greedily. "Please feel free, Elisabetta, to indulge in any of our food and wines we have prepared for you when you are free to partake."

"I think Discrete needs your help, Elisabetta," Elena said, guiding her in a different direction.

Vincenzo turned and bowed his head at Elena. Elisabetta just stood, smiling stupidly, not able to speak at all. "Thank you for your generosity," Elena answered for Elisabetta.

Elisabetta nodded, "Yes, thank you," and hurried away.

Elena knew she would have to watch her naïve young friends and the predators that would try to make them blush. She hadn't expected it to start as soon as they walked through the gate. The string ensemble began to play one of Vivaldi's known concertos, and the music floated around the garden. Their gifts and the mystery of how the cloistered young women lived were an aphrodisiac to the audience's imagination. The music laid down a magical canopy for those imaginations to run rampant.

Elena listened in on a conversation with a group of noblemen behind her.

"Yes, that one with the soft pink flower," said a young man.

"You mean Elisabetta. She is a lyric soprano of the lightest quality," responded a darker, older voice.

"And her throat is as pretty close up as one imagines it would be."

Elena recognized the young Vincenzo, whom she had just met, just as vocal as his robust father, a benefactor who'd she had seen at several post-Coro recital receptions.

She'd heard the noblemen use these minor introductions, wheedling them against one another in past outings. They were in a competition. This meant the girls were in a bit of a lion's den. They had to adapt quickly in conversation and flirtation. The nobility understood that not all the talent could be used at the Pietà, and the beds were continually turning over. It made sense for those beds to be turned outward to continue the legacy of the Pietà into society. This gave the nobles negotiating power. Whoever might happen to be there to ease these sheltered flowers into their grasp could indeed catch one of the prizes. If nothing more than to say they had.

Elena kept listening as she searched the garden, signaling to the other singers who were engaged in conversation. Francesa occupied some of the younger singers nearer the refreshment table, where three older women, presumably mothers, smiled and chatted with them. Elena waved a hand at Francesca, who nodded back. Candida looked up toward Elena and gave a big smile. But it wasn't for her.

"Oh, the allure of a young woman's single smile is compelling. But those who can wield a string instrument and ease a softness of voice to caress the ears of men hold great power indeed," said the older voice in the group.

The men chuckled in chorus. She'd heard enough. Elena moved away to gather the other vocalists and prepare for her performance.

Maestro Scarpari stood in front of the vocal ensemble and faced the crowd. "And now a more dramatic piece featuring our most experienced soloist, Elena."

The crowd welcomed her with gentle applause. Elena let the long notes reach across the garden. It was a drastically different experience to face an audience after being tucked into the Pietà's grille, where they were only allowed to lower their heads enough to see hat tops from the chapel balcony. Their focus was on the music and the picture it drew in their minds. This engagement exposed their emotions and yearning, intertwining them with the well-practiced notes, which spilled over the balcony's edge like a waterfall. It was said that audiences received this gift with awe and adoration. But the Coro girls never saw it.

Now she investigated their faces. Any musician, let alone a less experienced one, could quite easily lose themselves in their surroundings, letting their minds and hearts wander unless they practice intentional focus. She forced her face to remain serene as she scanned the crowd, caressing the melody in their direction. She had learned to make deliberate eye contact in these more intimate gatherings. Proximity was a truth-teller. She looked from face to face, stopping at a familiar one. Deep, solemn, brown eyes gazed back. She pushed her feet firmly into the ground, her stare unrestrained and bare. Ludovico Rossi did not falter.

Elena had thought of him for years after that first meeting on the alms walk, his strong arms carrying Agata inside after her fainting incident. No one had ever had such an effect on her. She recalled how she'd stumbled to find words. Though a small exchange, he sat there in her mind, a quiet friend she assumed she would never have the chance to know. Her heart's yearnings were no longer hidden behind the grille. Had everyone seen them? Her thoughts strayed into some girlish whirlwind for the rest of the set. Maestro's arms lowered dramatically, and the entire garden applauded.

Elena felt exposed. As soon as the performance finished, she looked up and saw Signor Rossi taking swift steps toward her. She took a few brave steps away from the ensemble toward him.

"Elena, isn't it? It's lovelier in person with such proximity, such exposed feeling." He sounded as nervous as she was. "Your singing, that is." He cleared his throat as if to clear his discomfort.

"Yes, Elena della Pietà." She thought she sounded shaky and immature. *Of course, that's who I am,* she scolded herself. That was all their last names: from the Pietà. "Thank you" was all she could manage.

"I have not seen you at one of these outings before," Ludovico continued.

"I've gone to a few," she responded. "Admittedly, the excitement is more than I care for. And do you go often to these parties, Signor...?" She couldn't reveal she remembered his name; she didn't want to appear juvenile or wanting.

"Excuse me, my name is Signor Ludovico Rossi. I'm pleased to make your acquaintance. I, too, do not care for large crowds nor frivolity. However, Signor Capello is a good friend. In fact, I'd prefer if I could have the quiet of song in my home, but the Sunday Vespers service at the Pietà makes me get out and enjoy it." He twitched his nose and locked his hands behind his back.

"Truth is, it's strange to be watched in such a way, with the applause and verbal compliments. We aren't quite used to that."

Their exchange comfortably paused as they looked upon those locked in conversation around them.

Maestro Scarpari announced from the front. "We will have one more ensemble piece for you. If my ladies could return to our stage."

"I have to go," Elena said, turning back to Ludovico, whose turned-down gaze made him look sad. She noticed the small gray flecks in his beard and the short hair over his ears. She wanted to memorize every bit to take back with her.

"It was nice to meet you, Signor Rossi." She let herself look fully into brown eyes.

As she turned to walk away, he reached out and grabbed her hand. She looked up at him with an unexpected thrill.

"May I write to you in the Pietà?" Signor Rossi asked.

"Yes." Elena nodded. Then she smiled. "I would like that."

She turned away, giddy, rubbing her hand to soak up his touch.

29
AGATA

Agata stood on the balcony of the *Chiesa della Pietà*, looking down at the empty church below, her heartbeat quickening.

"Go ahead, look over the edge. Look all over the church. Rid yourself of the unease. It's a distraction. You are here to glorify God," directed Apollonia. The Maestra paced in circles around her.

Choral singing had trained Agata to understand pitch and blend with the voices around her, but it also offered an excuse to hide under the quiet of her voice. There was something serene in the way the notes of a chord layered together as she tucked snugly into them, letting them envelop her. Agata unlocked her sweaty palms from her skirt's familiar sides and grabbed the rail, daring to look up and down the rows of red pews below. The thought of singing for all to hear frightened her so much she had to physically push her feet into the ground when, instinctively, she wanted to hide with her back against the footrest of one of those pews, just as she had as a small girl running from Elena.

In the past, Elena had worked with Agata's insecurities, keeping her physical space private, hidden in the back halls of the practice rooms, before asking her to broaden her vocal range. Apollonia made it clear that she would not let Agata's shyness hinder her growth.

"I am not letting this fear take you over, Agata. My role is to help you reach the final stage of your education. I'm convinced you have more than you see in yourself to give."

So here Agata stood in the vacant balcony space, where the performing Coro both practiced and performed. She longed for that nice, tucked-away practice room and its tight four walls. But Apollonia had other plans: challenging Agata to face her fears every step of the process, including the ones she had taken to get there.

"I want you to re-enter class with the confidence of a Coro performer, not an unsure student."

Agata walked back to the entrance of the dark performance hallway and turned around to face her Maestra's expectation. She exhaled, attempting to look confident even while so unsure.

"Roll your shoulders back, Agata. Remove the grasp you have on your skirt! Don't walk, glide. Think about how you are a vessel of God who has honed and trained her skills. Remove anything that says: I can't. Think *I can* because He has made me able."

Apollonia asked her to repeat this several times from behind the Coro halls' closed doors, over the bridge that crossed the green door below her, and to a marker Apollonia placed on the floor at the grille of the balcony. She had the harpsichord moved as near the edge as possible, instead of its typical position, which was placed back nearer the wall.

"We will have our lesson here," Apollonia instructed.

Week after week, Apollonia pushed Agata from the same spot at the balcony grille. She had her take the same long, slow walk to the same place on the floor. When she got there, her voice still held on, clamped as if two hands literally choked her neck.

"Sing to the far wall, Agata," Apollonia cried.

Agata was tired of this thing that held onto her like the darkness she hid, rising inside again to take over. All she wanted was to be free of it.

"Sing!"

"I can't." Tears filled Agata's eyes and weakened her argument.

"You can, Agata. Sing."

"I'm afraid!" she yelled. A warmth rose out of her, a flood of pain and anger. She felt something unlatch in her, her throat freed. "I'm just a nobody they left. They all left."

"Sing."

The notes she knew so well rose out of her like a strong wind was behind them. They blew over the balcony across the space of the sanctuary to the church's high white walls and vibrated in her chest like a power with no end or beginning. Tears crept down her cheeks during the song and revealed themselves in a sob as it concluded, the force she tapped into overwhelming her.

"Agata, I knew it was there. You finally felt it."

"I can't believe it, the strength of it. I've always felt so weak, like I could never use my voice. It would never be heard," Agata sobbed.

"Outside these walls, you did not have a voice. Agata, none of us did." Apollonia paused. "Inside of them, we do. But now, you control it. It's yours, and nobody can use it for you. They can't sound like you. It's your imprint alone."

Agata saw the tears that filled the corners of her Maestra's eyes.

"Let your anger and hurt and pain come out of it in the strength it carries. Let it echo all over the building and into the hearts of strangers, and let them carry the message of it back into the streets where you would never be heard on your own."

Apollonia spoke emphatically, as one who'd had years of practice doing what she instructed.

"Let's do it again," she directed.

Agata felt a business in the air that came with the cool of early fall. Change was afloat in the Pietà. She and her fellow third-year counterparts, including Candida, Elisabetta, Chiaretta, and Giulia, were in their final months of training. Those who passed their classes and made their audition could become official members of the performing Coro, the true Poinsettia Girls, the following spring. Agata sat down at her desk, alone with her pile of copying to accomplish. September always made her contemplative. It was the month her mother died, now twelve years ago. She pulled out the mysterious piece of music she had discovered from Maestro Vivaldi a few months back and stared at it as if asking it to speak to her in some way. She had yet to determine what it was for. Before she could get too buried in her thoughts, that special knock came at her door.

"*Bondì*, Agata, it's rest hour. Do you ever stop working?" asked Candida.

"Do you ever stop talking?" asked Giulia, coming up from behind them.

"All of this work. I don't even know if I want it anymore," admitted Elisabetta.

The other three girls snapped their heads in her direction and shifted their glances to one another.

"I heard that every spring, a noble family takes turns hosting a day on the Giudecca in a place called Eden Garden. Doesn't that sound like a dream?" crooned Elisabetta.

Agata turned around from her work. "We have auditions before then. That's what we are focusing on. Anyway, how do you know these things?"

"Her lover has told her in one of his many letters," teased Candida.

Elisabetta blushed and bragged in the same breath, "Vincenzo is going to ask his father if they can host it so that he secures his invitation. Then it is just a matter of his dad convincing the board that I should be there. Vincenzo said that would be easily agreed to."

"Unbelievable," Agata replied.

"You don't seem yourself lately, Agata," Candida implored. "You're unusually distracted."

"I've been busy, you know. Our rehearsal schedules, our looming audition… I've had many more requests for copying, and my lessons take a lot out of me." She saw Candida glance at her pile of papers with a quizzical eye.

Elisabetta changed the subject. "I still can't believe Anna Maria and Maestro Vivaldi."

"What are you talking about?" Agata asked. They were no longer whispering.

Giulia joined the conversation with her response. "You don't know anything, Agata, because you are always stuck with your head in the clouds." Giulia continued. "Vivaldi has been offered a director position at the court of Mantua and asked to take Anna Maria as a travel companion."

"But they aren't getting married," added Candida.

Agata looked back at the pile of papers. *Maybe that's it—the man in the red jacket was telling me goodbye.* It made her feel grown up, and somehow, she noticed that she had arrived at a destination she thought was many more miles away.

There was a knock on the door. The girls stood rigidly, looking from one to the other. The door pushed open, revealing two water-logged hands. Poeta poked her head in.

"You girls need to keep your secrets quieter. I can hear you from the hall. Don't you two have your own room?" Poeta looked at Candida and Elisabetta standing behind her, holding the heavy door open with their backs.

"We came by to give Agata some notes on string rehearsal," Candida fibbed, getting up and walking toward the door. Elisabetta followed her and gave Agata a little wave, mouthing, Bye.

"Well, I was leaving anyway," said Giulia. "I've got an extra private on the organ."

"Seems like you've had lots of those lately," Candida responded.

"Don't worry about me. I know I will make it into the Coro next year. The rest of you, well..." Giulia stuck her tongue out and flounced off.

When they were all out of view, Poeta stretched her arm in the door, dangling a letter playfully. Agata stood up to grab the paper, but Poeta pulled her arm and put herself in the room instead.

"Is this the *fifth* letter from your lute boy?"

Agata blushed and rubbed her lips together, trying to hide her smile.

"You are responding to all of them. I think it's about time I get paid for my discreet messenger efforts. Reading aloud this one would do," Poeta teased.

"Poeta! Gabriele is not my lute boy."

"After five letters, he is more yours than you realize. Or you do, and you're afraid."

After all these years, maybe Poeta understood Agata better than anyone else in the building.

"Is that what happened to you and Signor Alioni? The deliveryman?" Agata responded, trying to tease back. She knew nothing of men and relationships, but she found the topic more curious that last year than she had before, though she had hidden her desire to talk about it to anyone else.

"Whoa, oh no, I found out early on he is married. That doesn't mean I can't enjoy his attention. And I do. I'm not ashamed to say it," Poeta expressed flirtatiously. "Agata, you are allowed to have feelings, to enjoy the attention of a young man. You've achieved a lace collar, more than most do in here- go live your life. You don't want to be stuck here forever. "

Agata let Poeta's playfulness flutter around the room. She wasn't sure how to respond to that.

"Maybe it would help if you could see him in person," Poeta taunted.

"Yeah," Agata tried to laugh it off. "I guess it would, but that's not even possible."

Poeta raised her eyebrows. "I'll let you read your letter then, while you are still alone. But I get to read anything that has the hint of an offer."

Her comment elicited a smile from Agata. "Okay, Poeta," she agreed.

Agata closed the door and fell into her bed, feverishly ripping the envelope open. She unfolded the tri-pleats of the paper, not taking time to smooth them out.

She took an inhale and, in her mind, heard Gabriele's voice:

Dear Agata,

To this day, I can't believe it was you I ran into when I first entered the Pietà. All those years, I wondered where you went. It was as though you were this ghost from my memory that I had almost convinced my mind had made up. If it weren't for my family and the connection between ours, I might have been able to let you go.

Speaking of family, Sophia says hello. She has grown into a young woman who is only half as annoying as she was when she was little. She is engaged to be married. Just a few days ago, Mama was helping her clean out our old toy trunk for her to take her trousseau in, and she came across these puppets, or should I say our puppets. Do you remember them, Aggi? Mr. Mustache remained a loyal employee until his passing and was also faithful to me when I took over the lute shop after my father died. Sophia was reminiscing about you as she ran her fingers over the old lute strings of the fish. I gave in. I had to tell her I saw you. I think you two would be great friends now.

Aggi, the thing is, I have a child of my own now. He's just two and is running all over the place. My mom has been the best help. She was, after all, such a wonderful mother herself. The loss of my wife was significant, and I was so heavy for so long. Then fate brought me face-to-face with you. It's time for me to find companionship again and a mother for my boy, and I hope for others more to come. Aggi, we have always had a connection, but when I saw you in that hall looking so grown up and beautiful, I thought maybe it was God who put you in my path.

Elisabetta's earlier sentiment suddenly made sense to Agata. "I don't know if I want to work this hard anymore." But it also scared her. Agata ran her fingers over the page. Did she want to join the Coro? Or did she want him?

30
ELENA

E lena closed the door of her room and slumped against its sturdy back. *"Oh, sweet rest hour,"* she murmured to the empty space. She scanned her small *dormitorio*, ready to curl up in bed on the far wall, when she saw a letter waiting on her otherwise empty desk. Suddenly energized by its presence, she hastened to grab it. It was lying seam-up, so she could see it had been opened, which meant Madonna had both read and approved of its contents. Her heart thumped loudly, amplified by hope and possibility, as she turned it over to distinguish the writing on the front of it. A gusty laugh escaped her. She recognized the tall, narrow loops and formative middles of his handwriting. His first three letters arrived once a week, then two a week, and now he'd sent his fourth letter. She had memorized the shapes and curves of his handwriting with the trace of her finger—she'd know them anywhere.

Elena held the recent reply from Ludovico Rossi taut in her hands and fell into her bed, anxious to hide in the depth of his voice she'd played in her mind. His letters had begun informative, and his tone meek. In the exchanged habits and patterns of their daily lives, a recognition of their shared solitude emerged. Words of affection layered in. And the longing for an idea became the desire for a single man. Ten years had passed since his wife's death, and Signor Rossi never remarried. To nurture his lonely soul, he faithfully attended the weekly concerts at the Pietà as his wife had loved, calmed by a certain soprano voice from above. Her voice. By his third letter, he confessed he'd attended weekly with the hope of seeing Elena's name on the program. When he was finally face-to-face with her at Signor Capello's garden party, he realized his feelings for her.

Elena heard the stories of girls being whisked away by wealthy noblemen, never to be heard from again. It was a dream no one dared to indulge in, that a foundling could be a part of society, a woman with her own home, a status greatly elevated from her humble beginnings. Could this be her fate as well?

Her thoughts churned through the reality of it. The Pietà held a dowry for each inmate; she had earned a fair amount with some outings and extra hours from teaching private lessons, but it was the board who approved every match. What would they think of one of their own marrying her, the reliable, quiet, plain soprano? Would she be accepted? Marital security came with sacrifice, and there were no assurances of happiness with this choice. Would he be happy choosing her? Any would-be husband of a former foundling had to sign an agreement saying that his wife would no longer sing or play any instrument outside of the Pietà's walls. Elena would be bound to relinquish her gift of music forever. All this time working toward a goal just to let it go. And all this time contemplating it. Would he actually ask for her hand in marriage?

The door squeaked open, and Cristina waited until after she closed it to ask: "Is it him? Did you get a new one?"

Elena couldn't move from where she'd settled, lying back on her bed with a look of pure bliss.

"So, he did," Cristina concluded, sitting deep into her bed across from her. "I'm so happy for you, Elena. Has he asked yet?"

Elena shook her head. "No, I am trying to sort through all of it."

"You need to acknowledge that you have to let this all go if he asks. You'd never be able to sing again."

"I know. I've asked this of myself," Elena replied. "My vocal pursuits, the Coro... They have been such a significant part of my journey and my identity. Before all of this, I could never imagine not singing. But lately, I feel as though there is something else out there for me to grab onto, a new part of me longing to develop. But to find it, I'll have to let this go."

"It's going to happen. And I am really going to miss you," Cristina said with a little break in her voice.

Elena grabbed her hands, squeezing them in a hug, hopeful.

A low August sun seeped into the walls of the Pietà. And with it, a new Friday for the Coro to don their poinsettias. Outside of Sunday Vespers and weekly Saturday concerts open to the public, a quarterly concert was given to the governor, board, and most generous patrons of the Pietà. Unlike the other concerts open to the public, the Mansionaire Chorister, a sung Mass, featured all levels of the Coro, in addition to the public performing with the Coro. This concert showcased the improvement of all three levels being trained and, in turn, gave the younger girls practice performing in front of an audience.

Warm beams of light filtered in through the small windows of the bridge that connected the Coro to the church. These streaks of light energized the frenetic backstage mood inside the long hall, where dozens of girls waited in white dresses with their small lace collars and red bows that wrapped their smoothed hair. The older ones, current Poinsettia Girls, stood among them in their pressed white blouses with velvet red skirts and wide lace collars hugging their shoulders. Their hair was smoothed back away from their faces, framing the signatory Pietà poinsettia tucked behind their ears.

Elena stood among them, tightening a bow that had come loose in a first-level's hair; her hand was shaky from lack of sleep. Did Ludovico plan to attend? She thought it was too bold to ask him in her last response. They were ten letters in. Now, fidgety and unfocused, she wished she had made that inquiry so she could settle into expectations.

Amid the excitement over dresses, ribbons, and anticipation, whispers spilled out among the younger girls as the audience filed into their seats below. The Discrete whirled around them, flattening skirts with their hands, smoothing hair, and just plain shushing. Elena tried to brush aside her tangled thoughts by moving around with the Discrete, touching shoulders and head-tops to calm herself.

The youngest girls led the procession into the balcony, their sweet voices blooming into the sacred open space and falling like gentle petals on the ears of the board members. With every stanza, a layer of darker voices and more complex harmonies folded in behind them until the balcony space became a thicket of red-and-white blooms. Elena's tension eased as the familiar voices of old and the brightness of youthful voices she knew from their first willowy breaths circled her in a single wind.

To watch Chiaretta display her rare violin skills on par with a performance Coro duet partner and hear Candida's cello shine in a quartet piece filled Elena with a pride she hadn't allowed to envelop her before. And then Agata, her beloved protégé, stood and sang with such conviction and strength alongside a vocal trio, which confirmed in her that it was right to keep at something as long and faithfully as one could, and then, once one felt that release, to let it go. Apollonia had taken Agata to the next level.

The concert ended with a choral selection that brought the younger and older voices together, and a wash of tears left her spirit feeling freed. On a normal Saturday concert or Sunday Vespers, it was considered unmannerly for any applause or cheering to occur. But that evening, Governor Sovarizo jumped up with an exuberant "Bravo!"

The audience rose with him and released a burst of applause and cheerful vocalizations. While she had never dared to before, Elena looked down and caught an applauding

Ludovico staring up at her. He raised his arms when their eyes met with an unhindered smile through his dark beard. Elena was inclined to run up to him and give him an embrace; she was so filled with joy.

The pre-performance jitters dissolved into anticipation of the reception. Elena let the girls file ahead of her to form a reception circle while the board and audience members made their way up a back stairwell to join them. The kitchen staff hurried in trays with small bites of bread and cheese to a long table behind them.

The younger Coro members stood with their knees locked and smiles on their faces. Elena reminded them, "Bend your knees a little, and remember to say thank you for coming."

The low rumble poured into the balcony as board members and benefactors chatted their way in. Elena overheard fragments about the quartet's timeliness and Chiaretta's proficiency. Madonna moved to the center of the room and began applauding, asking the Coro members to join her.

"Thank you again for your generous support, our dear board and patrons. Now, our Discrete will lead our first and second-stage Coro students to dress and take their lunch. Please enjoy our meager bites and your conversations."

Elena tried to appear calm and unhurried as she watched the room break into conversation. She admired the theatrics of a purposeful Vincenzo Capello walking in with his father and quickly separating from his known love interest,

Elisabetta. Elena watched the coy duck of Elisabetta's head as she returned his greeting.

She turned to laugh with Agata, who stood next to her.

"That looks practiced." Elena laughed again.

"Is it that easy to tell? I don't know how I'd handle that," confessed Agata.

"It's not as hard as it looks," Elena said, coming close to her. "The small talk, the formalities… You've proven you can master anything with some practice."

"Oh, I'm not sure I want to." Agata laughed. "I'm focused on preparing myself for auditions. This looks in such opposition to meeting my goals."

"Your goals, I would say, are reached. You are there, Agata! I am so proud of you! I knew there was a voice in there."

"One more audition," sighed Agata.

"You get in and later have the opportunity to pursue other interests," she teased.

Agata raised her eyebrows.

"There is someone you enjoy talking to, and you don't seem to have any trouble finding words?"

"Not you too. Who else knows?" Agata asked.

"Not everyone. Margarita, Poeta, Madonna…" Elena's voice trailed off.

Agata gasped. "Madonna?"

"Madonna knows everything. You know that," Elena replied.

"There's a man over there who seems quite taken with you, Elena. He's coming this way," Agata replied.

Ludovico Rossi walked with heavy steps right up to her. She was reminded, though, that despite her intense feelings for him, her interactions with him in person had been brief— a wash of nervousness flushed through her.

"Good afternoon, Signor Rossi. This is one of our talented third levels and my dear friend, Agata."

Ludovico Rossi bowed his head. Elena blushed at his gracious demeanor.

"I am pleased to meet you, Agata. I expect we will see more of you on the balcony stage soon."

"It is my hope as well, Signor Rossi. I hope you enjoyed the performance today," Agata responded right on cue.

"I never leave without feeling impressed. Week by week, the Coro seems to get better." He looked at Elena with a tender, familiar gaze. Elena was lulled into sentiment by the affection in his eyes.

"Agata," said Elisabetta, waving just a few feet away. "I have someone I'd like you to meet."

"I'm so glad to meet you, Signor Rossi. If you'll excuse me."

Elena reached for her hand. "I am so proud of you, Agata."

As soon as Agata walked away, Signor Rossi turned to Elena. "Elena, I don't know how much uninterrupted time we have now, so I will be direct," he spoke intently. "I have written the board and made an offer that they have accepted. So, I am free to ask you, as it is your opinion that matters to me most." He cleared his throat, his eyes never leaving hers. "You have spoken to my heart first in song and then in our letters. I want to spend the rest of my years with you at my side. I know the sacrifice I am asking you to make is not a small one. In exchange, I offer you a home to make yours, and my heart, which is already yours. Elena, will you marry me?"

Elena was shocked at his tenderness, at his request. But the answer flew off her lips without regret.

"Yes," she said. Instinctively, her hand went to her mouth; she wasn't used to public displays of emotion. Happy tears clung to her eyes, and like a dream, they made the room blurry and soft. "I would be honored to be your wife."

The chatter around the room softened, and a gentle round of applause replaced it. Elena smiled at her dear friends, mentors, teachers, and students, and despite being so good at keeping things in, her dam of tears broke. Her dream of a family would come true after all.

31

AGATA

A final note swelled to the walls' height in the small choral classroom, pure and vestal as the girls that delivered it. Agata's soprano voice sat at the top of the chord, and she acknowledged every layer of it—reveling in the balance of voices around her. Compared to private lessons, which left her feeling challenged and exposed, choral singing was like a deliberate locking of arms, one note tuning to the next, many voices connected by a single chord. Such was the same in all classes, things to be worked out and to improve upon, but in the togetherness of bare expression and adaptation, she found sanctuary.

Maestra Apollonia lowered her arms just as the bell rang throughout the hall, indicating the end of rehearsal.

"Good work, choir. Please take time to look at our new song from today in your scheduled practice room time," Maestra Apollonia directed.

Two weeks had passed since the Mansionaire Chorister. After an evening of congratulations and flirtations, Agata observed an increased enthusiasm among the girls who were all hopeful about their futures. Their giddy whispers floated through the halls, at the beginnings and ends of class.

"Did you see how handsome Vincenzo Cappello was?"

"And the way he walked right up to Elisabetta?"

"He was so forward."

"I want someone to be that forward with me."

Some she thought were overly felicitous about their potential romances. She, too, felt caught up in the concert and the recognition they received afterward. But Agata was riding a different high, rapt in the moment of performing right behind the famed balcony grille, shoulder to shoulder with two of her fellow Coro students and a live audience below her. She overcame something that, for her, had been a terrifying feat. But an interference exposed her resolve. She wanted to revel in what she had achieved, but the sentimental mood circling in the third-level Coro shook her contentment.

She walked out of choir rehearsal quickly, hoping to disengage herself from potential dreamy rehashes. The rumbling of love matches and engagements pushed Agata back into the former dream state she'd lived within during her first years at the Pietà. The images of black cloths and funerals had long left her alone. But as she descended onto the wooded kneeler for daily mass, she looked at the crucifix, remembering her little home church's pale pink interior in San Canciano. She felt the warmth of Nonna's heavy, rust-colored skirt stuck to hers. They'd sit with Agata sandwiched in the middle—the Betranozzi's shielding her other side. Signor Franco would wink at Agata as she looked over, and Benedetta would reach for her hand and hold it throughout the mass.

She felt a jab from her left. Elisabetta cozied up to her shoulder, looking inquisitive. "Psssp," she said, pointing, eyebrows raised. It was time to stand and take communion. Agata followed Lorenza out of the aisle and knelt in a gesture of respect. In her new life, she maneuvered step after scheduled step, moving as she was expected to. She wondered what it would be like to walk out of mass freely and feel the wind on her skin. Could her legs still break into a run if Gabriele taunted a race to the canal?

"Amen," she said to Don Bollani. Her memories dissolved with the communion wafer.

Agata nodded goodbye to Elisabetta and walked back to her room, thankful to find it empty. She thought that after living in the excitement of the other girls and their prospective love interests, she might have an answer for her own story. The truth was, she hadn't responded to Gabriele in weeks on the topic of their future, and she knew she owed him that. She lifted her mattress and grabbed his last letter, folded neatly on a stack with his others. She unfurled the roll of paper and sat on her bed to smooth the furled edges slowly and deliberately. She took a deep breath to clear her mind of the turmoil of questions and focused instead on his voice.

Then fate brought me face to face with you... Aggi, we have always had a connection, but when I saw you in that hall looking so grown-up and beautiful, I thought maybe this was God putting you in my path.

Gabriele. She recalled the mischievous grin he wore when they'd joke about the people passing on the *calle* beneath them as they sat at their bedroom windows, that whisp of thick hair that wouldn't stay out of his eyes. In the seconds that passed between them that day in the Coro entry, she noticed the curves of his face were more defined. He had little, dark whiskers on his chin. She imagined walking into the front door of the Lute Shop as a young woman, the little bell calling out brightly and the sawdust filling the air. She would be in color, a blue skirt, and a newly woven shawl wrapped around her shoulders; she'd have proper shoes on her feet instead of the barefoot ones of her youth.

Hidden in the hanging lutes and messy shop counter was safety and comfort. She felt it again when she saw him in the entryway of the Pietà. Agata ran her fingers over the page. What if she could go home again and forget the stress of auditions and performances —would she be free?

The door whooshed open, and Agata jumped up to sit at her desk.

"Hi, Giulia." She gulped. "Did you have an organ lesson?"

Agata sat and discreetly placed the letter underneath a stack of her copies. Giulia looked at the mountain of papers on their desk and then back at Agata, annoyed.

"Oh, I'm sorry," Agata responded and gathered some of the scattered music, adding it to her pile. "I picked up a fresh batch to copy a couple of hours ago, and then I got distracted with one of the pieces."

Giulia answered with a huff as she sat on her bed and removed her shoes.

"I know. I take over the desk. Our desk." Agata gulped.

Giulia finally looked at her. "To answer your question, yes, I was in organ rehearsal."

"With Madonna?" Agata asked quickly. It was an innocent assumption; Madonna had taught Giulia for years.

"Actually, no. Madonna has her hands full with *so* many other things." Gulia cleared her throat as if dropping a clue.

Agata couldn't place how to pick it up.

"Assistant Prioress Prudenza has been giving me guidance on my future here at the Pietà. Prudenza is one of the only people here who sees Madonna's shortcomings. Look, I have to be the next performing Coro organist. We all see that the current one, Dorotea, is getting old. And I can't let anyone take it from me. I just met with the new organ teacher, Michelina della Pietà, who plans to take me on." She stared at Agata, more wildly defiant than usual, like she was daring her to push back.

"Prudenza?" Agata asked. "It seems like sound advice, but I would be careful getting in between Prudenza and Madonna. The Prioress is loved by everyone here, including the board. I'm sure if you just talked to her about your concerns…"

Giulia interrupted, "Agata, maybe you should consider minding your own instrument progression. I think your singing has always been stuck. Is that really Poinsettia Girl material?"

Agata creased her brows—Giulia's words stung.

"The truth is, Agata, if you still haven't guessed it, we all carry our secrets and form alliances that benefit ourselves alone. No one is going to do it for us." Giulia looked at the inkpot on the desk and back at her." Could Giulia know of her correspondence? Of what she was about to do?

Giulia flopped over toward the wall. "Ugh," she huffed.

Agata turned around in her chair and worked her quill around the ink pot. Giulia's words unsettled her, but strangely, they didn't make her want to run and hide. It was Giulia who couldn't sit still. She put her shoes back on and stomped out the door, which she likely would have tried to slam, but it was too heavy, and a light brown hand intercepted it from shutting all the way.

Poeta moved her entire body inside Agata's room. "Ok, so it's all settled. Are you ready for tonight?"

"Yes. I'm ready, or I will be, I hope, "Staggered Agata.

"You've got nothing to be nervous about, obviously, this man is smitten. I'll handle everything else."

Agata could only exhale and nod. "Ok," Agata replied ruefully.

"Don't worry!" Poeta replied. "I'll see you tonight!"

32
AGATA

The glow of the candle floated under her door. She had been waiting for hours since tucking under her covers, hiding her day dress, while Giulia was in the washroom, readying for bed. Agata grabbed her sweater off the hook before the candle revealed her dress and creaked the door open. Poeta gave her a nod and moved quickly for her to follow. She looked back at Giulia, who had rolled into the wall. Agata hoped she was sound asleep. For being such a quiet place, the Pietà was terrible at keeping secrets.

The two women slipped down the rounded stairwell and descended to the laundry room. Even in the dark, it smelt of metal and *sapone*. A sliver of light crept through the usually busy workspace. The side door was held open by a water bucket. Poeta stopped and pushed her toward it.

"Be quick," Poeta reminded her. "We only have a few minutes."

Agata peeked through the door and saw the silver moon illuminate the man before her. Gabriele was facing the water, his dark curls hugging the back of his neck. How was he so recognizable, the boy she remembered now the man before her? She stepped quietly over the bucket onto the small dock. Gabriele turned his head and took steps toward her, "Agata," he greeted. He went right for an embrace, which should have made her uncomfortable, but she was conscious of how she'd react after all these years without embraces and did her best to relax in his arms.

"Thank you for meeting me. I've looked forward to every letter from you," Gabriele said softly. Agata separated to answer him.

"As have I. To think of Sophia all grown up! And the Lute shop, Nonna's bakery…" she slowed, even saying her name still hurt.

"I know this must be overwhelming for you, Agata. But to think, you could see all of it again. You could come home."

Agata just nodded her head.

"I would be a patient husband. I don't expect you just to come home and work; my mom is still around to help ease you in with my daughter. God, she'd be so happy to see you."

"Have you seen him?" Agata looked at him directly to understand the truth.

"My father," she added.

"No, I know. Yes, but it's been a long time. He used to mill around the square, marching up and down the *calli* between our shops. But it doesn't matter, Aggi. I can protect you. I will protect you," he emphasized.

He took his hand gently underneath her chin and lifted her eyes to meet his. She could trust him, she knew that. But… His lips met her hers with a single tender kiss, and he rested his forehead upon hers.

"It's time. We've got to get you back," Poeta interrupted in a loud whisper.

"Write me, Agata. Soon, let me know." She didn't know how to verbalize all her emotions into a response. He grabbed her hand once more and kissed it, holding it between both of his.

Poeta moved the bucket quietly. Agata kept his gaze until the door was shut.

Poeta knew Agata well enough that she didn't harbor her with questions on the walk back, only providing candlelight for her thoughts.

"Thank you, Poeta," she said back at her bedroom door.

Agata remained wide awake the rest of the night.

"Agata, I need you to give me more focus—it's flat." Apollonia stopped and stood to face her.

"I can't today. It's not working," exclaimed Agata, flustered. She took a few steps away from her music stand and her Maestra.

In the last month, all her private lessons, from violin to harpsichord to voice, were geared toward preparing her for the final push to the Coro audition. But voice was always so hard. Was it because her true feelings revealed themselves in her singing voice? She could hear them flying out when the actual words, the speaking words, were not plain and easy to decipher. Apollonia did not give in to bad days or revisit fears. And she did not ask what personal demon was bringing them on; that was Agata's job to handle.

Agata stood with her back to her teacher, attempting to compose herself. Her clarity was submerged in fuzzy images clouding her vision, like the caliga on a winter day—the lace collar, the grille, her quill and ink, the pile of music on her desk, Gabriele, San Canciano, Papa...

Apollonia interrupted, "What's going on with you today? Your emotions are interrupting your airflow, Agata."

Agata grabbed both sides of her skirt, inhaling loudly. Her future was vacillating somewhere between elusive and unclear. How could she make all the pieces come together?

"You're right. I'm sorry," she said and faced her teacher.

"I'm wondering if we need to abandon this and start with something entirely different." Apollonia thumbed through a pile of music in a harried search for an alternative, and then she paused. "This audition, Agata, is a check-in. You affirm the choice made by the audition board that you are the expectation, the example for all other girls wanting to get in. You have already proven your capability. You'll need to impress them and show your range, but you must sing out from the emotion inside of you. When they hear you, that's what will convince them because the audiences come in search of hearing something they feel but can't express themselves."

It struck Agata at that moment. She knew exactly what she was supposed to sing.

"I have a piece," Agata muttered.

Apollonia looked up from her pile of music, intrigued.

Agata had kept Vivaldi's composition for her a secret. She spent hours in the practice room, trying to understand what clue it might have for her. At some point, she let go of seeking its purpose and let the fall of the notes comfort her. The only other person who knew about it was Discrete Margarita. And she said Agata would know what it was for and when to use it.

She sang the composition for Apollonia.

"Agata, where have you been hiding this? This somehow depicts every intricacy of your voice," Apollonia responded.

Agata knew it was not the music choice Apollonia referred to but the way she expressed it. Vivaldi's piece gently guided Agata's voice from an old place to a new one. And just like when he led her to the green door, she was crossing a bridge from a destination she was meant to leave behind.

Agata and Apollonia both smiled at one another, sharing a moment of proud satisfaction, but not for long before Apollonia predictably repeated, "Again."

33
MARGARITA

Venice was always cold in January. Margarita whispered to herself as she fumbled, getting her nightgown over her head. The cold had settled quite comfortably into her elbows, and she started to question whether a roommate request would have been a good option. It wasn't just her old age. Change had settled into her bones. It was unavoidable. She knew that. Her years at the Pietà had given her a stored record of reflection, which she used as a guide to those entrusted to her. She'd watched the girls grow from children to adults, many of whom she'd held as nameless babes in her arms. She'd watched the Prioress change from a timid but determined young woman into a judicious leader. She'd watched the male directors, overwhelmed with the pressure of writing and dealing with girls in their adolescence for a greedy audience, decide it was easier to quit. She'd watched herself, once a beauty in her own right with a distinctive mezzo-singing voice, become a woman who walked with a bend in her back, barely able to put her nightgown on.

She finally dressed and moved into the quiet hall. The Pietà ran cyclically from hour to hour, shuffling thousands of feet in movements marked by bells and masses. Margarita witnessed the clock tick off more of what seemed the same year after year, but in its nuances, great things occurred.

Change was an inevitable certainty in the Pietà's sanctuary, and she delivered expeditiously.

Margarita saw a red skirt ahead and dainty fingers tapping its side, and it was exactly who she was hoping to run into. "We never got a chance to discuss all your writing," she called out.

Agata turned around with her shoulders shrunk in, looking like she was caught.

"I wasn't talking about the copying," Margarita hinted coyly.

Agata moved closer and whispered, "Elena told me you knew. I've got an orchestra rehearsal. Maestro Scarpari is here today."

"We can save it for another time. In fact, what are you doing later tonight? I'll come by your room after Vespers."

Agata shrugged. "Okay, sounds fine." Her tone was unsure.

Margarita didn't explain, preferring to nudge the mystery. "Now, I've got somewhere to be." Margarita gave Agata a wink and shuffled off.

She wasn't upset by the letters sent between Agata and Gabriele. In fact, it made her light to know that love was alive in Agata's heart after watching sorrow and loss occupy her spirit for many years. She'd witnessed the struggle, which was harder for those who remembered their birth family. Margarita was in between quiet errands when she saw Agata hand Poeta her first response to Gabriele. Of course, Margarita had marched right down to Poeta when the errand seemed off. Poeta tried and failed to deny it. Though

Agata's staunch protector, there was recognition between them that Margarita was as well. She took a step back, and for a couple of months, Margarita watched the letters go back and forth, with imagination enough to understand where they were headed.

She handed the last response to Madonna a few weeks back. "Are we going to lose another one?" Madonna had asked.

Margarita enjoyed a little mischievous chuckle to herself when a terrible pain in her arm stopped her from going any further. A cold sweat trickled down her back beneath her heavy dress. She gathered herself and looked around, concentrating her breath to a slow cadence. It wasn't going to stop her today. Everyone would be patient with her pace; she'd have to be too. And she had a job to finish.

She had made it her business to keep a special eye on a few others in her position as Discrete. One of those others was the Prioress. Like Agata, she had watched Madonna enter the Pietà as a girl who had known her family outside of it. Madonna faced her own demons to make the leap from young teacher to Prioress, all while reconciling her past outside the walls. Margarita was a confidant to the Prioress, and in many ways, she looked at her like the daughter she'd never have. She dispensed admonishment or encouragement depending on the circumstances Madonna encountered over the years. Margarita also recognized that there was only one woman at the top. It was inevitable that some would feel more deserving. In a place where recognition was acknowledged by position, backloaded by years of questioning their purpose in this great big family of girls, some tended to act out. So, Margarita implemented a plan.

Without anyone else's knowledge, Margarita and Innocentia, Madonna's personal assistant, maintained a schedule that kept either herself or another Discrete always hidden in the background whenever the Prioress had to meet someone alone. She could never be falsely accused of anything and could always provide a witness. And who wouldn't believe an old, venerable woman?

Whisk, whisk, whisk. Margarita heard a brisk skirt moving near her, and she ducked behind a pillar where two halls merged. Sure enough, Assistant Prioress Prudenza walked down the long central hall as anticipated toward Madonna's office. She had a mission in her step. As a gifted cellist, Prudenza's talents were utilized as an advanced private teacher for the Coro's upper levels despite her elevation to Assistant Prioress years ago. There weren't many of her students who were happy about that, but in the Pietà, that question would never have been asked of them. Expressed personal opinions or feelings were not encouraged. Discrete and Madonna observed Prudenza taking advantage of this in her teaching methods. She was feared. She was tolerated. But she was not liked. For years after the mishandling of Candida, Margarita took a careful interest in Prudenza's activities.

She watched Prudenza march into Madonna's office, where the board meeting was about to start, and stood outside, listening in.

"We have a busy agenda today. Let's begin with some of our happy reports and changes within our Coro," Madonna instructed.

Governor Sovarizo jumped in. "I couldn't be more pleased for my dear friend, Ludovico Rossi. We have all approved of his generous offer to Elena and considered her dowry as part of that proposal. She has worked hard for the Pietà and has quite a savings built up to take with her. We need someone to motion approval to release these funds."

"I motion to release the funds for Elena della Pietà," Signor Mocenigo initiated.

"I second it. What a fortunate match. For them both," the normally quiet Signor Fosacarini added.

"It is also becoming apparent that there is a growing affection between Vincenzo Capello, the oldest son of our generous donor Signor Capello, and our third-level Coro student, Elisabetta. He has requested a private visit from her to the Capello home. I think an offer might very well be near," Sovarizo relayed.

"Do we feel we need to address her, ahem, 'fainting issue' before money is on the table?" asked Signor Mocenigo in his usual sullen tone.

"I don't think that's necessary," Madonna responded. "It has been years since her last episode, and it wouldn't affect her duties as a future wife or mother."

"Who do we recommend for her chaperone? I fear a Discrete may not be able to keep up with the whims of a young man in love," Signor Troy chuckled.

"I recommend Francesca. She is sensible, smart, and a non-threatening presence," Madonna answered.

"I agree with all of that," Governor Sovarizo replied. "All in favor?"

"Si," the room chanted back in unison.

"I have a request that I asked Governor Sovarizo to allow time for," Prudenza interjected.

Margarita put her ear to the wall. She did not want to miss a beat.

"You may go ahead, Assistant Prioress," Governor Sovarizo responded.

Margarita heard Prudenza's haughty exhale through the door. "It is with a heavy heart that I've observed some disturbing interactions between our dear Madonna and other students, as well as indiscretions that involve one of our auxiliary staff members."

"Prudenza, what is going on here?" Madonna demanded.

Signor Papafonda, the organ carer, stood outside the boardroom, staring at Margarita. "I'm not sure why I'm really here," he confided. *The poor man sounded like he was literally shaking in his boots, caught unaware*, thought Margarita to herself.

At that moment, Giulia, Agata's roommate, walked up to the door with her head held high. She took one look at Margarita, and her countenance flattened. The door swung open, and the two were asked inside. Margarita took a step back to remain unseen.

"For years," Prudenza continued, "Signor Papafonda has generously cared for our organ. It is a special instrument, with only one of its kind in the building, and requires sole attention, as only one person can play it at a time. As you also know, our Madonna is an accomplished organist herself. It appears that her personal practice time coincides with Signor Papafonda's time slot for tuning the organ. It would also imply that she has sought out alone time with this man, which we know that in this house full of impressionable girls is a mockery of our chaste way of life."

Signor Troy, who notoriously advocated a high value on morale, questioned Papafonda. "Is this true, Signor Papafonda? Have you found yourself alone in the company of the Prioress on more than one occasion?"

"Well, yes, weekly," Signor Papafonda admitted, tumbling his hands in circles over one another.

"Weekly, he says. And would you say that you felt she sought out your company?" Signor Troy leaned out of his large chair into the table.

"Madonna is always friendly. We usually have a chat, and she sits down to play. I understood it was how her schedule worked," he replied.

"When you spent these weekly exchanges together, please confirm, was there ever anyone else present?" Prudenza furthered the questioning.

"Often, one of her students, like Giulia here, would join us," Signor Papafonda admitted.

"Is this true, then, child? Have you witnessed Madonna with this man alone?" Signor Troy asked emphatically.

"Yes. One time, I saw their hands...meet on the keys," Giulia said shyly.

Prudenza interjected, "I'd also like to point out that our dear, brave Giulia is also one of Madonna's students. She confided in me, as she felt uncomfortable with the relationship she'd witnessed over the years and afraid of Madonna's strong opinion holding her back."

Prudenza continued, "I thought it wise to suggest one of the new teachers here be assigned to her, to continue her growth. Madonna has denied this. Giulia feels it is because she has not spoken outwardly of this secret relationship."

At that point, Margarita heard the Prioress respond in a clear, raised voice. "Giulia, how can you accuse me of such things? I have made time in my schedule because I enjoy my lessons with you. I am not so far ahead of myself to know that there are others with extraordinary things to offer you musically. I am far ahead of myself to know that I must be very careful with all my interactions, and thus, hold myself to a high standard. Which is why I have employed a small committee to watch over me, to both keep me accountable and prevent any false witness." She paused.

Margarita only heard quiet on the boardroom doors on the opposite side.

Madonna spoke quietly. "Would you let them in?"

Innocentia opened the door and met Margarita with a twinkle in her eye. Margarita rolled her shoulders back and nodded at the five Discrete behind her. The old women in white marched in like they had their youth back in their steps.

The Prioress explained that for years, this small group of women had been tasked with watching out for her. One of them was always assigned to follow her, sometimes visible but often standing in the shadows, behind pillars or adjacent walls.

Margarita stayed standing. "My fellow Discrete, please lay your logbooks out on the table."

Ten wrinkled hands carried the appointments, run-ins, and conversations of Madonna's every day at the Pietà. Those wrinkled hands heaved their books on the table.

"Signor Rossi, board, Prudenza, what days specifically were you looking for?" Margarita asked, licking her finger. It was hard not to gloat.

Prudenza had played her cards wrong. Madonna had relayed her Assistant Prioress' harsh dealings with the foundlings in a separate logbook after the Candida incident years before. The board unanimously decided that while they "Appreciated" her many years of service, the cycle of retaining and acquitting young women must serve in the best interest of the Pietà. It was time to name a younger candidate as Assistant Prioress, one ready to be molded for the future seat of Prioress. Prudenza had a unique skill set that might be better used with the older women in one of the many nunneries across the Veneto. They gave her a choice of three.

The board was lenient with Giulia because of Madonna's favor for her. It was determined that Giulia was consumed by jealousy and loneliness, as playing the instrument did not provide her with the same social interactions or opportunities as the other girls. It was also agreed that Prudenza had taken advantage of her weakness and that it was her pressure that Giulia responded to. The young organist was sentenced to two weeks in solitary confinement with only bread and water.

Governor Sovarizo was uncharacteristically grim. "Someone motioned to end the meeting."

All the men came to thank Margarita for her shrewd and perceptive undertaking.

"It's been my pleasure," Margarita said, satisfied with the recognition of her work.

It was a common fact—one Margarita knew well. No one should underestimate a woman with lines on her face and hands; they indicate secrets kept and wisdom stored.

There was only one task left to complete. But first, she'd head back to her room and sleep the full nap hour.

She was spent.

34
AGATA

Agata sat at her desk in the quiet of her room, diligently copying out the text. The soft light of the candle dispersed a gleam that filled her with the greatest contentment in her busy day. Teaching, choir, private lessons, and practice room time all dulled in comparison to sitting in the luminosity alone.

For months, she had recognized this little freedom at day's end as an opportunity to get lost in new melodies she rewrote and the newer one emerging in her head that taunted her with a single phrase she wasn't sure what to do with. The night work increased her need for candles, but she made enough money with the extra tasks to compensate for them.

It was only the first night of several that she'd be without her roommate, Giulia, who was stuck in confinement for two weeks. Since no one was allowed to roam the halls after Vespers, there wasn't even a risk of interruptions from Candida, although knowing her, she'd find a way around that. With the whole room to herself, her thoughts took advantage and reverberated loudly around her. The last letter from Gabriele stood on top of the pile, staring at her for an answer.

Knock, knock, knock.

"*Bona Sera*, Agata. Working hard, I, see?" Discrete Margarita stood at the door, her candle brightening the room.

Agata softened at the sight of her.

"This came through the laundry room door this morning." Discrete handed her a letter from Gabriele. She looked up to her Discrete. Although it was a single piece of parchment, she felt the weight of it in her hands.

"Leave that here." Discrete grabbed Agata's elbow gently. "We're going to take a walk. I have something I need to show you."

Agata couldn't fathom what that might be so late in the evening. She tucked the new letter beneath the old one and gave her door a firm shut.

The dark hall nearly swallowed up their light. Both the Commun and Coro sides of the Pietà were tucked into their rooms with their nightgowns on. The two women walked without conversation. The only noise was the abnormally heavy breathing of Discrete beside her. Agata looked down at her to ask if she was feeling okay, but before she could, Discrete locked her arm in hers and pulled her to the top of the stairwell. Agata looked up to the shadow reflected largely on the curved wall as they descended the stairs. It revealed the likeness of a tall young woman, her shoulders confident and squared, and the severe bend of an old woman whose days had been long spent next to her. She turned around to see whether they were being followed. There was no one. She put her hand at the bottom of Margarita's back, ready to guide her off the last step.

Margarita let her.

They passed through the front hall to the entryway, the same space she first entered in the Pietà, the same space where she had first been reintroduced to Gabriele. They walked toward Nurse Clementina's office and the hospital hall. Margarita stopped and nodded at Agata, who opened a heavy door. Agata was surprised to see Francesca, the current record keeper, at her desk.

"Good evening, ladies," Francesca greeted them with a hushed, calm tone. "I've been waiting for you. If you follow me."

Francesca led them through the hospital wing, guiding their steps past a room where little whimpers and whispers could be heard. The newest foundlings had been rescued from inside the green door and laid in the hands of the women in white. Agata slowed, stilled by their rocking and humming, such sweetness amid such despair. Francesa led the two women down another dark hallway that Agata did not know existed. The air shifted from cool and crisp to dank and musty. They stopped at a closed door, and Francesca pulled her keys out to unlock it and guide them in. Their shared candlelight revealed a large room whose walls were lined with stacks and scrolls, arranged high up to the ceiling. At the room's center was a large table with several items laid out, lit by another single candle.

Francesca exhaled. "I will leave you to it. Please leave everything you don't need on the table and close the door. I will be in later to secure it."

Agata quickened to the table; it was then that she recognized her lace mask. It was so dainty and small that it fit in the palm of her hand. She let out a short, mirthful hum.

She turned to Margarita to explain. "This is the mask Benedetta made for me, my Nonna's very dear friend. I had to give it back on the night I was checked into the Pietà. Ohhhh, I remember feeling so lost when I had to give it up."

She then pulled up a black material and shook it out to reveal its shape. It was her black cape. She smoothed her fingers along the ties, one of the last things her Nonna would have touched. Tears filled her eyes. She hugged it as if she could bring back the feeling of her Nonna's plush arms around her. But she had grown up; likely, it would be her holding her Nonna up now.

She placed her hands on the next item, a paper rolled out and secured to prevent it from rolling back up. It wasn't anything she recognized. She looked at Discrete for permission.

"Go on," Discrete urged.

Agata swallowed, her heart suddenly nervous. She placed her finger on the page and read out the first line. It was a list.

"Agata Maria Farusi. Maria? I didn't know I had a middle name."

"It was your Nonna's name," Margarita informed her.

"But my Nonna's name was Guilelma. I remember it distinctly."

"Your other Nonna, whom you never met. Keep reading."

"How foundling entered: 'Walked in by A. Vivaldi.'" Agata giggled. "I had no idea who he was. To me, he was the man in the red jacket. He was quiet, but I felt secure with him. And to think..."

"Keep reading," Discrete urged.

The list went on to record her physical distinguishers: height, weight, and mental health.

"Scared, overwhelmed, shocked." Agata shook her head. "That I do remember."

"Date of baptism, the priest, Don Bollani, who performed it. Oh, look. A second file is attached to this one. Maybe they got it mixed up?"

Agata read the name: "Maria Farusi." She looked up quizzically.

Date entered: 17 January 1691
Reason: Syphilis
Death: 27 January 1691
Length of stay: 11 days
Cause: Physical and Mental deterioration from syphilis.

"Wait, my grandmother died here? And I am named after her? How come I never knew this?"

"You were young enough when you entered, and you don't remember your middle name. Likely, your mother had her hands full enough with your father; she didn't talk about the fate of his mother. These things generally go down with their deaths, unspoken, unknown."

Agata stared at the file, processing both its contents and the Discrete's words.

"I took care of her, Agata, *your* grandmother. I was a young singer in the Coro, but I was always drawn to those in need, and the number of syphilis patients we received at the time left the hospital overwhelmed. Of course," Margarita chuckled, "They no longer let the Coro singers volunteer in the hospital. But your papa, Pietro, was just a small boy, and when he and his father carried her over, oh, I felt for him. He returned every night and sat on the steps outside the hospital window to ask if she was okay. Many nights, he slept there in the cold. His father gave up trying to bring him back. One day, she died, and that was the last I saw of that sad little boy." Margarita paused.

"And then I met you. I recognized the same intensity in your heavy brows, the ferocity of your love for your mother and your Nonna."

Agata let soft tears wash down her face, awestruck by the story of her family.

Discrete continued, "The loss of his mother was a heavy weight your father carried all his life. I know how you've struggled with whether to be afraid or angry with him. And I don't blame you for those feelings. His behavior was not aimed at you, but you needed to be free of him. He was a man full of pain. Not only did he lose his mother, but also his only daughter, to the same place because he could not get a hold of it."

Agata shook her head in disbelief. Discrete quieted, giving her the chance to let it all sift through her.

"There's more." Margarita pointed. "You should continue."

Agata picked up the scroll next to it and unrolled it slowly.

"Go ahead, read it."

"It's a letter from Benedetta! She knows I'm here. Oh, this must have been years ago. She wanted to tell me Nonna died." Agata looked at Discrete, and a feeling of betrayal swept through her.

"My dear, you were ten years old, brand new to the Pietà. We felt that if we read it to you, it would have prevented you from detaching and acclimating to your new life." After a pause, she added, "She also brought you this." Margarita tapped her thin brown finger on a wrapped package.

Agata breathed deeply as she pulled the package toward her. It was surprisingly light, as if empty. She opened it, slowly folding back the paper. It revealed a feather. Agata swallowed.

There was a small scroll beneath it. She unfurled it slowly and read its contents out loud:

"Put your name in writing, and let your voice be heard, and the generations to come will still be able to hear it. —G"

Agata felt a wave of emotion pour over her and spread across her body. All the years of wondering why were expressed in a tearful release. As it washed away, a new clarity revealed itself. The feeling that there was purpose in her life, even without those she had wished beside her. She was still known and cared for by them. Margarita cried deep tears alongside her. She came around the other side of the table and unlocked Agata's arms, which she'd wrapped around herself, and placed them on her waist. Their embrace squeezed away years of pain. Discrete pulled back to look at her.

"It was your Nonna's words and the quill she used to enact her wishes. Her greatest desire of all was for you to be taken care of and free of the pain your father did not know how to rid himself of. Here are the letters that first came to the Pietà that Maestro Vivaldi brought with him. They include the directive that upon her death, the sale of the bakery and all its proceeds go to your upbringing here in the Pietà, where she knew you would be safe."

"Can I take it with me? The quill?" asked Agata.

"I knew you would," Discrete responded.

They left the little room and its boxes of secrets arm in arm. There were no more words necessary to fill the warmth between them. Agata walked Discrete back to her room on the first floor and stood outside of it.

Discrete placed her warm hands on both sides of Agata's head.

"You're okay now, Agata."

With what seemed a great effort, Discrete stood on her tiptoes and kissed her forehead. Agata placed her hand on top of hers and nodded, welling up with more tears. Discrete moved her arms and patted Agata's hand. Agata understood her cue and pushed the heavy door open for her. She watched her pass into the darkness, her candle weak and dim.

Agata hurried up the stairwell, ready to abandon her weeping to her empty room. She unwrapped Nonna's quill and held it up in her palms. A slew of memories came flooding back, sweeping her up. She laid the feather across her work and blew her candle out, letting her pillow soak up the great well of tears churning out years of hurt. After she could cry no more, a solace descended upon her in the dark, and she understood something she couldn't see before.

She thought of her papa, the sad little boy who grew up to be an agonized musician. Agata knew something her father didn't. His mother had been in the hands of a great company of women who restored and renewed every soul that came through their door. Maria Farusi hadn't been alone. She passed her life away in the presence of love. And that love bestowed upon her trickled down through the Pietà's women's hands to her granddaughter. Agata had been raised by her family after all.

35
AGATA

Funerals were rarely held in the Pietà's church. Most of the women who lived there left long before old age took them. Some, like Elena, collected their dowries and married. Others were discharged to nunneries, such as Prudenza, when it was agreed that their duty to the Pietà was complete. A chosen few, like Margarita, were honored with a service.

Margarita della Pietà died peacefully in her bed the same night she reunited Agata with her Nonna's quill. She was still wearing her day dress.

Margarita knew the Pietà as her home for seventy years. She followed the same progression of steps as the current foundlings, was schooled on the Coro side, and advanced through auditions to eventually become not only a Poinsettia Girl but also a vocal soloist whose memorable mezzo-soprano voice reverberated over the balcony grille. After many years of service, she advanced to Discrete or aide, and that was how most girls and women came to think of her—as their helper.

She was mourned properly in a service full of older girls and women in their lace collars and younger ones in all-white dresses. Madonna played a musical tribute on the organ, and Agata swore she saw her wipe her face as she finished. She alone wore a black headpiece in honor of the significant loss to them all. Don Bollani conducted an emotive mass, and while there was much to laugh over and remember, the service was wrapped in tears. A quiet took over the building for a few weeks, and everyone honored her in their whispers.

November arrived rainy and gray, and a new seriousness took over the building. November in the Pietà meant audition time. As such, it was nearly impossible to get into a practice room. Students of all ages were found in every available nook, their fingers feverishly moving, their airways cycling. As a third-level Coro student, Agata was fortunate to have three weekly sessions secured in a practice room. She was days away from auditioning for the performing Coro. After rehearsing her song several times, she stopped to listen to the music whirl through the halls. She didn't feel the frenetic energy she had in auditions past; she could sing Vivaldi's composition as she wrote it herself. The sad strings of a cello floated through the wall next to hers, and she listened to how her friend had grown.

Agata and Candida exited the practice rooms at the same time, and two second-level students waited in the hall, anxious to take their spots.

"Good luck, girls," encouraged Agata.

The two old friends walked away. Once they were out of earshot, Agata spoke, "Impressive, Candida, really impressive!"

"Well, thanks. You are singing a song I hadn't heard before, a beautiful one," Candida replied.

"It is a special one," she murmured, conscious of talking in the hallway.

"I guess Elisabetta is beside herself. She finally received an invitation from Vincenzo. I hope he proposes. I don't think her heart is in this."

"Hmmm," replied Agata dreamily.

"Agata?" Candida stopped to look at her. "I've noticed you get quiet every time the subject of marriage comes up. Are you happy for Elisabetta? Do you not approve of having the chance to find life outside of here?"

Agata put her arm in hers, pulling her along. "Of course, I am happy for her," she whispered. "I've asked myself the same question. What would it be like to have a life outside of the Pietà, my home, for most of my life? Could I be happy away from it?"

Candida gave her that look that she regularly gave Agata when she wanted more.

"Let's go. It's about time I showed you something." They moved short of a run; their hands held to Agata's room.

Once the door was closed, Agata lifted the mattress. She pulled out a small stack of papers tucked away in the middle of her bed. She showed the stack to Candida, who swiped them from her hands. The hidden papers were Gabriele's letters. The two plopped down together on her bed.

"Agata!" Candida feigned anger over Agata's secrecy and took several opportunities to read her favorite parts out loud.

"Shhh, not so loud!" said Agata.

"Oh, somebody knows about these. How else would they have gotten here?" Candida would not be content without knowing every detail.

Agata confided, "Poeta, Elena, Margarita knew…." She got quiet as tears filled her eyes. She hadn't said her name since the evening she spent with her. The evening, she died. Candida put her arm around her.

"And I met him, in person," Agata confessed, biting her teeth over her lower lip.

"Who are you? The quietest person in here has the best secret life. Mine is so dull!"

"And he kissed me."

Candida was beside herself. "I've never been so jealous. Oh, I'll never be kissed," Candida flopped down on the bed and boo-hooed a fake cry.

Agata relayed the whole story of their night on the dock and the big reveal in the secret file room with Margarita. Candida cozied up knee-to-knee with her.

"I know it's hard. You relied on Margarita to help you navigate all your decisions here. But this is one you must make," Candida was frank with her.

"I know," Agata agreed, soaking up the safe space so close to her friend.

"I think that's exactly what hung over me all these years—that I wasn't given the opportunity to make my decision about leaving my home and my Nonna."

"There's so much I didn't know about you, Agata. However, I suppose that applies to all of us. When we aren't allowed to speak, our secrets stay hidden. Clearly, I need to sneak in here more so we can talk," Candida teased. "What will you do?"

"I've grown to love being here. I love playing music. I love writing music. But out there is San Canciano, the people I spent my life grieving for, weeping for. Is it wrong to leave that behind, that which I wanted back for so long, to leave them knowingly?" It felt so good to talk it all out, and she kept going. "I don't know how to answer him, and he deserves an answer."

"Agata, you haven't even mentioned Gabriele's name in that list. I've never heard you say you want to be married." Candida put the letters down and stretched out. "Of course, if you go, I'll be stuck here all alone," she jested, then flopped over and put her hand on Agata's arm. "If your choice has anything to do with needing family, well, you have me. We are sisters. I don't have any hidden letters or private invitations. I plan on playing my heart out until something blaring tells me otherwise, and I can only do that behind these walls. Agata, it sounds like you might have your answer. You just can't be afraid to make it."

Auditions came and went. The building was full of anticipation, young women waiting for decisions that would decide their futures. Agata, exhausted from processing all the emotions she'd encountered over the last few weeks, had fallen quite easily into a deep sleep when she heard a short knock at her door.

"Agata," a voice whispered. She blinked her eyes open to find Madonna standing right over her.

"Get dressed quickly. I will be waiting right outside the door."

No one ever questioned the Prioress. Agata forced herself out of bed and felt for her dress, which was hanging on a hook. She looped her lace collar over her loose and sleep-mussed hair. As she stood in her room fumbling to put her hair up, she wondered whether she should be nervous; upon meeting her in the hall, the Prioress's mood convinced her she needn't be. Madonna moved swiftly downstairs to the hallway bridge that led to the Pietà's church. Agata, mystified, lagged half a step behind her.

The church was normally glowing with light for the Pietà masses and concerts. But that night, it was lit modestly with two candelabras placed on either side of the altar. Madonna put her hand on the small of her back, a rare comforting gesture.

"Go ahead and take a seat up front."

Father Bollani, in a white robe and gold vest, stood forward from his regular spot at the front of the church. As though for the first time, Agata noticed the years had left him fuller and his hair thinner, but tonight, a peaceful mirth glimmered in his eyes. A dark-headed man sat in the front pew on the right. He stood and turned around to reveal his beard and kind eyes.

"Good evening, Agata. Thank you for joining us," Signor Lodovico Rossi said in a gentle, familiar tone. "It was important to her that you would be here."

As she took her seat in the pew across from him, Maestra Cristina stepped out, holding her violin with a warm glow on her face. They mouthed *hello* to one another as Cristina raised her bow, ready to play. Signor Rossi stood with the first note to face the rear of the church. His face was anticipative, and his eyes glistened. Agata felt a chill move down her spine. She followed his cue and stood to join him. Two figures in all white waited at the back.

Elena. The sight of her walking up the aisle made Agata break down in tears of happiness. She wore her plain white Coro day dress and a simple veil over her eyes. Agata noticed she was missing her lace collar. And no sight of a fresh Poinsettia. On Elena's arm stood the Prioress, who guided her to the front, steady and strong. As the two women neared them, Agata saw that Elena's smile held tears on her cheeks. The usually serious Madonna gleamed as she permitted herself a smile.

The ceremony was simple. Short vows were exchanged. Don Bollani pronounced them as man and wife to the three witnesses in the church with the exuberance of addressing a full room.

"I am proud to introduce Signor and Signora Lodovico and Elena Rossi," Don Bollani beamed.

Madonna squeezed Elena's hands tight, breaking the protocol of touch. The endearment was felt in the room. They exchanged words of gratitude, and Madonna gave Elena her blessing.

Madonna also shook Lodovico's hand. "I know you will take care of our very precious friend," Madonna said.

Elena turned to Agata and threw both her arms around her in a sudden embrace. In a single act of affection, their shared tears revealed their closeness after years of hushed expressions in quiet halls and practice rooms.

"Agata. I am so proud of you. I will still be here for you. I will write to you. I've already arranged it with Madonna. I will accompany Ludovico to the concerts and watch you sing from behind the grille."

Agata couldn't find words worth speaking; the tears spoke her truth. The two friends shared one last glance and held each other's hands.

"Goodbye, Agata. My dear friend," Elena cried as she spoke.

Lodovico took Agata's small hand gently in his. "Thank you," he smiled generously and squeezed his other hand over the top of hers. Agata looked up and knew he was the right one for her beloved mentor and friend. Lodovico put his arm out for Elena to loop through his, and together, they walked out of the Pietà as husband and wife.

Elena looked back, and Agata mouthed, *I'm okay.*

Agata walked back to her room and sat at her desk. It was close to midnight, and though her tired body wanted to crawl back into the warmth of her bed and fill it with her tears, she knew what she needed to do. With the light of one match, her solitary room became luminous and warm. She picked up her Nonna's feather, letting it tickle the fingers of her other hand. This gift of love was the clue she'd been searching for. It was time to write down the song she'd been singing, her song. But before she could write the time signature, she dipped the quill in the ink and began something new:

Dear Gabriele...

EPILOGUE
MAY 1735

A soft glow filled the Pietà church balcony from all corners in a crescendo of vibrant harmony. The horizon of red and white lined the balcony grille, illuminating the room with their lanterns. Agata, the esteemed soprano soloist, stood visibly in the front row.

"Good evening, ladies and gentlemen," Maestro Scarpari announced.

"I give you Agata de la Pietà and her composition: *Novo Aprili in F.*" He handed Agata his conductor's baton.

The crowd below was full of familiar faces, and their felt anticipation was unparalleled. Although Gabriele never wrote back to Agata, he knew his sister would enjoy corresponding with their old childhood playmate. Grown-up Sofia was accompanied by her new husband in the audience. She beamed with pride. Elena and Lodovico took their regular seats at the front, the warmth of their smiles reaching Agata on the balcony. Her eyes caught a slight movement in the back corner pew placed along the wall. It was an old man whose dark eyes shone with tears; his long, gray hair hung around him in thin strands. He was clearly moved by the music. He looked directly at Agata. Could it be?

It didn't matter anymore; I no longer fear him. I hear my Mammina's voice. I feel my Nonna's hands. I am nourished by

Margarita's and Elena's proud smiles. I have courage from Poeta and the reliance of the Pietà, whose white halls and small rooms are home to me now. They have held the secrets of my creativity. And I've learned that the work has taken away my twisted feelings and hurt and hurled them somewhere they can't taunt me anymore. I found my voice, Nonna, just like you asked. Our signatures will go down in history forever, our wishes heard, our cries poured out, our voices strong. I am Agata della Pietà.

GLOSSARY

Bovolo: small round bread shaped like a snail

Bondi: good day

Buono fame: good hunger, refers to reputation

Caffeterria: cafeteria

Caligo: fog

Calle: narrow street

Co quando la fame vien drento par la porta l'amor va fora pai balcony: When hunger comes from the door, love goes out through the window. Meaning: financial hardship can strain relationships and cause love to disappear.

Ciacole: chatter

Cichetti: small snacks

Chiesa: church

Dolce: dessert/sweet

Dolce manière: sweet way

Figlie di Commun: common daughters

Figlie del Coro: daughters of the choir

Fondamente: walkway along canal

Fornari: baker who specializes in baking bread

Libro Segreto: secret book

Maestro/a: teacher

Marangona: the main bell at whose sound practitioners of the various crafts (marangoni) began began and stopped work.

Notaio: notary
Pan bianco: white bread
Piccolo: little
Piccolo Ragazza Choir: little girl choir
Pistori: baker who kneads and shapes bread and pastries
Polpette: meatballs
Presipio: nativity scene
Ragazinne Coro: little girls from 10-12
Sapone: soap
Scafetta: revolving wood door
Sei mesi sei mesi: Proverb, 'six months in six months out'
Serenissima: serene city
Sopa de spessati: pea and pancetta soup
Soto Voce: low voice/quietly
Venite adoremus: 'O come let us adore Him'

AUTHORS NOTE

The Ospedale della Pietà was founded in the fourteenth century in Venice for the care of abandoned infants. It housed and educated foundlings for thousands of years. The disintegration of the orphanage came with the arrival of Napoleon's forces. I owe much of my research to Jane L. Baldauf-Berdes, who painstakingly compiled all the lost documents of the Pietà into a two-volume anthology. Most of these were scattered and rediscovered years after the war.

Baldauf-Berdes' anthology also includes a list of all the male teachers who played professionally for St. Mark's to teach at the Pietà, even the organ tuner Bartolomeo Papafonda. How could I not insert him in my story with a name like that? But I am here to talk about the women. All the foundlings, teachers, and Maestro di Coro (conductors) I've written about were contemporaries of Agata and would have passed one another in the halls. While not much is written about their detailed lives in Baldauf-Berdes' anthology, next to the inmates' names are referenced their instrument, the years they were part of the Coro, and perhaps a token easter egg: songs they soloed on, wrote themselves, or even punishments for minor infractions. Agata della Pietà was a soprano who composed *Novo Aprili in F.* That was all that I could find written about her when I began writing her story. Recent findings reveal a record of many other compositions by her, as well as other hints about her life, possibly including a physical deformity. She was one of three known composers throughout all the years the Pietà functioned. While the Agata in my story had a detailed backstory, it is likely that she was dropped off at the green door as an infant. I wanted to put myself in the shoes of comparing the contrast between a life outside the Pietà and the one inside it. I look forward to reading how others, inspired by Agata and the Pietà, will offer more ways for us to learn and appreciate this unique place, and to discovering more research that will allow me to continue her story in future projects.

Baldauf-Berdes provides a graph of the stages and ages the foundlings would have accelerated through to enter the Coro. I did my best to make sense of it and flesh out the hard work that would have been required for anyone to navigate this rigorous, competitive process. The Pietà was also meticulous about its funds and had an active board of nobles who managed them. Each inmate, whether a performer in the Coro or a silk cleaner in the lower levels, earned funds that were recorded and kept for them. There *were* offers of marriage made from noblemen's sons, and the Pietà provided them with a dowry from these very savings accounts. The women of the Coro (Poinsettia Girls, as I refer to them) would have also had opportunities to sing for private parties like the garden scene in Act 3. The public was open for Saturday litany, Vespers on Sundays, and masses on important feast days. Because it was technically a mass and not a concert, the young women never received whoops, hollers, or even applause. Only light tears and prayers were an acceptable response.

The steadfast rule was that no music could be performed in the Pietà unless written and performed for it exclusively. Can you imagine what that meant for at least two services a week for hundreds of years? Antonio Vivaldi spent much of his career as a violin teacher at the Pietà and wrote thousands of pieces during his tenure there. I had to mention the one name most people could identify, yet I didn't want him to be the focus of the story. I was captivated by the idea of young women being recognized and developing their talents with government backing. While it's hard to grasp why such a talent was not utilized as Maestro di Coro, it is understood that he was somewhat rebellious, aloof, and perhaps a little painful to deal with.

The building was rebuilt in the mid-1600s and stands as the four-story white building facing the Lido today, now known as the Hotel Metropole. The Pietà itself is now known as The Provincial Institute for Children, still functioning as a charity assisting women and children in need. It stands directly next door to the Chiesa della Pietà (the church where the Coro performed) in their lace collars and live poinsettias for every concert. You can find the green door still located in the alley between them.

Acknowledgments

It takes one person spending a lot of time with themselves, listening and rephrasing the words that circle in their heads to write a novel. But it takes several voices within singular moments stretched across years that give us the words to speak. These moments and memories accumulate, the good ones intermingled with the ones that weigh on us, forming a narrative that ignites the stories we must tell. I am thankful for both.

Ray, my husband, you've been my biggest fan since we were sitting across the table in the library at Fresno Pacific University, making me gush while I tried to read. You still make me gush, and you propel me to keep moving forward. I am endlessly thankful for you.

Ethan and Emilie, your creativity and individuality, as expressed in the music you made that seeped through the walls of our home, have brought me a lifetime of joy and spurred the ease of my own creative pursuits. Thank you for all of your creative help and encouragement in getting my first endeavor off the ground.

A special thanks to Heather and Dave, who dared to read through early versions and offer insights I could not see on my own.

Thank you, Roy and Tracey, for that date night in Paris, the start of it all.

ABOUT THE AUTHOR

Jennifer Wizbowski spent her childhood days lost among the spines of her favorite books. Inspired by the daffodil fields of Wordsworth and the babbling brooks of Shakespeare, she earned her bachelor's in English literature, a minor in music, and a secondary teaching credential, then wrote freelance for local business journals, taught in classrooms, and authored a Teen and Tween column for a parent magazine—all while raising her family.

As those years ended, she knew it was the right time to pursue her lifelong aspiration of bringing her own books to life. She now devotes herself to illuminating everyday women's stories often lost in the shadows of history, revealing how they became heroines of their own time and place.

FOLLOW THE AUTHOR:

WWW.JENNIFERWIZBOWSKI.COM

WWW.HISTORIUMPRESS.COM